“Mr. Terrell. I have been looking for you.”

A tall, thin man with chopped black hair emerged from the dark shadows in the municipal garage.

“I am your escort,” the man grinned. “We have little time.”

“I’m not going anywhere with you,” Terrell said, starting to turn away.

The man pulled out a blue metal automatic pistol. “I must insist—or you die here in a Berlin garage.”

Russian. The man was KGB, Terrell thought. This couldn’t be happening. He’d been so careful.

“Now, Mr. Terrell,” the agent grunted, jabbing him with his gun and nodding toward a nearby stairwell.

Stiff with fear, Terrell stumbled across pavement and tripped on the stairs. The gun barrel hit him again. He worked his way up the stairs on his hands and knees.

The bare concrete walls around him reminded him of prison. They would lock him up, make him talk about GABRIEL.

The agent shoved him against a black car. As he tried to stand up, he felt the sharp pain of a syringe in his neck. Suddenly weak, he grabbed hold of the door handle to keep from falling. “I . . . I don’t have it,” Terrell gasped.

“You don’t have what?” the KGB agent hissed.

“The tape. You . . . don’t have anything without the . . .” he said and collapsed.

GABRIEL'S FLIGHT

HANK BOSTROM

LYNX BOOKS
New York

GABRIEL'S FLIGHT

ISBN: 1-55802-085-3

First Printing/August 1988

This is a work of fiction. Names, characters, places, and incidents are either the product of the author's imagination or are used fictitiously. Any resemblance to actual events, locales, or persons, living or dead, is entirely coincidental.

Copyright © 1988 by the Jeffrey Weiss Group, Inc.,
and William H. Lovejoy

All rights reserved. No part of this book may be reproduced or transmitted in any form or by any means electronic or mechanical, including by photocopying, by recording, or by any information storage and retrieval system, without the express written permission of the Publisher, except where permitted by law. For information, contact Lynx Communications, Inc.

This book is published by Lynx Books, a division of Lynx Communications, Inc., 41 Madison Avenue, New York, New York, 10010. The name "Lynx" together with the logotype consisting of a stylized head of a lynx is a trademark of Lynx Communications, Inc.

Printed in the United States of America

0 9 8 7 6 5 4 3 2 1

FOR
J.T.

PROLOGUE

Thousands Die in Nuclear Mishap

CAPE TOWN, SOUTH AFRICA, April 18 (Reuters)—Shortly after two A.M., South African time, a nuclear device detonated in northeastern South Africa. The explosion occurred several miles north of the town of Brandvlei in an arid and desolate area known as Bushman Land. First reports indicate fatalities have been in excess of two thousand, and casualties may be twice that many.

Spokesmen for the South African Defense Ministry have provided only brief statements in the first hours of the tragedy. Some one hundred square miles, including the township of Brandvlei and a small military airfield, have been quarantined, and the numbers of dead or injured cannot be confirmed. One unofficial source said that an army field exercise was taking place at the time of the accident.

Officials would neither confirm nor deny that the army unit in question possessed tactical nuclear weapons. Informed observers have recently speculated that South Africa, in codevelopment with Israel, had achieved a tactical nuclear capability in defiance of world nuclear pacts. The same observers have also questioned the nation's policies regarding nuclear armament and South Africa's ability to control effectively such weapons systems.

Currently, reporters are not being allowed near the area, and reports coming from the north are chaotic. By six A.M., airlift operations were being organized from most military commands in the country.

WASHINGTON, D.C.

ONE

Colonel Steve Hamm was sitting at his desk, going through a stack of reports concerning the estimates of five subcontractors supplying parts to Chrysler for the M1 battle tank. It had been two years since Army Personnel buried him in the Pentagon's bureaucratic backwater. They said he'd get used to life in the slow lane after active field work. They were wrong.

His phone buzzed. "Yes, Gabby?"

"General Kuster on line three, Colonel," answered Fiona McAndrews, a meticulous, no-nonsense lady. Hamm had relied on her for years and brought her with him from DIA.

"Thanks," Hamm said, punching the blinking button. "Afternoon, General. How goes it?"

"Fine, Steve. How're you doing?" Kuster's voice sounded strained, not the booming command tone Lieutenant General Eugene Kuster was known for around the agency.

"Trying to follow your advice and keep my mouth shut. Works part of the—"

"I wish you'd done that earlier. You'd still be where I could get my hands on you." Kuster had sided with him, as far as he could, when the good old boys had come down on Hamm with their leather heels.

Hamm liked Gene Kuster, one of a few general officers who still knew what the objectives were and managed to keep them in perspective. "You inviting me to lunch or something, Gene?"

"How is life in the inspector general's office?"

"I'm chasing masterminds of evildoing in military materiel procurement. Recently, I caught a guy gouging us on coffee mugs. What could be more exciting? A little out of line with my education and training, but what the hell, right?"

Kuster was not in a light mood. "Hamm, can we meet in my office at about five? Something's come up."

Hamm knew an order when he heard one, and though Kuster was no longer his direct superior, he said, "I'll be there."

He arrived at DIA headquarters in Arlington Hall five minutes early, but he would not have been so punctual if he had known the topic. It did not help, either, to have Jackson Coriolanus sitting in on the meeting.

Coriolanus belonged, heart and soul, to the Central Intelligence Agency, and his officious nature had grated on him since their first contact in Vietnam Special Operations. When Hamm saw the little man sitting in one of Kuster's visitor chairs, he paused a moment, turned around, and started to leave.

"Hold on, Steve!"

Hamm grabbed the brass doorknob of the outer office door with his big right hand.

"Goddamn it! Colonel!" Gene Kuster yelled, his stony voice rising out of a barrel-sized chest.

Hamm looked back. "I don't need this shit, Gene." He knew whatever involved Coriolanus was always trouble.

Kuster sat tall behind his oak parquet desk. His long, horsey face did not have its usual good humor spread over it. The silvered hair was unkempt, as if he had been running his hands through it. The slight disarray in such a meticulous man puzzled Hamm. In their long history together, Kuster had rarely let his appearance or his speech reflect his inner thoughts. "This is damned important, Steve. Get your ass back here."

Hamm went back into the private office, closing the door behind him. He did not take orders graciously—one of the reasons he was now in the inspector general's section—but he respected Kuster. He sat down. "What the hell's going on?"

Coriolanus considered himself the official, tight-lipped spokesman for the Central Intelligence Agency. He wanted to deliver the news. "Your buddy's turned on us, Hamm. Gone over to the other side."

He wondered what "buddy" Coriolanus was assigning to him. The man sat erect in his chair and used a linen handkerchief to polish the tiny gold eagles of his cuff links.

"Does he have to be here?" Hamm asked Kuster.

The general nodded.

Hamm nodded.

"Bob Terrell has disappeared," Kuster said.

"Shit! When?"

"This morning. By this afternoon, the FBI had him tracked as far as Mexico City," the general said.

"Possible kidnapping? Bob's pretty hot property these days."

Coriolanus laughed. "Try treason and murder. He left a body behind."

Somebody was getting something wrong, and Hamm was damned sure it was the CIA agent. "Maybe he's—"

Coriolanus jumped in again. "He took a file with him, Hamm. A big, bad file."

Hamm stared at the CIA agent, and Coriolanus stared right back at him. The man was a bantam rooster in Ivy League disguise; he never backed down from a challenge. Hamm returned his attention to Kuster.

"That can't be right."

"We want you to find him and bring him back," Kuster said. "You know him well, and you have the best shot at it."

"I don't work here anymore."

"Temporary-duty assignment." Kuster pushed a sheet of paper across the desk.

He did not pick it up. He leaned forward and scanned the TDY order, then saw Admiral Joseph Dilman's scrawl over the signature block. That was a hell of a turnabout. "The chairman of the Joint Chiefs? He likes me like he likes VD. What kind of levers did you push?"

"The President read through your file at my suggestion and saw your association with Terrell. Just like me, he thought you were the man for the job. Dilman didn't have a choice."

"And I didn't either, did I? Forget it, Gene."

"Good goddamned idea," Coriolanus agreed. "The Agency will take care of it."

"Shut up, Jack," Kuster told him. "Now, dammit, Steve, listen up! Your whole damned career's on hold. This may be your only chance to salvage it."

Hamm flipped a thumb at the special order lying on the desk. "That's what this is about—my fucking career?"

Coriolanus grinned. He was beginning to enjoy himself. "Hell, Hamm, you don't even have a career. Why don't you grab your pension while you still have that?"

Kuster leaned back in his chair. His eyes took on a flinty, angry edge. "I thought I knew you pretty well, Steve."

"Sorry."

"It's about your knowledge of Bob Terrell. It's about a file code-named GABRIEL. It's about national security. When have you ever put your country last, Steve?"

Never. Not yet, anyway, he thought. "What's GABRIEL?"

Kuster gave him a grim-lipped smile, as if Hamm had taken the first step in the right direction, merely by asking the question. "High-tech war plan. It could be operational—it likely is operational, in fact, and it could be turned on us."

"You don't know for sure?" Hamm asked.

"This was tightly held in the Strategic Planning Group, Steve. Terrell's numbered copy is missing, and it appears as if he destroyed any other copies. We only know that GABRIEL, in the wrong hands, is decisive. The operative word is *devastating*."

Hamm closed his eyes to think. Bob Terrell would not have gone off any deep end unless GABRIEL really had catastrophic potential. Hell, Terrell had been working with destructive concepts for years. "I.D. on the body?"

"Lawrence Pelagio. Doctorate in mathematics and computer science. He was the system designer on the project," Kuster said.

"You said devastating."

"Truly." Gene Kuster's volume came down, and the one word held every touch of sincerity that Hamm remembered about him.

"Politically or militarily embarrassing, Gene?" he asked.

"All of the above, if Terrell goes public. Whether he goes public or not, if the Soviets get hold of it, you get to learn how to say, 'Yes, master,' in Russian." Kuster clasped his bony hands together on top of the desk blotter. "Forget Pennsylvania Avenue and the Joint Chiefs, Steve. I'm asking."

"I get to do this my way?"

"Try to be somewhat reasonable, Steve. My ass is on the line, too."

"I want one of your Lears. I want DeMott for intelligence analysis."

"Give my secretary your wish list."

"All right," Hamm agreed. "I don't like it."

"None of us does," Kuster said.

''For starters, I've got to figure out the motive. Bob won't go to the Soviets.''

''The hell you say!'' Coriolanus blurted. ''That plan's worth millions to Terrell, and it's worth billions to the Kremlin.''

''Stay out of my way, Jack.''

''If you're going to be involved, we've got to set up a liaison network,'' Coriolanus argued. ''Agency resources have to be utilized in this, and I need to know what's going on.''

''I'll drop you a note from time to time,'' Hamm promised.

''I could recommend that this be run out of my office.''

''I don't see your name on that order,'' Hamm told him, smiling. ''Gene, we'll be in touch.''

TWO

Sometimes, she felt like screaming.

And then Diane DeMott would force herself to remember that she was an objective person, making recommendations based upon facts and perceived patterns, and not reacting to emotional stresses of the moment. An intelligence analyst in her position, especially a woman among the savage egos of a male-dominated department, did not leap to unsubstantiated conclusions.

She worked in the Estimates division of Intelligence Processing.

She sought patterns, logic, rationale.

But, goddamn him, anyway!

Right out of the blue, he was back. There had been no forewarning, no planning, no invitation.

No rationale. Very damned little in the way of explanation, too.

She shoved the stacks of green-striped computer paper to the corner of her desk. Her latest project—Red Banner Northern Fleet spring exercises—had been abruptly terminated.

All in the flash of a phone call. An hour ago she had absentmindedly picked up the handset on the second ring, her mind still in the middle of the Barents Sea. "DeMott."

"It's Steve, Diane."

It took her a few seconds to put the Red Banner Fleet on hold and connect the name. Though they had seen each other occasionally in the two years since he had been forcibly removed from DIA, the frequency of their calls was not what it had been when they were sharing most of their nights together. "Steve? The stranger? The one with telephonitis who—"

"Look, babe, I haven't got much time. I'm on my way out of town. Whatever you've got on your desk, shove it in the wastebasket. You're working for me."

"*For* you!"

"*With* me, then. You'll get a memo on it in a couple of hours. We'll use your office, so see if you can find me a chair. Right away, I want—"

"Hey! Hold on!"

"Diane, we'll have to talk when I get back. First thing you do, get a line on Bob Terrell's latest activities."

"Bob, you said? *Our* Bob Terrell?"

"Yes. Particularly his frame of mind. And don't talk to Nancy just yet. Don't talk to anyone, in or out of the agency."

"How in the hell am I supposed to—"

"Use your contacts. None of the usual sources."

"Dammit, Steve! Tell me something—anything. Are you back? Is Bob in trouble?"

"I'm back on loan. And Bob is gone. He took off."

"Oh, shit!"

"I'll see you in a couple of days." Hamm hung up on her.

The first thing Diane did after his call was to telephone Kuster's office, which was a couple of steps around the chain of command, skipping the assistant director of Processing and the chief of staff. The general was out, but his secretary told her, "If it's about your temporary assignment, Miss DeMott, I'm typing the memo for you now."

"Can you give me the gist of it, Mrs. Clare?"

"You're to be the intelligence analyst and executive officer for Colonel Hamm on a special operation. It's a temporary assignment. The rest is need-to-know from the colonel."

When she replaced the telephone, DeMott felt as if she had regressed in age to her teens. She was being told what was good for her, but not the reasons for it.

Once, she had looked forward to the maturity of a few gray strands among the ashy blond; now, it was irritating to look in the mirror and see the streaks radiating from the temples, but she still refused to color it. There were tiny lines at the corners of the eyes and at the outer edges of the lips. The flesh under the chin was looser, and she found herself jutting her jaw forward to maintain tension. The veterans around DIA probably thought she was too aggressive. Two degrees, six years teaching, and nine years as an analyst—and they pulled rank on her?

Disgusted with her introspection, DeMott grabbed the federal phone listings and began running her fingernail down the long columns of names.

Rich Schumacher was something of an expert in defense policy and planning. He had a mind that reveled in complicated formulae. Diane DeMott had once pictured it as a mind with nothing but numbers in it. There were no pastoral scenes, no memories of life on the Ohio River. There were just rows and columns of numbers.

Schumacher had taught calculus at Columbia University at the same time DeMott was teaching political science, and they had had an affair that lasted several months. That was ten years before. Now he was a top-level civilian in the Defense Department, a senior aide to the undersecretary responsible for strategic planning.

Since her snooping was supposed to be on the quiet side, DeMott had to use some back doors, and she had remembered Rich Schumacher as soon as her searching finger had crossed over his name.

She met him at a restaurant on the west end of New Hampshire Avenue. In the distance, through the large plate-glass windows and through the trees, some dotted with magnolia blossoms, she could see the Potomac.

Schumacher grinned at her as he sat down. He had a fetching grin, but no longer any hair on his head.

"Do you know," he asked, "that I am not a

business-breakfast person? Lunch, all the time. Dinner occasionally, but never breakfast, because it occurs two hours before my mind gets going. How are you, Diane?''

''I'm well. Busy. And you?''

''Quite well. Married, did you know?''

''I didn't. Congratulations. Do you have a family?''

''Two boys, nine and eight. I guess I'll give it all up, though. You look ravishing.''

''Thank you. That makes my day brighter.''

''Married?''

''Still looking.''

''Still letting the job get in the way, I'll bet. And you did say business on the phone, didn't you?'' Schumacher took the menu handed to him by the waitress, but then immediately returned to her. ''Just a couple of eggs, poached, and coffee. I didn't know you were in town, Diane. What department?''

DeMott ordered toast and marmalade and waited until the waitress departed. ''DIA.''

''I'll be damned! A spy!''

''An intelligence analyst, Rich.''

''Same thing. And you want me?''

''I want to poke in your brain a little.''

He ran his hand over his pate. ''Gets a little more sun now.''

She smiled her understanding of age, and they devoted a few more minutes to catching up. She was happy that Rich appeared contented.

After their breakfast arrived, Schumacher asked, ''Now, how can I help keep the national security secure?''

''It may be a very minor matter, Rich. It's something that came up as a peripheral item to another project I'm working on. Do you know a Dr. Robert Terrell?''

''Terrell? It has a familiar tone to it, but I don't place the name.''

''He does something in strategic planning.'' Diane knew Terrell had worked for Team Three—also known as the Soviet Response Team—of the Strategic Planning Group.

''Probably where I heard the name. What's his problem? Or what's your problem?''

''I don't know that there is a problem, Rich. I'd just like to know a little more about him.''

''In what way?'' Schumacher asked.

''The kind of work he does. His reputation in the department. His attitudes. That kind of thing.''

''Is this leading somewhere?''

''I don't know, but I don't want to raise any alarms. That's why I'm asking you.''

''You realize,'' Rich told her, ''that this is a detail not filed in my head? You'll have to give me a couple of hours. And your phone number.''

DeMott went back to her office at eight-thirty and made more calls, but none of the respondents offered her anything new about Bob Terrell.

Schumacher called her at eleven. ''You know something I don't know?''

''Why? What's wrong, Rich?''

''I don't know what's wrong. Hell of a position for my office to be in. I was checking on your man. It's Dr. Robert Boyd Terrell, of the Defense Department's Strategic Planning Group Team Three. Like most of the think-tank types, he's an academic. Harvard doctorate. He has some Peace

Corps time. Taught at Georgetown University, spent a few years at Georgetown's Center for Strategic and International Studies before Defense offered him enough money to move across town. He lives in Arlington Heights. Wife and kids."

DeMott knew all of that. "You know what he's working on?"

"If I did, it would still be classified, Diane."

"What do you think my clearance is?"

"I don't know, but it wouldn't be high enough."

She took a deep breath. It was not the time to antagonize Schumacher. "You're right. And that's not my interest. I'm checking his reputation."

"It's good, as far as I can tell. He's highly intelligent, respected. Bit of a liberal, I understand, but nothing the hawks can't put up with. His stature seems to have improved dramatically in the last couple of years. He has some wide-ranging influence with the Pentagon brass. Works ultrasecret projects."

"No recent changes in behavior?"

"Not that anyone told me. But then, no one over there is saying much today."

"What you mean?" But DeMott could guess.

"A great big blanket of security just dropped all over the Strategic Planning Group. It's closed up tighter than a drum."

"And you can't get through it?"

"Not even me, my dear. We're scheduled for a briefing at one. If there's anything I can pass on to you, I'll give you a call."

"Thanks. I owe you another breakfast."

"Make it lunch, will you?"

When she hung up, DeMott decided she did not know much more than she had already known.

SPG was shut down because Terrell had disappeared.

It was difficult for her to believe. She liked Bob Terrell, and Nancy Terrell was her best friend. There was nothing in their lives that would lead to this.

She should call Nancy.

DeMott almost picked up the phone, then decided she had better talk to Steve first. Where in hell was he?

Then it came to her quite clearly.

He was chasing Terrell.

Steve Hamm was an ex-intelligence operative, one of the best. He was also a good friend of Bob Terrell's.

The bastards in the Pentagon ordered Hamm to find his friend.

THREE

"Where the hell have you been for four days?"

Hamm grinned at her. Diane DeMott looked fresh for late afternoon. He himself felt gritty, the dust of Mexico still lingering in the pockets and seams of his uniform jacket and size seventeen neck collar.

Hamm was a big man at six-two and two hundred pounds. He had once told Gene Kuster, when they were off making the rounds of bars in Tokyo, that his size made him an easier target. His body showed a number of scars that proved his point, the worst of which ran along the underside of his left jaw—the result of a skin-burrowing 7.62-millimeter slug. The hardened, dark tissue, like a mole tunnel, was not all that visible when he held his head level. Most observers found themselves focused on his eyes, which were the color of blued gunmetal. A little on the cold side, and suggesting a core of deadliness, his eyes countered a ready smile.

"You look good," Hamm told her. "Come on. Let's close up the shop and go get dinner. I'm starved."

She frowned. "It's only four."

Leaving the office on unofficial duties before the appointed time to leave the office was a no-no for dedicated bureaucrats. Hamm thought that most bureaucrats fell in the undedicated category. "I'm still eating in another time zone."

He offered his arm, but she chose to ignore it, and they walked out to the parking lot, where Hamm had a motor-pool Chevy waiting. He opened the door for her, then walked around to the driver's side.

"You going to tell me where you've been?"

"Sure. I just don't want to talk in a place where there's so many ears trained to listen."

"What? Steve, those are people you worked with for years."

"Every time I go in the building, Diane, I see old friends. Some say hello, some look the other way. Dennis MacNamara, the guy I worked with for six years? I stuck my head in his office. He said, 'What can I do for you, Colonel Hamm?' I'm blacklisted, and reputations suffer in my presence. This operation probably won't do you any good."

"But you asked for me?" she wanted to know.

"Of course. I only work with the best."

The compliment held her until Hamm turned off on Seventeenth Street and found a parking place within two blocks of the Sans Souci. Hamm had not made reservations, but they were early and the line was shorter than usual. He led her to the end of the line and inclined his head to talk to her. Each of them provided briefs of the two months since they had last talked on the telephone.

Diane reached up to finger the six rows of decorations on his uniform jacket. "I don't object to the uniform, Steve, but someday, why don't you give up the military haircut?"

He had never worried excessively about his appearance. "Because all the gray will show."

"Ah, but then you'll become the distinguished Colonel Steven Hamm."

" 'Distinguished' is not quite the word my colleagues in uniform will ever use when they're recounting my exploits," he said.

They had been waiting twenty minutes, and the line had tripled in length, when an army brigadier general entered the foyer, escorting a redhead half his age. The general eyed the line for a minute, then picked out Hamm and sauntered past the ten couples ahead of him. "Mind if we slip in here, Colonel? We're in a bit of a hurry."

Hamm did not budge. His blue eyes took on a steel edge and the line of his mouth went rigid. "Yes, I do mind. The end of the line's back there, General."

The general, whose name tag identified him as "Oliver," reddened. His eyes dropped to Steve's nameplate. "You got a burr under your saddle, Colonel Hamm?"

"I do for anyone mistaking privilege for right."

His face starting to purple, Oliver said, "I know

about you, don't I, Hamm? You're the one on everyone's shit list?''

''The list gets longer each day,'' Hamm acknowledged.

The general was working up a fever. He said, ''You haven't had a Korean assignment in some time, have you?''

Hamm mused, and his mouth relaxed into a grin. The general had stepped out on thin ice. ''Oliver. Benjamin Oliver, isn't it, General? A tank regiment? I'll bet you haven't had an equipment and appropriations audit in some time, have you?''

The general's cheeks were mottled bluish-purple when he spun on his heel and marched for the front door. The redhead ran after him.

DeMott watched them leave and laughed nervously. ''Could he do that? Get you transferred to Korea?''

''I doubt it. And he knew I doubted it. There's over four hundred fifty generals and admirals in D.C., and he's only one of them. I think I still have a couple of friends over in the Personnel division.''

''And could you audit his command?''

''No, not on my say-so. But he didn't know that. Not a very good general. He didn't have a reading on his enemy before he fired his only shot. No line of supply and no reserves.''

''How come you're always the enemy, Steve?''

''Because they piss me off from time to time.''

''And look where it's gotten you.''

He grinned ruefully. ''True. But I just can't help myself, hon.''

''Someday you're going to run into someone who can ship you overseas.''

''Well, I've been there, too.'' In more than

twenty years of military service, Hamm had learned to accept the inevitable. He did what was necessary, but when it was unnecessary, he let others know about it. Hamm had little patience for favor- and influence-peddling for personal gain, and in a town like Washington, D.C., which floated on a sea of favors, he was a drowning man.

They moved ahead, and the maître d' knew Hamm. "Ah, Colonel!"

"Got a table a long way from anyone else, Jaime?"

When they were seated at a small table that was more remote from its neighbors than most, DeMott said, "I see that you still overtip."

"And they remember me. You pay for what you want in my world. Of course, mine is a very small world." He grinned. "What have you found out?"

She played with her water goblet while she reported. "I talked to twenty-three people on the phone, and I met with another twelve. Some of them knew Bob, and some of them knew about him. Up until April 19, none noticed a change in his behavior or his attitude."

"And after the nineteenth?"

"No one I talked to knew he was gone. There has been nothing on the news, and the SPG has all its locks in place. I didn't try to get in over there."

"All right. That's what you've learned. What do you know?" Hamm asked.

"Only what you told me, you tight-mouthed S.O.B!" She gave him a sneer. "I even tried Kuster, and he told me to wait for you. I tried Dennis Jordan, and all I did was raise his level of curiosity."

The waiter interrupted and Hamm ordered salad,

prime rib, and burgundy for both of them. He remembered that DeMott liked her beef medium rare. After the waiter disappeared, he told her, "Bob got up with his alarm at six o'clock on the nineteenth, had breakfast with Nancy, and left for work. When he did not appear for a scheduled session at eleven, the normal search calls went out. Nancy did not know where he was. His secretary had not seen him. The FBI was notified, and Director Vanderman determined that he had departed Dulles International, at two-thirty, on a Mexicana Airlines flight for Mexico City. He used his own passport."

"No duress?" she asked.

"He was unaccompanied, and telephone interviews with the cabin crew suggest he might have been a little nervous, or agitated, but not obviously under the influence of either drugs or alcohol. I personally interviewed the chief steward on the plane, too."

"Not a kidnapping."

"We don't know where he went after deplaning in Mexico. I just spent four days traipsing around to all of the places Bob and I visited when we went down to that international conference in '84. I found a hotel where he had spent one night, but I didn't get a lead out of it."

"Jesus! Why, Steve? Why did he run?"

"I don't know yet. First, we've got to get a detailed look at the structure of the Strategic Planning Group. The Department of Defense is in a damned poor position when the disappearance of one man can jeopardize so much."

"And second?"

''His copy of the GABRIEL file is missing, and all other copies have been destroyed.''

''Explain GABRIEL,'' she ordered.

Hamm paused while their salads were set in place. He smeared his Roquefort dressing around and tasted a tomato. ''GABRIEL is a contingency war plan developed by Team Three.''

U.S. and U.S.S.R. strategists were always developing contingency plans for anything from silent warfare to tactical warfare to strategic warfare. A silent war was one that did not have the appearance of a ''first strike.'' The contingency plan could be in the form of biological warfare—the introduction of a disease that would assume epidemic proportions; the undermining of nuclear and other energy sources, resulting in chaos and economic collapse; a severe disruption of the basic food chain, bringing on starvation; or an economic strategy aimed at destroying confidence in the stock markets. The KGB and the Soviet leadership had imagination, as did a few of the American deep thinkers. On the Soviet side, to some extent, those strategies were always taking place by way of disinformation tactics and other active measures of the First Chief Directorate's Service A.

''Specifically,'' Hamm continued, ''the GABRIEL plan was under Bob's supervision. It's a computer-based scenario—''

DeMott interrupted. ''Bob doesn't know about computers.''

''No. That's right. The systems designer was Dr. Lawrence Pelagio. His body was discovered in his laboratory at eleven-fifteen the same morning Bob took off.''

DeMott had been with DIA for long enough that she was not shocked. "Cause of death?"

"Looks like a heart attack. The pathologists are still trying to determine whether or not it was unnaturally induced."

"I can't see Bob Terrell killing anyone, especially in a sophisticated way."

"Nor can I," Hamm agreed.

"What about Pelagio's background?"

"I've been through his file—which I'll give you—and I've talked to some people. He was first a whiz at mathematics, then a whiz in computer science. Bred in the Midwest—Iowa, I think it was—and he leaned so far to the conservative side that his right hand could touch the ground. He was well liked by quite a few generals, from what I can tell."

DeMott nodded, then asked, "What more can you tell me about GABRIEL?"

"Only what the deep thinkers are telling me, which is what they think is enough to get me by, and yet not reveal the essence of the plan. They're paranoid about it, and trying to hide it. After all, GABRIEL was *only* an exercise in strategic thinking, and there was no suggestion that it would *ever* be recommended for operational readiness. It's a strategic plan, Diane, involving the use of nuclear devices. The GABRIEL file not only develops the scenario, it contains the computer programs, as I understand it."

"And that is cause for abnormal alarm?"

"According to Kuster, the President and the Joint Chiefs are near alert status. The National Security Council came unglued. The CIA thinks he's going to the Soviets with it."

"No way." DeMott was adamant.

"That's what I said. But I honestly don't know. I couldn't have predicted Bob's taking off this way, so now I don't know what I can predict about him."

"What about computer programmers? They must have had some working on the project."

"Twenty-two programmers were used, each working on a distinct part of the program, and none with an overall view. Pelagio collected all of their work and compiled the final program. He erased the computer files maintained by each programmer. With time, they might be able to reconstruct each segment, but they aren't certain how it all goes together. Still, Admiral Dilman has ordered them to begin the reconstruction. We may need it in order to develop countermeasures . . . if the opposition finds Terrell first."

"What does GABRIEL really do?" she asked.

"No one wants to give me specifics. I'm still an outsider."

Demott sat quietly while the prime rib was served, then asked, "You've been ordered to recover GABRIEL?"

"Yes."

"Even at the expense of Bob's life?"

Hamm did not answer. She had been in intelligence long enough to know what that response meant.

"I've got to go see Nancy. She must be worried sick."

"All right, Diane. But you can't tell her any of this."

"I know," she said quietly.

Nancy was her best friend.

* * *

"So, you finally found him?" Jack Coriolanus's tone was even and reasonable, but his dark eyes contained a degree of suppressed fury. Both were usual traits for Coriolanus, and both had been developed early on, at a time when he already knew he was going to trace the footsteps of his idol, Wild Bill Donovan.

While he had had a New Haven, Connecticut, address and family money in his favor, Coriolanus had had to overcome a Greek heritage and a small stature in order to achieve his employment objective. The Central Intelligence Agency was somewhat selective in the late fifties, heavy on an Ivy League and WASP clique assembled by Allen Dulles. A straight-A average at Yale and an ardent patriotism helped with the first obstacle, and a fierce athletic prowess overcame the barrier created by his size. He had held bantamweight boxing championships at Yale and in Golden Gloves in earlier years. He was accomplished in karate and judo. Continual exercise kept the musculature oiled and the stomach flat. With his five-six height and expensive, impeccable wardrobe, Jack Coriolanus gave the impression of well-compacted stick of dynamite, moments away from detonation.

Coriolanus was also a survivor. He had lasted through the John McCone and Richard Helms eras, and, more important, through the purge that followed William Colby's appointment after Watergate. With deft moves—new friends acquired and favors granted—he had consolidated his power bases.

Gayle Moore fidgeted. Beads of perspiration stood out on his temples. It was one of Coriolanus's small delights to have six-foot, broad-shouldered men stand before, and above, him and display the body language of nervous fear. Coriolanus knew the fear arose from a combination of his physical presence and his status within the Agency. His title was Special Assistant to the Deputy Director of Operations, but his informal influence reached beyond that title in both lateral and vertical dimensions.

"We didn't even know he was out of the country," Moore said.

"So, no one bothered to check? You guys have been playing pool for four days? Or volleyball?"

"Sir, we staked out his house in Georgetown and his office at the Pentagon. We had a watch on Arlington Hall Station. Nobody seems to know where he's based. I don't know. . . ."

"Sat there for four fucking days and didn't even wonder why Hamm didn't show? Jesus! Do I have to do all the thinking around here?" Coriolanus let a little of his incredulity escape into his tone. He added a dose of sarcasm. "Being coach of this goddamned team would be a breeze, if I had some goddamned players."

"We've got him now," Moore said, but his tone was iffy, as if he was not certain how long that status would continue.

Coriolanus was truly awed by the lack of self-confidence in the new generation of agents. "So what's he doing?"

"Uh . . . having dinner at Sans Souci. He had an argument with an army general in the foyer."

"Who won?"

"Hamm, I guess. The general left without eating."

"Congratulations. That sounds like Hamm. He with anyone?"

"With a woman named DeMott. She's an—"

"I know what she is." Coriolanus had occasionally wondered whether Diane DeMott looked as good in bed as she looked out of it. Someday, he would take the time to find out.

Moore fidgeted again, working up his courage. "Could I ask a question, Mr. Coriolanus?"

"What did you have in mind, Moore?"

"Why are we following Hamm?"

The new bunch of operatives always failed to see the more global picture. "Because Hamm knows Terrell. We follow Hamm, we get Terrell."

"Okay, I see that."

"And because there's an off chance Hamm already knows where Terrell is. Terrell went to Mexico, right? You want to give me odds Hamm has been in Mexico?"

"No, sir."

"We've got to keep tabs on Hamm. You lose him again and you'll be in the basement, licking postage stamps, assistant to the damned mail girl."

Moore's throat worked noisily. "Yes, sir. We'll hang on to him."

Coriolanus looked at the man before him, one of the best the agency had to offer in recent years, and did not feel reassured. He had known Hamm for too long. The son-of-a-bitch had lived through a lot of complex operations. "So, I'm going to tell you something, Moore. Your only chance with Hamm is to stay a block away. Get too close, and he'll turn on you."

"Well, hell, sir, we're on the same side."

"He doesn't care who he kills." Worse, Coriolanus thought, Hamm did not care whom he embarrassed.

The assistant to the DDO thought of himself as a realist. He knew Hamm was a competent operative, not to be underestimated. But he also knew the man was a rogue, not to be trusted. He had learned that in the last twenty years.

And this rogue had a big mouth. It was one of Hamm's major flaws.

Another of his shortcomings was that he did not follow orders.

That goddamned piece of paper from the President did not mean a thing. It just cramped Coriolanus's style.

Coriolanus looked at Gayle Moore.

"This should be our operation, and we're going to treat it as such."

FOUR

The first time DeMott met Nancy Terrell, she and Hamm had gone to dinner at the Terrells' place in Arlington Heights.

The house was a two-story colonial with four fake columns on the front, but the interior was not phony. Nancy Terrell had simple and elegant taste, and she had decorated well: muted blue stripes in the wallpaper, pale blue carpeting, antique furnishings that were family heirlooms. There was nothing overly ornate or crowded, just polished and oiled craftsmanship. DeMott liked a Queen Anne card table in walnut finish. On first, external impressions alone, she thought Nancy Terrell was a woman she would like.

Nancy Terrell was a pretty woman, with dark,

finely chiseled features. She was dressed in white culottes that contrasted nicely with her tennis tan. She was bright and outgoing, but DeMott had the feeling she might have been happier in an academic setting, rather than the governmental one in which she was.

The children, Fred and Beth, came up from the basement recreation room to say a polite hello, then disappeared. Somewhat typical teen-agers, DeMott thought, and Elizabeth, the older at sixteen, displayed early physical maturity, but also a touch of disdain.

The old-fashioned adults sat in white wrought-iron furniture on the flagstone patio beside the pool and drank Bob's weak martinis before dinner.

Robert Terrell wore chinos and a gold-checked sport shirt. He appeared at ease and fit, as if he wore his job well and used his swimming pool daily. His demeanor was somewhat professorial, yet lively and good-natured. He wore his hair trimmed slightly over his ears, in a style that DeMott thought Hamm should try. Steve had told her that he preferred to be called Robert, unless the caller was a close friend.

Hamm said, "Christ, Bob! How is it possible to make a martini weak? Don't you buy real gin?"

"I'll have you know, Steve, that this concoction has been admired by people who are very close to people who are heads of state. You don't mess with a proven formula."

"You sent it out for independent lab tests, did you?"

"Your problem," Terrell said, "is based in your military breeding. Your taste in alcoholic beverages revolves around a standard consistent with torpedo propellent."

Hamm grinned. "I've known some damned fine navy men who had access to torpedoes."

Terrell turned to DeMott, and his hazel eyes were lively and magnified behind the thick lenses of his glasses. "See what you've gotten yourself into, Diane? You've linked up with a man who thinks masculinity is defined by weapons systems. His videotape library will be heavy on John Wayne and Audie Murphy. I think he must have pearl-handled revolvers stashed somewhere in his home. Swords crossed over the fireplace."

"Better than what you ex-hippies have stashed," Hamm said.

"Careful, dear," Nancy cautioned, "Diane may be too young to remember Audie Murphy."

"I wish I were," DeMott said.

"Who's Audie Murphy?" Hamm asked.

Terrell was not through. "If you pull down the sun visor in his car, you'll find a picture of Patton."

"It's MacArthur," Hamm said, "not to put down Patton, though."

"You guys always bait each other like this?" DeMott asked.

"Oh, this is mild, Diane," Nancy Terrell said, smiling to show her enjoyment. "I'd appreciate it if you didn't mention foreign policy, or around ninety percent of the names in the current administration."

DeMott confessed, "Steve didn't tell me there were forbidden topics. All I knew was that the two of them had spent time together in Africa."

"Africa did something to their heads," Nancy

Terrell told her. "Some kind of role reversal. Bob came home from their first trip together mumbling about strategic stress points, and Steve came home and told an undersecretary at Defense to shove his head up his ass."

"I did not!" Hamm protested.

"You were quoted in the *Post*."

"I was misquoted. I told him to pull his head out of his 'deleted'—as the *Post* wrote it—and look around at the real world. He hasn't done it yet. In fact, he's been promoted."

"That's because he wasn't quoted," Terrell said. "You have to know how to get along with the media. In your case, a quotation results in a demerit on your Two-oh-one File."

"I get along fine with the media," Hamm argued.

"Oh, sure," Nancy said. "You've had more column inches than Bobby Seale ever did. None of it good."

"But all of it accurate."

"See? You still haven't caught on, Steve. This is not an accurate town," Bob Terrell said. "You want another drink?"

"I'll need about five refills before I finally have a drink." Hamm reached over to touch DeMott lightly on the forearm. "Tomorrow, hon, send this man a case of Beefeater's, will you?"

"I'm not your secretary!" she said.

"I know that. You're my friend in need. I have a need." His wink told her what the real need was, and it matched her own.

Terrell walked around with the pitcher and refilled glasses, then held up his own and offered the toast. "To friends."

* * *

DeMott remembered that first meeting as she pulled her Alfa Romeo into the drive. She shut off the ignition and sat for a moment. Except for a lawn mower buzzing three houses away, it was strangely quiet for midafternoon. The drapes in the house were drawn, as if the Terrells were away, off to Disney World.

She got out of the sports car and crossed the lawn—which needed mowing—to the front door, then rang the bell. She pressed the button twice before the door was opened by a trim young man in a dark suit, white shirt, and muted tie. He was either from IBM or the FBI. She took a guess which one.

"Yes?"

"I want to see Nancy Terrell."

"I'm afraid she's busy at the moment."

"She'll see me."

"It's not a good—"

DeMott pulled her DIA identification from her purse and held it out to him, and that put the young agent in a quandary. Who should he call for the right permissions?

"Who's there?" From the back of the house.

"It's Diane, Nance."

Over the agent's shoulder, she saw Nancy emerge from the family room. DeMott slipped easily past her barrier—he seemed afraid to touch her—and met Nancy halfway down the hall. They hugged each other, and Nancy's grip suggested she was near panic. Her eyes were red-rimmed, dark circles under them, and her hair had been hastily brushed this morning. She was wearing slacks and a blouse that had not been pressed.

Nancy stepped back, her eyes locked on DeMott's, looking for understanding, or perhaps an answer. ''You know?''

''I know. I wanted to come out earlier, but things have been somewhat . . . hectic. Where's Fred and Beth?''

''There's a Little League game, and Beth is taking guitar lessons now. They have FBI escorts, Diane. It's terrible!''

Glancing into the living room, DeMott saw a card table with tape recorders and other monitoring equipment placed next to the sofa's end table, where the telephone was located.

Nancy took Diane's hand and led her back to the family room. It was a comfortable room, soft and upholstered in beige and blue. It was also a mess. Newspapers and magazines were dropped haphazardly on the floor; empty glasses and plates with dried, half-eaten sandwiches were littered about on the tables.

''Why the escorts?'' DeMott asked.

''They think Bob will try to kidnap them. Can you imagine that?''

It was beyond her imagination. ''No, I can't. Nance, how are you holding up?''

''You want something to drink? To eat?''

''No. Let's sit down.'' DeMott settled onto the sofa and dropped her purse on the floor.

''I can't sit. I'm so hyper I can't even sleep. I get up, walk around, open a Coke, take a sip, sit, get up, pace. And I can't even keep my house clean.'' Nancy walked behind the sofa and stared out the sliding-glass door at the backyard.

The FBI agent came to stand in the doorway.

"Why don't you run down to the drugstore or something?" DeMott asked.

His face said he was offended at the suggestion. "Miss, I'm supposed to stay close."

"Not this close. Go take a swim." She pointed out at the pool. "Or better yet, go mow the grass."

He went back to the living room.

DeMott shifted on the couch to look at Nancy's back. "Did you have any idea that this could happen, Nance? Did Bob say anything?"

"Not a word." She was on the verge of crying again. Nancy was a New England girl, raised in security and a close-knit family life. She knew, in general terms, what her husband did for a living, but this kind of reality was a dream. "You know he never talked about what he did. Not to anyone. Oh, God, Diane! They took him!"

"The indications are that he left on his own."

Nancy Terrell spun around to look at her. After a moment's hesitation, she said, "You've always been honest, haven't you?"

"I've always tried."

Nancy closed her eyes and shook her head from side to side. "What am I going to do, Diane? What am I going to do? I haven't even told the children yet. It's just another damned business trip."

"I'll help all I can," DeMott said. And then she decided to say more than Hamm had allowed her to say. To hell with him. "Steve's been assigned to find him."

"Thank God for that!" she said.

Nancy did not understand some of the consequences of the intelligence profession.

* * *

Hamm did not have to wait long to finagle a pass through the barriers placed around the Strategic Planning Group. After a short interview with Admiral Joseph Dilman, chairman of the Joint Chiefs of Staff, in which his shortcomings, his potential, and Dilman's disgust over his present assignment had been reviewed in detail, Dilman had reluctantly approved a meeting at the Strategic Planning Group.

He had an appointment with the director of Team Three at nine-thirty, and he arrived at nine-fifteen. Hamm loathed people who thought that being late for appointments was fashionable.

Thc Strategic Planning Group, always a bastion of security, had a new look. Somebody had brought in an additional contingent of marines from the marine corps barracks at Eighth and I streets. They were a ceremonial unit, but available for emergencies, and now they manned checkpoints at the entrances and wandered the halls in armed pairs.

He was properly saluted in crisp, ceremonial fashion, but had his pass, his I.D., and his temporary DIA credentials checked three times before he was escorted by a gunnery sergeant to Foster's spacious but untidy office. It should have been adequate, with a big couch, half a dozen chairs, a desk, a credenza, and a conference table, but felt crowded. Every horizontal surface was coated with both dust and stacks of files and books.

Dr. Samuel Foster was in his mid-sixties, white-haired with a matching goatee and huge eyebrows—which met over the center of his nose and trailed across his forehead to point at his ears. His face was pale and deeply lined. He sat sternly and quietly behind his huge paper-strewn desk, but Hamm was still able to detect the aura of agitation in the man. He and his office were under fire, and he did not like it. Team Three devised war plans; they did not expect ever to be under siege.

Hamm learned no more than he already knew. Foster had detected no obvious changes in Terrell's behavior.

"What about his project, Doctor? Tell me about GABRIEL."

"Classified." Foster was clear on that point.

"Neither you nor I has the time to screw around about this, Dr. Foster. Do we involve the President in this little discussion, or do you tell me what I need to know? I'm here to get your ass out of a jam."

Foster glared at him, picked up a phone, and dialed it, then spun his chair around so that Hamm could not read his lips as he talked. A super-cautious man. The routines of his job had been woven into his psyche.

Three minutes of heated mumbling passed. Whoever he was talking to—Dilman, or Dilman's flunky, Winfield Storch?—had to get his words in edgewise.

When Foster turned back to him and slammed the phone in its cradle, he was less happy than he had been. "GABRIEL is a contingency war plan."

This was going to be like pulling dead stumps out of baked earth. "Not many of those around this place, are there?"

"You have to understand, Colonel, that I don't have a great amount of concrete facts. As director, I oversee some forty projects currently under way."

"All of them with the same susceptibility to flight?"

Foster's back went rigid. "What do you mean?"

"Seems shortsighted to me when a secret is so closely held that the disappearance of one man can compromise the national security."

"As I understand, Colonel, your task is not the security measures in place at this institution. You are simply to recover Dr. Terrell and the file."

Simply? Hamm thought. "All right, Doctor, let's start with April 19. One man had control of the file—"

"There were two men—"

"And one of them is dead."

"There were dozens of people working on this, Colonel."

"None of whom knew what they were working on, isn't that right?"

Foster picked up a stubby pencil and twisted it in his fingers. "I didn't design the organization."

"But your bosses are treating you as if you did it, I'd bet." General Kuster's first priority had been to collect each of the numbered copies of each contingency plan under development by the Strategic Planning Group and get them in a vault. They would not be released again until some serious thinking about SPG's structure had been accomplished.

The director did not bother responding to the obvious.

"Tell me what the hell GABRIEL does."

Tapping a thin file folder on the edge of the desk, Foster said, "I've reread the memos to my office. GABRIEL is a little . . . unique."

"In what way?"

"Normally, the various teams of the Strategic Planning Group work in words, in the abstract. They take the germ of an idea and help it blossom into a scenario. They take a fantasy and shape it into a possibility. If someone in the Department of Defense likes the possibility, it might be farmed out to another group for development. Occasionally, Defense will ask us to take a plan and give it more substance.'' Foster spoke as if Hamm were somewhat on the dense side.

''Somebody liked GABRIEL?''

''Naturally.'' His tone said that Team Three never had a bad idea. ''Larry Pelagio came up with the concept, it was bantered about, and then submitted to Defense. They wanted it developed.''

Therefore, it was Defense's fault, from the beginning. Hamm waited in silence. Merely keeping one's mouth shut was often a good interviewing technique.

Foster waited also, but gave in first. ''That was two years ago. The original concept concerned an enhanced methodology for gathering intelligence about an enemy's tactical and strategic moves in a time of war. Currently, we use HUMINT—intelligence from human sources—and ELINT—from electronic monitoring—to accomplish that task. Information obtained from satellite surveillance, SR-Seventy-one overflights, the interception of radio and microwave communications, and the like is culled, then refined into intelligence estimates that give battlefield commanders and rear-echelon planners the best possible options for their decision-making.''

''Go on,'' Hamm urged.

''GABRIEL, as it was proposed, went beyond just trying to listen in on communications. Listening has its drawbacks. Messages are coded, and the codes must be broken. Advanced technology has made possible some other obstacles to monitoring. High-speed message transmissions can be accomplished in a fiftieth of a second. Radio frequencies automatically switch from one frequency to another in random patterns. Fiber-optic transmission has opened an entirely new dimension.''

Hamm knew all of this, but played the rapt pupil as long as Foster was gushing.

''The GABRIEL proposition started simply enough. Rather than sit back and listen, we would get *inside* the enemy communications network. GABRIEL, using computer technology, would put us in a position where we were tapping enemy messages before they were encoded, before they were put on the radio. Right inside the Kremlin itself, without the Soviets even knowing we were there.''

Foster had finally identified a specific enemy. Hamm said, ''That's a concept I like. But you said that was only the way it started. What happened along the way?''

''Well, let me back up a little.'' Foster was dragging his feet about getting to the nitty-gritty. ''The Department of Defense wanted to keep it very quiet. They provided the funds for us to develop the plan in-house. Larry Pelagio was named director of the project. And Robert Terrell wanted to enlarge his sphere of knowledge—he had been working with African planning on Team Five since the beginning of his association with the SPG. He came over to the Soviet Response Team, and I assigned him as Pelagio's supervisor, Team Three's liaison with the project.''

''And then?''

"And then, about fifteen months into the project, some other . . . potentials became apparent."

"Potentials?" Hamm asked.

"Some other utilizations for the programming that had been written."

"You want to explain those uses?"

Foster started to clam up. "My instructions are to tell you no more than that GABRIEL now has a nuclear capability."

Hell of a jump, Hamm thought, from communications tapping to nuclear threat. "What kind of capability? What does it do?"

"It seems to me, Colonel Hamm, that you know all you need to know. GABRIEL is extremely important. Your job is not to know what it does, but to recover it."

"Recovering it may hinge on my knowing what all of the ramifications are, Doctor."

"Sorry. You're not cleared."

"I've got to know, dammit!"

"Then go ask the chairman of the Joint Chiefs. I've said all that I am going to say."

When he left the building, striding along the long, polished corridors, Hamm was in the mood to knock down marines, but restrained himself.

Alexi Ivanovitch Naratsmov arrived at Dulles International Airport aboard Aeroflot's nonstop flight from Moscow. He passed quickly through customs, using the diplomatic line, and carried his single small piece of luggage directly to one of the bars that was spotted along the concourse. Finding a vacant standing spot at the bar, he ordered Scotch—a taste acquired in London—and waited while the plastic glass was filled for him. America was a hint of taste surrounded by plastic. It had always seemed so to him.

After he had paid with U.S. dollars from the large roll provided to him, he turned his back to the bar and perused the terminal. The swirl of travelers darting up and down, back and forth, did not interest him. The small, standing groups did. Some of them were meeting friends or relatives, some were seeing that friends or relatives got off safely, and some were present for other tasks.

It required only a few minutes to identify four possibles. Clean-cut men relaxing at convenient observation posts, watching just who got off an airplane from Moscow. They would be FBI or CIA, or both.

There was no one from the embassy present to meet Naratsmov. He preferred to travel without recognition. As far as the Komitet Gosudarstvennoy Bezopasnosti, the Soviet KGB, was concerned, he was a legal rogue, a member of Department Twelve of the First Chief Directorate. The department was comprised of free-lance veterans, given their heads to achieve political ends by their own proven means.

Naratsmov would never be spotted as a Russian. There was no squat blockiness in his build. He was six feet, two inches tall, and very lean at one hundred fifty pounds. His hair was dark and lank and cut short, with a forelock that fell over his forehead. He was not a vain man, and he wasted little time on style. His barbering appeared haphazard, and the coat sleeves and pants cuffs of his ready-made suits were always a trifle short. The shortcomings were subtle, not often noticed, but he would not have cared if they were.

He had a twin sister named Alexandria who still lived with his parents in Minsk, in the White Russian Soviet Socialist Republic. Her stature matched his own, and he was afraid that she was destined for spinsterhood. Alexi himself held no interest in marriage. A wife and family would only intrude upon his real purpose in life. If a sexual need arose, as it infrequently did, Naratsmov had rubles, or dollars, or marks, or afghanis available to satisfy it.

From the time of his matriculation at the Moscow Institute, through his training at the Foreign Intelligence School at Yurlova, off the Volokolamskoye Highway, Alexi had committed himself to the Soviet system. The members of the KGB were a tightly knit sect, and those given the elite status of assignment to Department Twelve were above reproach. There was no other way of life. If a failure to promote the system became too apparent, there was always the wall behind the Lubyanka or the *gulag*.

Alexi Naratsmov had proven himself through his years of service. His record spoke for itself, and he had required only the briefest of instructions from Colonel General Nikolai Andresev, the chairman of the First Chief Directorate and deputy chairman of the KGB. Andresev had given him a photograph.

Alexi studied it, committing the face to memory.

"That is Robert Boyd Terrell, Colonel Naratsmov. His code name is Blue Heron."

Naratsmov nodded.

"Until the nineteenth of this month, he was a member of the U.S. Soviet Response Team, a part of their war-planning apparatus. On the nineteenth of April, he disappeared."

"He is very important, Comrade General?"

Andresev slid a folder distinguished by a black border across the desk to Naratsmov. "At any time, he would be important to us for what he knows, Alexi Ivanovitch. In this case, our various sources say the Americans appear to be in a frenzy to find him. That makes him doubly valuable. We must have him."

Alexi picked up the folder, noted Terrell's name on it, and dropped the photo inside. He offered one of his rare smiles. "And so you shall, Comrade General."

Now he waited patiently for a break in the airport surveillance. It would come, and he would disappear into American decadence once again. Actually, he intended to go to the Soviet embassy on Wisconsin Avenue, but he did not want the U.S. intelligence apparatus to know he was there.

Hamm paced the perimeter of DeMott's office. "We need to get you a bigger office, Diane. The landscape is monotonous." He stopped by the two holes in the wall. "What did you take down?"

She was sitting at her desk, poring over surveillance reports that had come into the DIA's communications room from all over the globe. For the first week, they had relied on the refined intelligence reports available on the computer terminal behind her desk, then realized they were not getting all of the information. Someone was siphoning off intelligence estimates indiscriminately, hiding them behind security access codes that were not being provided to them. Now, Hamm and DeMott spent four or five hours a day reading all of the raw data, the operative reports in the original forms. Paper was stacked along two walls of the office, in piles three and four feet high, many of the stacks threatening to collapse.

"What did you say?" She looked up from the flimsy report she was reading.

Hamm pointed at the holes. "What was here?"

"A couple of pictures that depressed me."

"Oh." He turned to look at her. She looked good to him. Her posture at the desk, leaning slightly forward, allowed one breast to touch the blotter, and her ash-blond hair draped slightly forward, shading her cheeks. "You don't look depressed."

DeMott sat back in her chair, resting her forearms on the padded chair arms. "Are we going to start this again?"

"Start what?"

"It was a good time in my life, Steve. And yours, too. I relish the memories, but let's keep them memories, huh?"

They had been lovers for eighteen months, with a great deal of affection for each other, camaraderie and common interest, but without a growing sense of *love*. "The memories are enough?"

"I like you better as a friend. For anything else, you're too damned unpredictable."

"Barbara once told me that. Twenty years ago." Barbara had been his wife of three years.

"She should have told me. It was wasted on you."

Hamm grinned at her. "Maybe just one time, for old times' sake? See if my memory is holding?"

"Go to hell or to one of your chippie girlfriends. We have work to do."

"Talk about depressing." Hamm waved at the stacks of paper. "Two weeks of nothing. I'm going down to Communications."

"Good. Get out of my hair."

"Not what I had in mind."

She went back to reading.

Hamm went out to the corridor and found an elevator that took him to the basement.

The basement corridors were lined with beat-up file cabinets and cardboard cartons of reports, White Papers, catalogs, directories, and miscellaneous—probably unnecessary—collections of words. The cramped hallways of Arlington Hall looked just like the hallways of any other agency in Washington. There was not a governmental department that Hamm knew of that had adequately planned for the storage of the tons of paper it produced. Computers were supposed to help, but the bureaucrats did not trust the computers. They needed a hard copy of each document, no matter what its importance.

The Communications section occupied a number of large spaces. The few hundred people working there fell under the command of the assistant director for acquisition, responsible for defining intelligence requirements and then managing the collection of data to be passed on to the assistant director of Processing. That division produced the intelligence estimates for all of the services and the National Security Council, along with crystal-ball reports out of its Current and Indications department. Until 1961, when DIA was formed to avoid duplication of effort, the individual services had produced their own estimates. Of course, the establishment of DIA had not eradicated the army, navy, marine, or air force intelligence agencies. That was a topic on which Hamm and Terrell had frequently argued.

He bypassed the big area where clerks collated and filed reports after entering the data into the computer data base and went on to the Signals Reception section. Voice and telex communications were received there, and the voice messages were transcribed onto paper. A navy lieutenant commander named Voros was in charge of the shift. He looked up from his post at a gray metal desk as Hamm came through the door. "Help you, Colonel?"

"Just wandering, Commander."

The man appeared pained that Hamm had the clearance to wander through his domain. "Very well, sir."

Hamm browsed about the big room as if it were a dime store, stopping to read the printed lines appearing on chattering teletypewriters. The terminals were set in long rows, and the clatter was mildly dulled by clear plastic soundproofing boxes. The endless paper spewed forth and piled up in wire baskets behind each machine. It was a full-time job for two people, just keeping the hungry machines fed with pin-feed paper. He paused occasionally behind operators with headsets who were typing madly on transcription typewriters as they took oral reports.

London. Berlin. Johannesburg. Moscow. Copenhagen. Manila. Seventh Fleet. The 1st Armored Division. The 2nd Infantry Division. Clark

Air Base. The sources were identified and the dirty laundry of the world was gathered into this room.

As he wandered about the communications center, Hamm noted also that one clerk or another would frequently approach Commander Voros with an item that was apparently hot news. Voros sometimes initialed the message sheet and sent it immediately off into the labyrinth. With some messages, he read them quickly and dropped them into a suspense file that stood on the credenza behind his desk.

Hamm thought that to be interesting.

He sauntered back to Voros's desk, walked around it, and started flipping through the sections of the suspense file. The sections were labeled alphabetically.

"Colonel, that's none of your business."

He found H and pulled out six message forms. "That's what General Kuster told you, is it, Commander?"

"Sir, I have my orders."

"Whose orders are they? That's what I was asking, Voros." Hamm shuffled through the random messages: Hapsburg—bus strike; Helsinki—mass murder; Havana—cabinet shuffle; Hanoi—Politburo member dies; Le Havre—disabled Swedish frigate.

And Hamm—Venezuela computer rental.

"Whose orders, Commander?" Hamm asked again. He read the terse memo. It had come in seven hours before.

"I'm not at liberty to say, Colonel."

"I'll bet. And that's exactly what's at stake, Voros. Your liberty."

The commander's face turned ashen as Hamm

walked out of the room. He did not bother going back up to DeMott's office, but called her from a telephone in the hallway.

"DeMott," she said, and he could tell her mind was still in the middle of something she was reading.

He did not identify himself. "Somebody in the agency is screwing with us, Diane. See if you can find out who it is while I'm gone."

"Gone? What do you mean, 'gone'? Where are you going?"

"Caracas."

FIVE

"There's an oil company in Caracas named VenCo Limited. It's owned mostly by American investors, and it owns a hefty IBM computer that doesn't get full use, so they lease time on it. Terrell bought himself eight hours of time."

Colonel Winfield Storch listened impassively to Hamm. He was a dapper man, crisp creases in his summer khakis, and sharp lines in his hawk-nosed face. The ribbons above his left breast pocket were earned mostly for merit: army commendation medal, meritorious service, Vietnam service, and the like. Framed glass boxes mounted on one wall held the actual medals. There was an enlarged photograph of Storch and his crew in front of a UH-1H Huey, the steel mat runway of An Khe in the background. Storch obviously liked his memories. Hamm could do without most of his own.

Hamm glanced sideways at the photo and Storch's frozen, beaming grin. What had he done that was worth smiling about? Hamm had never considered the man a natural chopper pilot.

Storch was a paper pusher, an excellent staff officer, but not much of a line officer. He had three months of seniority over Hamm, and he was the chief aide for special projects to Admiral Joseph Dilman.

Hamm had been ordered to report to the chairman of the Joint Chiefs, but what he got was Storch, and Storch still remembered a time or two in Vietnam when Captain Hamm had loudly questioned Captain Storch's combat effectiveness. Storch did not say anything about it, but the incidents were not likely to be ones he would forget.

"And you let him slip away?"

He had not been asked to sit down. He was wearing a civilian suit, and he stood at ease in front of Storch's desk. "It wasn't a matter of letting him slip away, Winnie. I got there a week behind him."

"Why?" Storch's dark eyes held Hamm's in a tug-of-war. The man enjoyed his position of power, though he was probably less than pleased at Hamm's use of his nickname.

Hamm was not going to make excuses about messages diverted in the communications room. For all he knew, Storch had ordered them diverted. Winnie was the kind of man who could bask in the light of Hamm's failure. "We haven't told our assets why we're looking for Terrell, and we haven't put a priority on it, so as not to alert the opposition—

who probably know anyway. The sighting was made by an inactive asset of naval intelligence. The man did not put a rush on it."

"What the hell was Terrell doing with the computer?"

"I don't know. Playing with GABRIEL, maybe?"

Storch pinched the bridge of his sharp nose. "GABRIEL requires a supercomputer, like the Cray. It doesn't run on an IBM."

"That's news to me," Hamm said. "It's one of the goddamned details I should have had from the beginning."

The admiral's aide ignored the comment. "The man's been at-large for nearly three weeks, Hamm. Admiral Dilman is wondering what is so hot about your technique, or your knowledge of Terrell, if you haven't picked him up yet."

Here comes the pressure, Hamm thought. He had expected it earlier.

"One week from today, the admiral will expect to have a full report of your activities and your assessment of where Terrell will go to ground. If you haven't recovered GABRIEL by then, he will have to go to the President with a recommendation for a different plan of action."

"Give me GABRIEL, Storch. I have to know what's in it."

The man's mouth was a thin, prissy line. Currently, it was what passed for a smile. "That's all, Hamm."

"Yes, sir." And *fuck you*. Hamm came to attention, though not with a snap.

"And wear a uniform the next time you report to this office. Dis-miss."

Hamm executed a precise military salute and received a half wave in response. He pivoted on his heel and left the office, staring straight ahead.

DeMott could tell Hamm was in a bad temper from the way his heels clacked on the linoleum as he came down the corridor toward her. She stood in the doorway and waited for him.

"How's the chief joint?" she asked when he reached her.

Hamm's eyes were in the iron-edged state she had seen so often. "I wouldn't know. I wasn't allowed into his presence." Abruptly, he changed topics. "We need a complete listing of every supercomputer in the world."

"Why?" The question came from Jack Coriolanus, who stood behind her in the office.

The CIA agent had been there for twenty minutes and had made at least three passes at her. DeMott's negative signals had not fazed him in the least. He kept moving close, touching the back of her hand, touching her shoulder, suggesting dinner at exclusive restaurants, expecting her to be overwhelmed by his interest. She had finally opened her private door to the hallway in self-defense.

Coriolanus's presence did not improve Steve's day. The corners of his mouth turned down in distaste. "I'm considering a career in computers, Jack. Saw this ad on TV."

"Not a bad idea for you. Before you go, however, I want to know what you found out in Caracas."

"Caracas? The one in South America?"

The agent waved a copy of the DIA message. "Our agencies share information, remember?"

Hamm set his bulk into a chair. "I found out things the CIA should have known days ago, what with all the resources around the world that you brag about."

"Just tell me, Hamm." Coriolanus stood with his shoulders back and his chin jutted forward, ready to make an offensive move.

"I found out Terrell had been there. I didn't find out where he was staying, if he was still there, or where he's gone, if he left. Okay? You can go now, Jack."

Coriolanus smiled. "So don't you think it's about time you threw in the towel? Shit! You haven't done anything in three weeks. Let the professionals take over, Hamm."

"You mean the professional who swore Bob was going over to the Soviets? He hasn't walked through any of their embassy doors yet, and you do have those doors covered, don't you? I mean, you're supposed to have them covered."

Coriolanus's face darkened nicely, DeMott thought. He did not like being reminded of an inaccurate evaluation. The CIA special assistant said, "You're giving him enough time to make that decision, Hamm. You're not living up to your billing. Call it a TKO, and get out of the ring."

"You live in a past full of Golden Gloves glory, Jack? You ought to drop the allusions and catch up with your age." Hamm stood up. His back was straight, his dander was up, and DeMott considered backing out of range of wild swings.

"I can still whip you," Coriolanus promised.

"You've never tried."

"Why don't you two kids go out on the sandlot?" DeMott suggested.

The two of them stared at each other, neither giving in for a full two minutes. Finally, Coriolanus said, "I've got work to do. Something *you* ought to try, Hamm."

After he left, DeMott asked, "What happened?"

He told her about the computers. "Dammit, we should have had them covered from the start."

"We'd still have missed him, then, if he went for an IBM. Why would he do that?"

Hamm stood in the middle of her office and thought that one over. "Bob doesn't know computers. Maybe he thought it would work."

"Which raises a bigger question," she said.

"I know. Why in hell does he want to make it work? And what is he going to do with it, if it does work? Dammit! Diane, I need to know what GABRIEL does."

"What do we do now?"

"Go home and go to bed."

"Not with me," she said, though she had strongly considered it in the past couple of weeks.

"That's kind of sad," Hamm told her, then walked out.

Hamm was not fully asleep. Lingering on the edge of a dream in which his memory helped to direct the action, he had drifted through dated and recent scenes in which he and Bob Terrell had been paired. The drunken night in Pretoria when Robert Terrell asked him to use the nickname "Bob." The intellectual sparring in Salisbury, Quelimane, or Nairobi, Hamm's conservative stance facing Terrell's more liberal position. Like high noon in a dusty Tombstone street.

The minute hand on the nightstand clock was five minutes beyond one when the phone rang. He checked the time through squinched eyelids as he rolled over in the king-sized bed and pawed at the phone. When he found it, he grunted, "Hamm."

"DIA duty officer, Colonel. Captain Hoke. I've got what I'm told is a priority message for you."

Steve Hamm sighed and sat up on the edge of the bed. He did not carry his weight very well at that time of the morning. The bed sagged under him. "What is it, Captain?"

"It's simply 'Terrell,' sir."

That was enough, and he was wide awake. "What's the source?"

"A man named Holloway." The captain gave him a phone number and an address in Laurel, Maryland.

"When did it come in?"

The captain's voice became uncertain. "Uh . . . twenty-three-oh-seven hours, sir."

"Who'd you call first, Captain?"

"Well . . . uh . . . sir, there's a list I'm supposed to follow."

Shit! Central Intelligence would already have it. "You'd better get that damned list rearranged, mister. My name goes at the top."

"But, Colonel—"

Hamm hung up and dialed long distance. The phone was answered after the first ring.

"Mr. Holloway?"

"That's me."

"I'm Colonel Steve Hamm. I'm with the army, at the Pentagon."

"About time you guys called. I've ended up in the middle of an old movie, waiting on you."

Apparently, he was still ahead of the other spooks. "I understand that you have some information about Robert Terrell?"

"Damned right. I saw him on TV."

"On TV?"

"It was an ABC news shot of a riot in Cape Town. I almost missed it at six—knew the face, but couldn't recall the name, so I watched the eleven o'clock news. Then I called my boss, and he suggested calling the Pentagon. It took you guys two hours to get back to me."

A delay Hamm would investigate later. "You're positive the man you saw was Terrell?"

"He's got this bushy moustache now, and black horn-rimmed glasses, but yeah, it was Terrell. I knew the eyes—they're deep brown. And the face—kinda wide and chunky, you know? Hair's a lot longer, hiding his ears almost completely. He's got a pretty good tan now, too."

He had had a deep tan the first time Hamm had met him. "How do you know him?"

"I'm with NSA." Which explained the Laurel address, near Fort Meade, where the National Security Agency had its gigantic facility for eavesdropping on the world. "I'm a supervisor, GS-Thirteen, out there. Back a few years ago, Terrell was out at our place, doing some kind of research. We spent maybe four or five days together while he picked my brain."

"And you're sure this is the same man?"

"My job involves details, Colonel. And since I had worked with Terrell, I sure as hell remember when he skipped."

Hamm had not gone to bed alone. He half turned to see Merrilee sitting up against the headboard, the sheet pulled up to her chin. She grinned tiredly at him. "Skipped?"

"I know nothing was ever reported, Colonel. But I'm also part of the intelligence community."

"Thank you very much, Mr. Holloway."

Hamm dialed Diane DeMott, but the answer was electronic, so he left his name. Turning on the light, he looked up the number for TWA, and tried that.

"How can I help you?" a sweet voice asked.

Merrilee dropped the sheet, slid over beside him, and started playing.

Hamm played back, his big hand cupping and caressing. "I want to go to South Africa. Cape Town."

There were a few background beeps from a computer terminal, then: "We don't have any direct flights, at eleven tomorrow—"

"How about in an hour?"

"An hour, sir?" She searched her magnetic memory and got him on a flight to Lisbon, connecting to Lagos, then Johannesburg, then Cape Town. Three different airlines. She told him he would be in-flight by three A.M.

Merrilee already had him airborne, and he had to hang up in order to reciprocate; that took some time.

DeMott called while he was shaving. "What's up, Steve?"

Merilee was sound asleep, curled up on the far side of the bed. She snored in a tiny, nasal way. "I'm going to Africa. You'll have to cover for me." He filled her in on Holloway's telephone call.

"Given Holloway's intelligence background, I think there's a good chance he recognized Bob."

"He's changed continents on us." She did not sound optimistic.

"First thing in the morning, Diane, get hold of that ABC tape and see what's on it. I want the name of the reporter, also. You can leave any messages with the consulate in Cape Town."

"All right."

By the time Hamm had thrown a few changes of clothing in a carry-on and dressed in a charcoal suit, which he realized too late would be inappropriate for the climate in South Africa, even in its winter, Merrilee had only rolled over once and gone back to sleep. He decided not to awaken her and hoped she would lock the door when she left in the morning. There was not a lot to steal in his small Georgetown house, but what there was, he would miss.

In the lower foyer, across from the small living room, Hamm slid open one of the drawers in an antique secretary and found his passport. On impulse, he dropped to one knee, pulled the lower cabinet door ajar, and fished around at the back of the bottom shelf. The secretary had a false back in it, two inches deep, and it served as his safety deposit box. He riffled through a few of the documents stuffed behind the false back and selected one of the extra passports he kept on hand. Bundled with the passport by a rubber band were the accompanying driver's license, pilot's license, Social Security card, and credit cards that fit the name—this set belonged to a Dean Whalen of Omaha, Nebraska. He replaced the panel and stood up, then opened the door to the garage. His agency sedan was unmarked, but obviously government in steel gray. His new Trans Am had less than five hundred miles on it, and the way things had been going lately, he would never put more on it.

He used Uncle's gas.

Jack Coriolanus received his copy of the message at one-thirty. The phone memo sat in a duty officer's In basket at Langley from the time of its reception at eleven-fifteen until the officer tracked Coriolanus to the pub out on Twenty-third Street where he and a few agency friends were rehashing old times. Coriolanus's friends tended to be his age and from New England.

When he finally received the message, Coriolanus swore a few elegant oaths, then made his first call to Darrell Holloway, his second call to his boss, the deputy director of operations for the CIA, and his third call to the office that made flight arrangements for the agency.

Then he grabbed a cab for Dulles International, bitching quietly to himself for most of the ride.

Alexi Naratsmov received his version of the information in a more indirect way. He was awakened in the middle of the night from a deep sleep in one of the guest rooms of the Soviet embassy on Wisconsin Avenue. It was a steel-and-glass structure that Naratsmov thought paid too much homage to American architecture.

It had also been his prison in the time he had been in the United States. He did not rove outside the embassy, and he missed the freedom of movement he had in Berlin, his usual residence. Here, he used the embassy simply because it was the home base of a sophisticated communications system.

The lieutenant who awakened him said, "Comrade Colonel, Gray Tiger is on the move." He used an American idiomatic expression that Alexi found sounded awkward in Russian. Soviet officials assigned to the United States picked up poor habits too easily.

Gray Tiger was Steven Hamm. "Tell me."

Once Naratsmov had learned that Hamm was active again, and in charge of the search for Terrell, he had reviewed Hamm's file, then ordered a sensitive beam microphone, which picked up vibrations at human voice frequencies, aimed at Hamm's town house windows. The house was regularly swept for listening devices, but this one was located a block away. Both Hamm and Terrell's files had listed many coinciding assignments, and Hamm had become his key to locating Terrell.

The lieutenant said, "Your target is apparently in Cape Town, South Africa. Colonel Hamm arranged to fly to Cape Town."

"When?"

"He is already on the way to the airport."

"Call Aeroflot for me," Alexi ordered, then began to dress.

Hamm did not go to National Airport.

Instead, he used three alleys, one parking lot, and a vacant McDonald's to elude the Chevy Citation that had been waiting for him outside his house. Then he drove the nearly deserted streets at a fast clip, taking K Street over to 395 south, dipping through the tunnel under the Mall, and bypassing to Capitol Street. He used the Douglass

Bridge to cross the Anacostia, driving with the window down, and breathing in the magnolia-scented breeze. The May nights were warm, his favorite month in the capital, after April. October was not bad, either. The rest of the months, he would just as soon do without.

Hamm checked frequently, but did not see another shadow. His recently acquired covert friends probably thought they would be able to pick him up at National. He had not bothered to check out the origins of the surveillance assigned to him, assuming the KGB would be interested in him after they had obtained a copy of his orders. And, he supposed, Coriolanus would want to keep track of him, too.

When he reached the Capitol Beltway, Hamm took it over to Andrews Air Force Base and drove directly to Operations. Inside, he found the duty officer, an air force major, and presented his I.D., passport, pilot's license, and special orders.

"What can I do for you, Colonel?"

"I want a Lear Twenty-five just about as fast as you can get it ready. Either seven-nine or nine-three."

"Colonel, the air force doesn't have—"

"Try DIA."

From the look on his face, the major might have thought Hamm was asking for an F-15, which he would have liked to do. "Uh . . . sir—"

"Read those orders carefully, Major."

"Yes, sir." As the major read, Hamm waited for the expected reaction. It usually occurred at about the time the reader reached ". . . at the express direction of the commander in chief . . ." He generally got a raised eyebrow at the signature, too: Admiral Joseph C. Dilman, chairman of the Joint Chiefs of Staff.

The major's mouth parted. Then both eyebrows rose. "I'll get right on this, Colonel."

"Thanks." Hamm began filling out a flight plan, pausing to remember the aircraft's new range at maximum cruise, while the major scanned through a vinyl-covered binder, then took another look at his license to verify the multi-engined jet rating. Strange rating for an army man, no doubt. He picked up a phone and issued orders.

When he hung up, he asked, "This is a priority-one mission, Colonel?"

"Correct."

"Do you have a co-pilot, sir?"

"No."

The major's eyebrows raised slightly, but he didn't say a word.

Hamm gave him his flight plan, then went down the hall to a small shop, bought a Thermos, had it filled in the canteen, and picked up a half dozen plastic-wrapped sandwiches. Hampshire Airlines did not have the amenities of a TWA and Air France. The head was a Porta Potty under a rear-seat cushion. By the time Hamm had checked in with the weatherman, retrieved his bag from the car, and picked up charts, the Lear jet had been towed to the ramp by a tractor.

"Thank you, Major."

"Have a good trip, sir." His expression was carefully controlled, but Hamm sensed his certain knowledge of foolhardiness.

The plane was not marked for either the military or the federal government, of course. It was cream colored with a single blue line down the fuselage and the blue logo HIC on the tail—Hampshire Insurance Company. It belonged to Defense Intelligence.

The ground crewman opened the door for him, and Hamm stepped up, letting the tech sergeant secure the door. The wheel struts sagged with his weight, and Hamm had to half crawl through the cabin because of the low ceiling. After stowing his carry-on behind a seat, he went to the rear of the plane and levered the cushion off the seat next to the Porta Potty. The exposed cavity contained a few items of a covert nature, and Hamm dropped his extra passport and papers into the well, then replaced the cushion. His true passport was in his inside breast pocket. The paperwork out of the way, he slipped into the curtained cockpit, laid his Thermos and sack of sandwiches on the co-pilot's seat, and levered himself into the left seat.

The twin GE's cranked right up, and Hamm called Ground Control. It already had his flight plan, and the priority number worked its magic. "Lear seven-nine, you are cleared for taxi to runway one-five."

"Seven-niner, Roger."

At three-ten, after a C-141 took to the runway ahead of him, Hamm switched his NavCom's to Andrews Control, and was cleared for takeoff. "Wind three knots at oh-one-oh, seven-nine. Have a good flight."

"Seven-niner, Andrews, thank you."

Hamm shoved the throttles forward, and the lightly loaded plane was airborne in under a mile. Pulling his gear up and trimming out while he banked to the south, Hamm found forty thousand feet nineteen minutes later, and settled into maximum cruise at a ground speed of five hundred thirty miles per hour. Flipping the toggle on the IFF—Identify Friend or Foe—he activated the transmission that identified his blip on a radar screen full of blips. He dialed in the VOR frequency for Norfolk on the Nav-1 radio and set his Omni bearing Indicator.

The airplane had originally had space for ten passengers, with nineteen hundred miles of range. Now, with the additional tanks, the maximum human load was six passengers, but the range had been increased to twenty-three hundred miles, nearly the limit for his crossing of the Atlantic from Fortaleza, Brazil, to Sierra Leone. His first fuel stop was going to be in Trinidad, about four hours away.

Locking in the autopilot, Hamm poured himself a cup of coffee and hoped that whoever had been listening—somebody always was—was looking for him at the TWA counter out at National. Some poor operative would get his ass chewed for losing Hamm.

Because Captain Hoke and Darrell Holloway had had no suspicion that their conversations might have been tapped, Hamm could not suppress either Terrell's name or location. He might, however, slip into Cape Town before they expected him and be able to do some tracking without an escort. That concerned him since the escort was likely to have a business address on Dzerzhinsky Square.

SOUTH AFRICA

SIX

At the single window of the cramped boarding-house room, Robert Terrell craned his neck hard to the right to see the feathered surface of Table Bay. A light breeze touched the wave tops and splattered them with dashes of white, a Swiss-polka-dotted blue. The freighters, tankers, and trampers anchored in the bay or moored to the docks were serene and unmoving. Most of the derricks and container-transfer cranes were at rest. One passenger liner was being nudged from her berth by two tugs.

He remembered another steamship, a seven-day cruise in the Caribbean with Nancy. The Pentagon had paid for that trip, happily picked up the tab for everything.

A fourteen-story building directly across the street, with a vertical sign advertising Cape Colony Insurance, blocked his view of the South Atlantic. Looking down the four stories to the street, Terrell could see the traffic jammed up by the five o'clock rush. The hordes of pedestrians on the sidewalks moved faster than the Mercedes, Cadillacs, and Citroëns abandoning the financial district. He had had the same limited view for the past week.

It was not the Cape Town he remembered from his last trip.

Lately, protests were erupting all around. A black would commit some small infraction of some law Terrell found difficult to comprehend, and a policeman or soldier would react vigorously. Yesterday's incident had not been much of a disturbance, but it had attracted one of the city's many reporter-and-camera teams. He had noticed the melee across the street and chose to ignore the gathering mob. In any commotion attracting attention, his objective was to be elsewhere. But he had needed to eat, and on his way to a local restaurant he had run directly into a camera crew. There was a possibility, even a small one, that the footage might be seen by someone who should not see it.

The day dragged while he paced his eighty square feet, counting the hours, trying to organize his next movements by debating with himself out loud.

"You were a planner for over six years, Robert. All you have to do is concentrate."

"It is not the same kind of planning. This isn't maiming and killing. This is running."

"Your problem, Robert, is that you don't know how to be a fugitive."

"Fugitive. I didn't start out to be a fugitive."

"I know, but that's the way it turned out, Robert. Now think!"

ABC had caught him at noon. That would be about . . . six A.M. on the East Coast. It would have been midnight, his time, before the footage had a chance to air in the States. He had some time yet.

He still had to go to the bank. He should have done that yesterday afternoon. That had been a stupid move, putting his cash and documents in a safety deposit box. It was the action of a man not accustomed to carrying around thousands of dollars. From now on, he would keep his documents more readily available.

Thinking about the money made him think of Nancy again, and Fred and Beth. He had started with twelve thousand, one-third of the savings, leaving the balance for them. Would she sell the house in Arlington Heights? What choice did she have? God, he longed to pick up the phone and call, just to let her know . . . what? "I'm alive, Nancy. I love you."

With his eyes closed, Terrell had a perfect picture of her, long hair shining black, her eyes animated and curious.

Then other images began flooding into his mind like a kaleidoscope, washing Nancy away.

It was twenty minutes before seven A.M., South African time, when Hamm crossed the border from Namibia, the Orange River his landmark. He was not exactly exhausted by the twenty hours aloft and the two on the ground to refuel, but the muscles in his back, arms, and butt ached. He had climbed out of the seat periodically, leaving the aircraft on autopilot, to use the head and to stretch, but it was still a long time to be confined in one slim cylinder.

He did beat the commercial flight by nine hours, which, he assumed, would throw off the timing of anyone following him.

The sun had been up for three hours at his altitude, and Hamm had been able to observe the veld and mountain and jungle unrolling ahead of him. When he mentally erased the rail lines and ribbons of highway and strings of electric and telephone lines, he could give it all back to the Xhosa and Zulu, when it had been really beautiful. He could envision the kraals of the mighty kings and the daylong, tireless, trotting marches of impi warriors, scouring the land for cattle to enhance the treasuries.

Then came men like Cecil Rhodes.

And there went the neighborhood.

It was too bad Chaka and Cetewayo, the greatest of the Zulu warrior kings, were so outgunned, Hamm thought.

The gazelle and the eland survived in protected preserves. The whites did not seem to be faring as well. Back in the mid-seventies, before he made light colonel in '77 and Gene Kuster called him in, Hamm had devoted twenty-seven months to gathering intelligence in the Transvaal, Namibia, Botswana, and Zimbabwe, crossing occasionally into Angola.

Sixteen of those months, off and on, had been in the company of Bob Terrell. And Hamm knew Terrell, knew the man preferred to go only to places where he had been before. His mind was more adventuresome than his body. It was not surprising to Hamm that Terrell had surfaced in Cape Town.

Hamm was staying to the coast, the Namib Desert and a chain of five-thousand-foot mountains off to his left. When he spotted Bitterfontein, he eased back on the power and began a slow descent. Already, the emerald green of the Cape was visible on his horizon, a wooded oasis against the shrubland and desert below. He was glad to be back, even though Terrell was the reason.

Hamm had no illusions about the course he might have to take. The GABRIEL file came first, and if Terrell had to die for Hamm to get it, then that was the way it was.

So much for friendship.

"Decker."

Hamm stood in a hellishly hot telephone booth outside the general aviation section of D. F. Malan Airport. It was overly warm for the onset of winter. Twelve miles to the northwest, he could see a haze over Cape Town. Maybe it would rain later in the day.

He recognized Decker's voice. A real up-and-comer at the company a few years back, he was relatively young to be holding a chief of station. "Roy?"

"Yes."

"Steve Hamm, here."

"Heard you were coming, Colonel, but I expected you to call later. You must have had some decent flight connections."

"Worked out well."

"I got the message from your office, of course."

Hamm wondered how secure the phone was. ''And?''

''And, what?''

''Did you view the tape?''

''Oh, yes. And I've talked to the reporter.''

He waited. Fucking CIA need-to-know game. He would string along. ''Well? What did the reporter say? Do you have the location?''

''We're checking into all that. You must be beat, Hamm. Why don't we meet later for lunch, say around one?''

Bastard. The Company types always assumed that anything three miles out of CONUS was their private party.

''Look, shithead, I've got no time for an agency civil jerk. I'm going to give you a phone number and then hang up. You get on your hotline, and ask for verification of Yardstick. Then you call me back. Ten minutes.'' Hamm gave him the number of the pay phone, slapped the receiver on its hook, and stepped out of the booth in search of a breeze.

The phone rang in eight minutes, and he picked it up.

''Uh . . . Colonel—''

''What do you have on a location?''

''Location, yeah. We've identified the street—Boersword, and I have people out with photographs of the subject, canvassing a twelve-block area. It's damned near downtown, and there's a lot of ground to cover.''

''How about the opposition?''

''They're aware. Some agitation in their consulate yesterday morning, and most of their actives have been seen around town, dogging our footsteps. But I'm not sure of the current status because I pulled my people away to work the streets."

Hamm was not surprised. It only confirmed some kind of bug on his house. "What about the locals?"

"We've made no contact with them. The NIS probably knows we're looking for someone." There was a long pause. Then Decker asked, "Colonel, why are we after this Ter . . . this guy?"

At least the CIA had not spread the real reason into its network. "Some important people want to talk to him."

"Yeah. Sure," Decker said, pissed.

"All right. As far as I know, I haven't been made yet. I'm going to keep it that way in case I need to move fast. Right now, I'm going to find a bed for a couple of hours. I'll check back with you later." He hung up before Decker could ask where he would be.

While the taxi aimed itself downtown, Hamm sat in the back and looked at the skyscrapers and the dominating, thirty-five-hundred-foot Table Mountain, and hoped he had a sufficient lead on Coriolanus and the Soviets. The KGB—First Chief Directorate's sphere of operations—would have sounded a general alarm and would have also assigned a specific operative to Terrell.

"Where we going, sir?" the driver asked.

"Try the Hilton." Hamm had a thing about decent hotels.

He wondered if Terrell was keeping a close watch over his shoulder, if he had thought about the danger of a Soviet interest in him. Damn! He would have to know. Bob was a realist when it came to the Russkies. There were no deficiencies in Terrell's thinking—or at least there had not been.

Hamm paid off the cab driver in front of the Hilton, passed quickly through a blast of heat, and entered the refrigerated lobby. He registered and went right up to his room. Shedding his poorly chosen dark wool suit, he first called room service for four eggs, muffins, marmalade, and a pot of coffee, then hopped into the shower. The grit was out of his eyes and off his cheeks by the time breakfast arrived.

Digging his small black address book out of his carry-all, he began to thumb through the pages, ticking off the calls he'd make, while scooping yolk off his plate with a muffin.

SEVEN

The morning sun was already warm when Terrell dressed in light gray slacks, a blue sport shirt with a muted gray tie, and a blue-checked sport coat. He stood in front of the window, looking down on the Thursday morning, late-for-work traffic.

"Well, Robert, you finally get to go north," he said out loud in that other voice.

"It's about time. I've been screwing around here, getting too comfortable. Suppose anybody saw me on TV? I never wanted to be on TV. I wanted to be in the movies once, with Roy Rogers, but never on TV. Just wanted to visit my friends."

"That's a long time ago, Robert. Roy Rogers!"

"I remember crying because Mom and Dad wanted to drag me up to our cabin, Evensong, way up in the woods outside Quebec, and I'd have to miss six weeks of Saturday matinees. Lash LaRue, he was good, too."

He packed his bag, leaving it open on the bed for later insertion of the Dopp kit. "Funny, the way it works out, isn't it? Probably got half the damned world looking for me, wanting me to go back to where I was. And the only place I want to go has been closed off to me. But there's bound to be someplace I can slip in. Bound to be."

"Eternal optimist, aren't you, Robert?"

At nine o'clock, he went down the four flights of stairs and walked the six blocks to his bank. The pedestrian crowd had thinned down to mostly blacks. The whites were at work in the buildings; the coloreds—last traces of the Hottentot and other mixtures—were performing their typical service and servant roles, leaving the avenues to the largely unemployed members of various tribes of the Bantu. Terrell wondered if he were unemployed. Certainly, they would not be sending his paycheck to Nancy.

The lady at the vault took his key and hers, opened his box, and left him alone to clean it out. The currency was in American dollars in a buff envelope, and he stuffed it in the pocket inside his coat. There was also the other passport, courtesy of the Venezuelan black market. He'd had two made in Caracas. On the way out, he stopped at one of the teller's windows and exchanged some dollars for rand.

During his walk back to his building, Terrell lamented again the fact that, in almost fifteen years on the fringes of a covert world, he had not learned more about the tradecraft of spies. Every face he saw was intently interested in him, and every aspect of body language around him was sinister. He knew it was not true, but it made him nervous, caused his hands to shake, and he felt better when he reached his room. It was an island of security, and he would have liked to stay in it. He had grown complacent in Cape Town, but in the end, it was just like Mexico City and Caracas. He was beginning to believe there was no refuge for him. "Like a bird, huh, Robert? And the nest is gone, blown away in the big wind."

"You're supposed to be able to build a new nest. We keep building nests, only to destroy them."

In front of his mirror with razor and scissors, Terrell shaved off his moustache. He snipped at the hair over his ears, cutting it way back, and with black hair dye he streaked his hair, losing some of the gray, and giving it overall darkness. He dumped his horn-rims in the wastebasket and donned a pair of old metal-framed glasses he had had for years. He selected the Albert Simmons passport, dropped it in his coat pocket, and slid the extra passport under the bottom cardboard of his shaving kit. "You about ready, Robert?"

"Albert, please. Or Al. I can live with Al."

He placed the kit in his suitcase, then descended the stairs for the last time—it was almost like running away from home, even though he had been there only a week—went out to the street, and hailed a cab.

It was noon by the time the cabbie accepted a modest tip and let him out at the railroad station. Again, Terrell felt the presence of spies everywhere as he stood in line to buy a ticket on the first train out to Johannesburg. As a white, he naturally bought a ticket in a first-class accommodation.

While waiting for the train to board, Terrell was able to objectify some of his thinking. There was a large number of policemen and soldiers in the station, but they were keeping wary eyes on the thousands of black travelers who no longer had to obtain travel passes. With some sense of partial, and probably false, relief, he realized he was not the only one under scrutiny. He joined the jammed flow of the crowd and rode it along the concourse. There was shouting and yelling and babbling in Afrikaans, some English, and a dozen tribal dialects. The jostling and shoving irritated him.

His carriage was second in line. Terrell boarded and settled into his compartment, shared with one lady and one man. A young couple arrived alongside the compartment, pushing an English-style pram.

The young man, dressed like an earnest stockbroker, kept looking at his watch as he kissed his wife, then helped her into the compartment. He lifted the carriage inside, blew her another kiss, then took off running. The woman had a distinctly English appearance: light brown hair and eyes, a clear complexion, and a sense of primness. She looked wistfully after the running figure, then selected one of the two available seats next to him, and began to retrieve cartons and diaper bags, stowing them in the luggage rack. A curly-haired baby gurgled happily inside the pram.

She pulled the carriage close to her and fought with a brake device on the rear wheel for a minute before Terrell leaned over and helped her. His hand trembled a bit when he pushed down the lever.

"Thank you, sir." Her eyes suggested she was wary of him, he could tell. They scanned his face closely, noted his hands.

"Anytime."

"You're American?"

"Yes."

"I've never met an American before. I'm Margaret."

The new passport. "I'm Albert. Al. You're from England?"

"A year ago. Chelmsford, which is in Essex."

As a fugitive, he had a feeling that it would be helpful if he appeared part of a small family, perhaps on holiday. Cover, the spies called it. He slid over one seat, next to Margaret, which alarmed her for only a few minutes. "Near London, isn't it? Tell me about it."

Hamm slept for two hours, waking from the nightmare of falling asleep at the controls of a diving Lear. Too many hours aloft, trusting the infallibility of electronic circuits in the autopilot, he decided. He rolled onto his side, then sat up.

Picking up the phone from its cradle on the bedside stand, he levered himself out of the bed and paced around the room while he called Decker. Through the window of his room, the sun glared whitely on the buildings across the street. Hamm drew the drapes across the window.

"We found his room, Colonel. He's skipped."

"Nothing in the room?"

"Not much. We lifted some prints, to double-check the I.D. Couple of empty beer bottles and some candy, a bottle of hair dye, and a pair of glasses in the wastebasket. The glasses match those on the videotape, and I've sent them out to have the prescription read. He'd been living there for a week.'' Decker was being very open with his information now.

Damn! A week. ''What color hair dye?''

''Black. And he's probably lost the moustache now. Maybe even the glasses.''

''He's real nearsighted, Roy. Something like twenty-six hundred. His lenses are like Coke-bottle bottoms. What about local help?''

''Maybe. What's the cover?''

''Let's make him a fugitive from a weapons charge. He's lifted a hefty bunch of National Guard weaponry, and he's out to sell it. M-sixteens, M-seventy-nines, and a dozen Redeyes. How's that sound?''

''Good.''

''It'll also explain our sudden burst of activity in the country.''

''I hadn't thought about that angle, Colonel. The cops and the customs people would be damned glad to help us locate a guy who might be trying to sell heavy firepower to the blacks.''

''Do it.'' Hamm hung up and sat on the edge of the bed. Something was nibbling at the edge of his mind, some hint of the familiar. Hamm had not been able to get a fix on Terrell's plan, but now it was coming to him, and it had something to do with Africa. At least, it had to do with Terrell's Africa.

He called room service and asked them to find him a big map of the continent.

Then he opened his address book and began to make calls.

After five calls he got to Sam Farley. In '65, he

and Sam had flown together in the same helicopter company in Vietnam. When Hamm went through a career change to intelligence in 1967, Farley had entered his own career as a mercenary, based in South Africa. They had bumped into each other from time to time over the years.

Hamm located him in Johannesburg. "Sam, Steve Hamm."

"I'll be damned! You in town?"

"Down south, on the Cape. I have a favor to ask."

"Go, man."

"I'm looking for a guy. . . ." He described Terrell. "He's been seen in Cape Town, had a room here on Boersword, but is now scampering."

"You want him bad?"

"Bad and quiet."

"Alive?"

"If at all possible."

"He got anything to do with the nuke that went off over at Brandvlei?"

"No."

Hamm had forgotten about the nuclear explosion. The official South African explanation was that an electromagnetic interference with the electronic triggering circuits had caused the detonation. It was a logical explanation; commanders with nuclear devices in their inventories had nightmares about electromagnetic anomalies in the atmosphere. As yet, though, there had been no explanation as to why an army unit on field exercises had a tactical weapon in its possession. The governments of Namibia, Angola, Botswana, Zimbabwe, and Mozambique were raising holy hell in the United Nations over the issue. They did not like the idea of having a close neighbor with the potential for catastrophic accident.

"What happened over there, anyway?" Hamm asked.

"Somebody fucked up."

"How bad is it?"

"All I get is what's in the papers, Steve. There's still a quarantine, and there's still a hot spot around ground zero, but the military is in the area cleaning up. I guess that, after three weeks, most of the area will be livable."

"Nice, isn't it, that we have a new nuclear power in the world?"

"I might move to Pakistan or Afghanistan or some other place I feel safe," Farley said, then went back to the topic at hand. "You on your own with this?"

"Wish I were, buddy, but I've got unwanted company."

Farley got the message. "Let me make some calls, Steve. I'll be back to you."

It took three calls before Hamm located Dave Messenger in Nairobi. Messenger was a former Air America pilot whose territory had been the entire Indian subcontinent. Hamm and Messenger had shared a lot of booze and a few hot times when Hamm had served as liaison to the CIA-supported transport service. At the time, Hamm was an "attaché" to the ambassador to Thailand.

"I hear you're shit-listed," Messenger told him.

"You know a time when I wasn't?"

"That's a fact."

"What are you up to?"

"Got me a Herc and two Otters, a staff of five people. Whole fucking air force."

"Charter service, huh?"

"The best around. You need transport?"

"Information." He went through the description of Terrell.

"My men have a grip on the grapevine. I'll see what I can shake loose."

"Appreciate it, Dave."

"I still owe you the big one." Messenger hung up.

Ninety percent of intelligence work was maintaining a positive balance of favors owed. Not the bogus backscratching that went on in D.C., Hamm knew, but the ones on which lives could hang. He had always been willing to help out others in order to keep the scale tilted in his direction. In Messenger's case, Dave had gone down in the Cambodian jungle with a Cessna 180 and an influential tribal chieftain's son he was transporting to an air force hospital in Bangkok. Lon Nol's avid fans were on the immediate horizon when Hamm put his UH-1H Huey on the ground and pulled them out.

Hamm tried a few more people without any luck before the bellman arrived with his map. He tipped him with more rand than necessary, ordered a pot of coffee, and spread the map out on the unmade bed.

Just picking out the familiar names on the map made Hamm remember some good times when he had been working with Bob Terrell. Despite their vociferous arguments over the direction of American foreign policy, their views regarding the encroachment of civilization on the African continent had coincided. Both deplored not only the poverty and famine present, but also the rape of the continent's resources.

Hamm stretched out on the bed and waited for phone calls. He figured Coriolanus would be getting in soon, spoiling for a fight.

And, if the Soviets were as far behind Terrell as Hamm had been, they would be watching every movement his side made. He could not do much about Coriolanus, but he could try to keep himself in the shadows.

Farley called him just after lunch.

"Got a lead for me?"

"Not yet. Some people I know are checking into your man's housing arrangements in Cape Town, and I've got the word out around the country. What I picked up, though, the word's out about you, too."

That would be Decker, or maybe the Russkies.

Hamm's backyard was filling up with people not invited to the barbecue. "I appreciate the info, Sam."

"You need any backup, give me a call. Keep your ass covered, Steve."

EIGHT

"So, you've been feeding him whatever he asks for?" Coriolanus kept his voice level, but his eyes expressed his fury.

Decker squirmed. "I didn't have a choice. I called DIA about YARDSTICK. They said Hamm had the—"

"You don't work for the fucking DIA!"

Coriolanus shook his head in disgust and turned away. He let the silence hang for a while, let the anxiety build for Decker, while he walked around the office. It was a large office, nicely furnished in mahogany pieces. The chairs had cane backs. Too damned nice for a screw-up like Decker. On one wall, Decker had hung his law degree from the

University of California at Los Angeles. Another damned West Coast lawyer, he thought.

Skirting the desk, he dropped into Decker's desk chair, leaned back, and carefully laid his Gucci-clad heels on the polished surface of the desk. He usually assumed control of the offices of men with lesser rank. "That's a bunch of shit, Decker. Your brief says nothing about liaison with sister services. And Hamm's a damned paper pusher in the army's inspector general's office. He calls again, you refer him to me. Better yet, take a message."

"But—"

"Or hang up, if you can't handle it." Coriolanus used his forefingers to rub his eyes and smooth the olive skin of his cheeks. It had been a long flight, with four transfers. "Now, sit down."

Decker had no choice but to take one of the two visitor chairs in his own office. He pulled one to the front of the desk, started to lean his elbows on the mahogany top, then thought better of it.

Through the large window, Coriolanus watched a black gardener tending to the shrubs laid out geometrically on the rear lawn and listened while the younger man detailed the short investigation. "So what's your next step?"

"Well, sir, Hamm and I are supposed to meet with Peter de Vroot at two o'clock."

"De Vroot? NIS?"

"Yes, sir."

With his elbows pressed against the chair arms, Coriolanus splayed his fingers apart and pressed his left fingertips against the fingertips of his right hand. He pushed hard, making the tendons of his wrists stand out. "Tell me, Decker, what the fuck went through your mind when you decided to involve a foreign service in an internal investigation?''

Decker sat up straight. ''Sir, I didn't deci——''

''Cancel it.'' Coriolanus dropped his feet to the floor and leaned into the desk. He did not bother to mention that, in the first few days of Yardstick, he had urged an international manhunt for Terrell, based on a charge of murder. Even when the autopsy of Pelagio proved that his heart attack had not been externally induced, Coriolanus thought the murder rap was a good cover to use in order to get Interpol's involvement. Hamm had shut down that tactic by suggesting to the director of Central Intelligence through Kuster that if Terrell felt that much pressure, he might go to the media with GABRIEL. He said that if Interpol and the courts were involved, then GABRIEL and its contents might become household words, like Iran-Contra. It was fine with Hamm, if that was the way they wanted to play it. The director was pissed, to put it mildly.

''But—'' Decker was beginning to look totally confused.

''Hamm doesn't want to involve Interpol, but he's pulling in NIS.''

''Well, that's a little more limited,'' Decker said. ''He just wants to use them as a locater service.''

''You defending the son-of-a-bitch? Where's Hamm now?'' Coriolanus asked.

''Uh . . . he didn't say.''

''And you didn't ask, did you? So, let's assess the damage you've done and figure out how we're going to get our men.''

''Men? You mean Terrell?''

''I mean Terrell *and* Hamm.''

The telephone on Decker's desk rang shrilly, and Decker started to reach for it.

The assistant DDO snaked an arm out and snatched it up. "Coriolanus."

"Where's Decker?"

"Busy. Where are you, Hamm?"

"What took you so long to get here, Jack?"

"We need to talk."

"I'll meet you in front of the NIS building."

"That's been canceled."

"For you, maybe," Hamm said, and hung up.

Coriolanus slammed down the receiver. "Shit!"

Peter de Vroot was completely bald, but had a moustache that Yosemite Sam would have envied. The man was bald as an American Eagle, but his follicles thrived on his upper lip. The moustache was fully an inch and a half high under his broad, deep red nose, and was densely compacted, tapering outward in S-curves to upraised points in line with his ears.

"That, Mr. de Vroot, is the best damned moustache I've ever seen," Hamm said, smiling.

The National Intelligence Service's director for domestic operations grinned, and his blue eyes twinkled. He used a thick thumb and forefinger to caress the tip of the moustache. "Prevents my rolling over in bed and smothering myself, Colonel. Lifesaver, in many ways. Now, from what Roy tells me, you have a bit of an un-procurement problem."

"That says it," Hamm greed. Decker had introduced him as an army weapons auditor, and he quickly went through the list of weapons missing from the National Guard armory in Alabama and provided de Vroot with a picture and snapshot biography of Bryce Calder—the name Decker had dreamed up for Terrell.

"And you believe these weapons may be in South Africa?"

"To be honest, we don't know where they are. But we do think that Calder may be here, attempting to sell them."

Coriolanus sat through the recital, his dark eyes reflecting his displeasure. He sat up straight, so as not to mar any of the creases in his thousand-dollar suit. Hamm had met Decker and Coriolanus outside the building, just before this meeting, and only a threat to call the White House had forced the CIA assistant to submit to the tactic.

"I'll have copies made and get it out to my people."

"Appreciate that," Hamm said.

The three Americans left the building and stood on the white sidewalk beside Decker's Chevrolet sedan. The driver hopped out to open doors, but Coriolanus beat him to it, leaning over to pull open a rear door. "Get in, Hamm," he ordered.

"I've got things to do. We'll chit-chat later."

Coriolanus stood upright, as far as he could, and his eyes emitted new levels of malevolence. "I want to know where you are and what you're doing."

"Sure you do. Problem is, you're on need-to-know status."

"Not for goddamned long," the special assistant said. "The bell's about to ring on your round."

"Fuck off, Jack." Hamm spun on his heel and walked to the corner of the block, signaling for a cab.

He got one right away.

As expected, he had plenty of company. Coriolanus had two cars waiting to follow him, and there was also an Audi 5000 with two men in it. The Audi could have originated with the Soviet consulate or with a suspicious Peter de Vroot.

Hamm went sightseeing.

They were minimal, touristy jaunts—a look at Table Mountain—clear out to Green Point, a dash around the harbor. Three cab changes between Cape Town and Bellville and back to Cape Town shook off the Audi and one of the company tails. Cape Town was a joint capital, with Pretoria, and had a population of close to a million people. On his trip downtown to look at the government buildings, in heavy traffic, Hamm hopped out of his southbound taxi, crossed the median, slipped into a vacant northbound cab, rounded the corner, and got out again. It resulted in the loss of his last shadow.

Hamm walked the last blocks back to his hotel. He thought about having dinner in the manner to which he was accustomed when living in hotels, but the dining room was not yet open, so he took the elevator up to his floor. In his room to make more calls and wait for responses to earlier calls, he ordered a tray of sandwiches and two bottles of Michelob from room service.

Sitting on the bed with his snack, his mind kept rolling back in time, looking for clues to Terrell's aberrant behavior. There had been many conversations on hypothetical case studies in which they both agreed on the basics and disagreed on the solutions. Terrell never identified specific ideas he might have been using in the SPG, but Hamm had always suspected Terrell's frame of reference for strategic planning leaned more toward deterrence than toward strike capability.

Given that assumption, what about GABRIEL? From what Hamm had learned, the GABRIEL software began as a sophisticated intelligence-gathering tool, and information meant superiority. It was a deterrent. Somewhere along the way, though, it had changed. Larry Pelagio had changed it, and Larry Pelagio was known around the SPG as a right-winger. So GABRIEL became less an intelligence machine and more a powerful weapons system.

Was that enough to push Bob to compromise the plan? Hell, there were strike plans laying around all over the Pentagon, and Terrell had lived with them.

No, there was something more—either in GABRIEL or in an outside influence—that had set him off. What was it? Goddamn Dilman, anyway. Hamm needed more data.

It was not money or ideology. Terrell had not gone to the Soviets. Not yet, anyway. The CIA and DIA intelligence collected so far, intercepted by Diane, indicated that General Andresev and his FCD people were pursuing Terrell just as intensely as Hamm.

There were a lot of "buts" involved. But something about GABRIEL had finally violated Bob Terrell's mental barriers. But he had been with it for two years. GABRIEL had already evolved into the second phase. Hamm needed to know more.

And the pathologists proved Terrell hadn't killed Pelagio. Maybe there was something connected with Pelagio's death? Had Bob seen Larry Pelagio on that last day, on the nineteenth? In backtracking, no one on Team Three could recall seeing Terrell that morning. Nancy waved him off after breakfast, and the next time he was seen was when he boarded the Mexicana flight.

If Dilman and Storch and the Team Three director, Foster, were not so damned tight-lipped about the GABRIEL file, Hamm might have more to go on. Out of the hundreds of war plans stuck in drawers around the Pentagon, what was special about this one? Something in the association between communications—which was where GABRIEL had started—and the delivery of MIRV warheads?

What did GABRIEL do?

He set his empty tray on the floor. Until he had more information about GABRIEL, he had to rely on the other pattern he had been developing. Hamm unrolled and studied the big map of Africa.

On it, he had circled each of the cities in which he and Bob Terrell had spent some time together. There were a lot of circles.

He was using a ruler to work out radii for air and rail travel time out of Cape Town when the phone rang.

Hoping it was Sam Farley, Hamm picked up.

It was Roy Decker. "Hamm, we need to talk."

It was not a secure line. "That's what you said. I'm busy."

"It's about you."

The landscape was gigantic and mostly barren, and Terrell was pleased to have Margaret to talk to and James II to prod into giggles with his forefinger. The way he had gotten wrapped up in his work in the last few years, he had drifted away from people. It seemed so clear to him now. Many things were much clearer to him now.

His academic love was history, and history was people. At the center, he had played fascinating games. Based on the history of a culture, how would the *people* react to the injection of a new and startling development? Terrell had successfully predicted the outcome in Angola when he worked in the African section, his first assignment because of his Peace Corps experience. And yet, he had gotten away from people; he had objectified them, made them pawns in the game.

Rising in the bureaucracy, he had become part of it.

While he predicted global power struggled, he engaged in departmental skirmishes. Who would head the African section? Who could influence this general or that admiral? Who was making more money, or had more prestige? Terrell learned how to work the system, and he landed the coveted GABRIEL project on Team Three, the Soviet response team.

His purpose, from the very beginning of his association with strategic planning, had been humanitarian. Though it had sometimes gotten away from him, he thought he had done a fair job of neutralizing the generals. Terrell believed America could lead the world in the demonstration of peaceful coexistence. That was his job. Acting the hawk, he could nullify the effects of some of the far right's first-strike mentality.

Then he discovered what real power could be, and he nurtured it, led Larry Pelagio into the right paths, pumped up the egos, smoothed the ruffled feathers, and came out of the process with GA-

BRIEL. Though Terrell and Pelagio often entered fierce and private debates over the objectives of the project, he had seen the original GABRIEL as a way to cancel Soviet aggression. If the U.S. knew exactly what the Soviets were planning, through unrestricted access to their communications, the Kremlin would run into a dead end on every military move. Terrell and Pelagio held world-class power in their hands, though they saw it in different lights.

The hints he had dropped about GABRIEL left seasoned generals and admirals with their mouths watering. A major intelligence and weapons system, all rolled onto one spool of tape. They just did not realize that it was a weapon of peace.

And then Larry Pelagio took it one step too far.

The tape was simplicity itself. Load it on the machine, and all of the power Larry Pelagio had envisioned was instantly at one's fingertips. There were more than one hundred thousand man-hours of programming in that tape, two years of overtime for twenty-some programmers. Pelagio had known what he wanted. Only Pelagio and Terrell, as his supervisor, had known what it all looked like when it was put together.

Terrell shuddered when he remembered how he had used the implied power of GABRIEL in the first fifteen months of the project. In briefings before Team Three colleagues and select Pentagon brass, he had provided general glimpses of the GABRIEL programming outcomes. It brought him two substantial raises in salary. It made him a target of Pentagon largesse—invitations to lavish dinners, theater tickets, a couple of junkets to Nassau, the Caribbean cruise. It raised the level of his influence. He would use that persuasive power to counter hostile intents.

Only Pelagio, as a master systems designer, could have done it, and he was dead. He probably died of the workload, Terrell thought. The stress levels were high, and the man was obsessed with completing the task. But it worked. Robert Terrell had been there when Pelagio brought the program up on the screen, keyed his way through the displayed menus, and was magically transformed into a very powerful man.

All the way through the nine months of the second phase of GABRIEL, Terrell had not really believed that it would work, that Pelagio could adapt the system into a nuclear trigger.

But he did it. GABRIEL was suddenly not another intelligence system, to be emplaced at Fort Meade as a companion to the National Security Agency's other systems. It was now a weapons system that would belong to the people at NORAD. Joe Dilman and his people would love it. And when Terrell saw what was happening, knew that it was too dangerous to give to people with little minds, he knew what he had to do.

There had been only one backup tape, and Terrell had destroyed it before leaving Washington, along with all of the hard copies of the programming.

There had been only one master tape. It was cumbersome and difficult to conceal. A big reel, almost fifteen inches across and three inches deep. He had carted it in an attaché case through Mexico City to Caracas. He had come close to destroying it several times, when he had thought that the CIA, or someone, was getting close to him.

He held on to it, though, because he believed that somehow he could rework the programming, take it back to what it had been in the first phase.

Terrell had spent seven hours at the console of a computer owned by an American oil company in Venezuela. He rented it for one long night. The machine was not large enough to handle the total program, he knew, but he had thought that it would be adequate for his purpose, which was to transfer the programming from the big reel to several hundred floppy disks. They would be easier to conceal, perhaps in many locations.

His seven hours at the IBM were fruitless. Either he did not know enough about computers, or it would not have worked in any case.

He could not keep the reel with him, either, not do that and cross the borders he intended to cross. Terrell knew that he—and others in his position—was under constant surveillance by the Soviet KGB. They would be seeking him with as much zeal as the CIA.

In the end, he wrapped the reel of magnetic tape carefully in a heavy cardboard box, marked it "Business Software," and mailed it to Evensong, the cabin on Lake Edouard in Québec that his parents had owned for forty years. His folks were in their late sixties now and rarely left the environs of Boston. It had been years since they made the summer trek northward. He had suggested to his folks that they sell it about five years ago, but they had refused. GABRIEL would be safely held in general delivery at the little store in Lac Edouard where Terrell had so often spent his youthful nickels and dimes.

GABRIEL would be safe in the arms of Madame

Gurnette, the postmistress and candy purveyor, until he wanted to retrieve it. After he took care of the other things he had to do.

It had been an immense relief for him, the minute he had shipped the reel off to Canada. In the last week, GABRIEL had been only fleetingly in his mind. Pained thoughts of the disaster in South Africa had kept him from considering how he would change the software back to its original form.

Except . . .

Except, why would he want to do that, anyway?

Sitting there in the overheated, rocking passenger car, there was suddenly a brand-new alternative for Robert Terrell.

"A way to stabilize the world," he mumbled, newly aware.

"What did you say?" Margaret Redding asked him.

Terrell smiled at her. "Sorry. Talking to myself, I guess."

NINE

Hamm met Roy Decker in the Hilton lounge at five-thirty. The tables were filling up quickly, and they sat at the end of the bar, against the wall, where there were fewer ears to overhear. The lounge was finished in simulated black-oak table tops and burgundy Naugahyde. The light level was close to that of an abandoned mine, and it was difficult to appreciate the decor, much less read Decker's eyes. The bartender poured Scotch for Hamm and bourbon for Decker, then discreetly moved away.

"You located me fast enough, Roy. I was supposed to call you, remember?"

The young chief of station shrugged. "It wasn't

difficult. You picked an obvious hotel. Coriolanus told me that you always do."

"When did you pick up on me?"

"I don't know. Couple of hours ago."

If there was not a tap on his phone yet, there would be some agent checking his long-distance calls on the hotel log. Well, it would keep him busy.

He sipped his Chivas. "You said it was important?"

Decker swiveled on his stool to face Hamm. "Maybe more to me than you. How long have you known Coriolanus?"

Perhaps there was someone besides Hamm who was disenchanted with the "cream of the CIA"? "Since 'Nam. My second tour in sixty-seven. Jack was already with the company, running the SOG I was assigned to." His Special Operations Group had been based in Saigon, but operated all over the delta, with occasional forays into Cambodia and Laos. With his rotary-wing and, later, fixed-wing qualifications, Hamm had found himself at the controls on many of those missions.

As his eyes adjusted to the low lighting, Hamm began to pick up more detail. The intense expression on Decker's face suggested he was wrestling with some piece of his conscience.

"What's he got against you?" Decker asked.

"You love him like I do, huh?"

Decker shrugged again. "I'd like to know."

"Maybe he doesn't like my style? In Jack's case, we didn't get along much from the start. Hell, Roy, don't get yourself crosswise with your bosses. You'd better stick close to the agency. The people that count have already written me off."

The agent downed the rest of his drink and slid the empty glass down the bar to the barman. Hamm took a refill, too, and they waited in silence while the drinks were poured. Thinking time for Decker.

When the bartender walked away, wiping down the table top, Decker said, "Shit! They already know I've come to see you. We've got two people in the lobby. There's two things."

"Okay, two things."

"Coriolanus is building a case against you for aiding Terrell. Impeding his investigation."

"Nice guy, Jack."

"Is it true?" Decker's eyes sought him out in the gloom.

"My job comes first. You've been through my file?"

"No."

"You're about the only one, but try it sometime. I may not be Super Patriot, but I don't let much interfere with my assignments." Hamm wondered where they were going with the buddy-buddy routine.

"That's good enough for me, I guess."

"What's your other point?" Hamm asked.

"De Vroot's people have a line on Terrell. They think he was in the airport about mid-morning yesterday, somewhere between nine and ten. Somebody remembered the face. I wasn't supposed to give you that."

Hamm set down his drink and stood up. "I owe you, Roy, and I'll pay up later. Right now I've got a date."

Decker ordered another drink as Hamm left the lounge.

He spotted Coriolanus's agents as he went

through the lobby to the elevator stack. Hamm thought it was a hell of a waste of resources in tight budget years. Typical damned bureaucracy.

In his room, it took him one minute to determine that it had been searched. The pencil he had placed on top of his map, point on Durban and eraser on Lubumbashi, was now bisecting Cameroon. Maybe Decker had been the diversion necessary for Coriolanus to get into his room. Maybe Decker was feeding him a false trail for Terrell. Should he believe Decker or not?

Hell, no.

Decker was a company man, evidenced by his fast promotion track. To have achieved chief of station anywhere at his age, the man had to have an ingrained sense of loyalty to the company. Decker was not going to change horses now.

Talk about impeding an investigation. Hamm could build his own case against Coriolanus, if he wanted to do that. But he had other things to do.

He grabbed the phone and carried it around the room with him while he packed. Whenever he reached one of his sources, he left the same message: "Don't call me. I'll call you."

Then he called DeMott at her office. "I thought you'd be off on a long lunch hour," he said.

"Go to hell. Why haven't you called me?"

"Been busy." Hamm quickly briefed her, not telling her anything that someone tapping the phone would not already know. "How about you?"

"Naturally, I've been sitting on my ass."

"Nice ass, though."

"Quit that, Steve. You on a secure line?"

"I doubt it. Do we need one?"

"Call me back."

Hamm grabbed his suitcase and went down to the lobby. The two operatives waiting for him busied themselves with a newspaper and a week-old *Newsweek* while he made his call from the end telephone in a bank of five phones.

"What do you have?" he asked her.

"Coriolanus might have his tentacles in DIA, but I found a useful ear out at Langley."

"I'll ask you how someday. What's your little bird told you?"

"Number one. You know the code name Chukker?"

Naratsmov, Alexi Ivanovitch. Department Twelve. "I know the trademark. A few assassinations tentatively charged to his ledger. Big on torture. He likes crotch shots."

"He's been in D.C. for a couple of weeks. The Company caught on to that fact after they spotted him leaving the country, bound for Ankara."

"There's more?"

"Apparently the Company has an asset on the cabin crew. The information is that he connected in Ankara en route to Cape Town."

"He's the opposition's lead man, then." It helped to know the characteristics of his counterpart. "See if you can't call up his file, for the next time I call in."

"He might be retired by then. Number two. Coded message for Anchor, from Batman."

To the DDO from Coriolanus. Hamm had always suspected that Coriolanus had selected his own code name. "Damn, Diane! You got hold of a real rare bird, didn't you?"

"My secret. I've got a few friends, too. Your

guy left Cape Town on a train at, or shortly after, noon, your time."

"That son-of-a-bitch fed me a line of shit about an airplane. Thanks, Diane. Remember that file." Hamm hung up, and while he checked out, one of the agents went to a telephone and the other left the lobby by the front door, probably to find his car.

Hamm slipped into a taxi waiting in the rank in front of the hotel. He dropped a double fare of rand on the front seat and requested speed. The driver hit the accelerator pedal hard, and they shot out into the evening traffic. The neon lights cast a multi-hued glare over the city and reflected off the hoods of cars. Within five blocks, he spotted the three cars tailing him. Mentally, he assigned two of them to the CIA. They were taking no chances. One would stay with him, or the other would. The third car would be NIS or the Soviets. Everyone was closing in.

It did not matter to him. He was not going to elude them this time, not in the city.

After the twelve-mile run toward Bellville, on the boulevard leading into Malan Airport, the driver swung off toward General Aviation and deposited him in front of the operations office. Hamm went in, paid his fuel bill and parking fee, then filed a flight plan for Johannesburg.

Twenty minutes later, wheels up at twenty-two thousand feet, he set his NavCom's and autopilot. Cape Town was a flat glow behind him, and Africa was a dark abyss ahead of him. Above, the Southern Cross was a reassuring beacon. A sprinkling of lights on his right would be Paarl and Stellenbosch. Hamm flipped on a chart light and spread his map out on his lap.

Terrell had about a six-hour lead if he had taken a train around noon, but Hamm was closer to the man than he had been for weeks. He estimated a train speed of about sixty miles an hour, counting stops, and added a couple of hours as a fudge factor. With a compass, he drew a new radius centered on Cape Town. "Goddamn, Bob! That puts you in the middle of nowhere."

Where was he going? Hamm projected ahead, giving Terrell another thirty hours of travel time, and drew another radius.

Within the arc were nineteen circles indicating the places where Hamm and Terrell had spent at least three days when they were doing their intelligence-gathering tours together. There would be other places that Hamm was not certain about; places Terrell had visited when he was with the Peace Corps.

He was certain of one thing. Terrell did not often go anywhere on his own. He was well-traveled, especially in Africa, but his first visits to any new locale were made as a result of being ordered to go there. He never minded returning to a city he had toured earlier, but that first effort was a struggle. They had talked about that once, on Terrell's first visit to Pretoria. That had been a long and slightly drunken night.

With a pen, Hamm started crossing off circles—Bloemfontein, Pretoria, Johannesburg, Pietermaritzburg, Kimberley. All too close, he thought. He crossed off three cities in Namibia. Terrell had never cared for the arid country.

Forget Botswana for the same reasons. Hamm found his target areas were leaning to the east.

Salisbury? Terrell liked it well enough, but had seemed uncomfortable there during the two months they had headquartered their study in Zimbabwe. He crossed it off.

Quelimane, Zambia? It gave him access to the sea, an additional route out, if rail or air became a problem for him. Hamm put a question mark over the circle.

Now we're in Central Africa, he thought. Tanzania. Dar es Salaam. Bukoba, on the lake. Terrell loved Lake Victoria. Bukoba was a nice out-of-the-way place to hide. Hamm lined out Dar es Salaam, then went back and crossed out Quelimane. Somehow, he thought that Terrell might feel trapped on a ship at sea.

He was near the top of the arc of his drawn radius. East of Lake Victoria was Nairobi. They were there for five weeks in the spring of 1976, then back in the fall of that year for a camera safari. Terrell had spent part of his Peace Corps time based in Kenya.

Nairobi, Kenya, was a good bet, if Terrell could make it.

Back up, he told himself. *Start cutting back, because Bob is not going that far, not by train.* Coriolanus would be thinking the same way Hamm was, and he would have the railroad schedules at hand. If Bob had taken, say, a Johannesburg train, they—Coriolanus would have to get local help to chase around the country—would pick a place along the route to intercept him.

Like Bloemfontein. Around midnight.

The clock on the instrument panel read nineteen-oh-three.

Hamm listened to the clipped chatter of an Air France pilot on his frequency, asking for approach instructions to Cape Town, then shut it out.

He forced himself to relax back in the seat and try to change the way he was thinking about Terrell. What was a prime characteristic?

Tenaciousness. Terrell could be very stubborn, much as Hamm could be very stubborn, when he got hold of an idea or a task. What if it was something personal, and GABRIEL was secondary? What if he had another objective entirely locked in his mind?

Hamm went back to his chart and ran his pencil tip along the route of the railroad track. Nothing. No city or village rang bells for him. With his pencil, he began to range out from the train route.

And there it was.

The stopover in Ankara, Turkey, had taken two hours longer than it was supposed to have taken, and Alexi Naratsmov cursed Aeroflot in general and suffered a rare phenomenon—impatience. He sat at a small table in the terminal, drank bitter coffee, and watched through the window as two technicians worked unhurriedly on some hydraulic function of the Illyushin airliner.

Naratsmov was not normally an introspective man, but the delay forced time upon him, and so he reviewed the successes of his past, which were many and varied. In Afghanistan, in Berlin, in London, in cities becoming too numerous to list, he had achieved his and the Supreme Soviet's ends through relentless persistence and the appropriate application of a blade or an electrode. His record was flawless. He would not fail now.

Naratsmov deplaned in Cape Town at seven-thirty in the evening. He searched the airport crowd behind the customs barrier for Josef Malengorov and found him immediately. Malengorov's face was a dark frown, impatient as he waited for Naratsmov to move through the diplomatic line.

After he was passed from the inspection table with his single carry-on bag, he joined the Cape Town *rezident* in the jostling crowd of the terminal.

"Comrade Naratsmov."

"Comrade Malengorov. It has been some time."

"Moscow, I think. In the fall of nineteen eighty-two."

"Yes," Naratsmov agreed. It had been a four-week refresher course for First Chief Directorate personnel assigned abroad. The pleasantries accomplished, he asked, "Blue Heron?"

Malengorov took his elbow and guided him toward a glass wall, while checking the watch on his thick wrist. "I have booked you on a flight for Johannesburg that leaves in . . . forty minutes."

"The man has been detected?"

The *rezident* displayed the slight nervousness of those, even ranking KGB personnel, who found themselves in face-to-face contact with Department Twelve. A tic in his left cheek was working overtime. "Not actually seen, no. But Steven Hamm departed for Johannesburg tonight, about an hour ago, flying himself, and Calypso followed soon after, in a chartered aircraft. I suggested to Moscow Center that your target was no longer in Cape Town. Center agreed." Malengorov appeared relieved at the prospect.

Calypso was Coriolanus. If Coriolanus were now involved, the chase might well be coming to a head. The scent was getting stronger. ‘‘They did not go together, Coriolanus and Hamm?’’

‘‘No.’’

The assignment of Steven Hamm to the Terrell case—he had read a photocopy of the special order—had been a mystery to Naratsmov at first. Hamm was an outcast of the American intelligence community. Had he been an operative of the KGB, he would now be cutting timber in the northern reaches of the Soviet Union. It was only his connection to Terrell that had revived his clandestine career. Still, he did not discount the man's talents; they were well documented in his file.

‘‘Hamm has the superior position in the case,’’ he told Malengorov.

‘‘Is that right? Then there must be dissent within the ranks, Colonel, for he was under zealous surveillance by CIA agents while he was in Cape Town.’’

A rift between Hamm and the CIA? It would follow what Naratsmov had learned of the ex-DIA operative.

And further, it was a development that might be exploited to his own advantage. Yes. Alexi checked his own watch. ‘‘Is there a place where we could get a cup of tea before my airplane leaves?’’

TEN

Jack Coriolanus had been in Decker's office studying train schedules when the call came in. De Vroot's sources had said that Terrell was spotted in the train station sometime between noon and two o'clock, and he was checking off the potential destinations for trains leaving Cape Town within that time span.

He picked up the receiver. "Mr. Coriolanus? This is Jim Draper. Hamm just left the airport."

Hamm had bought Decker's performance, then, taken the airline bait. Coriolanus reached for the stack of airline schedules. "All right, Draper, good. We're finally pushing Hamm into an action he'll regret. What airline?"

"None, sir. He was flying a Lear."

"Son-of-a-bitch!" He had not expected Hamm to have a plane available. "He file a flight plan?"

"Yes, sir. For Johannesburg."

Coriolanus paused. The destination agreed with one of several available to Terrell if he had left Cape Town on the twelve-twenty train. If Hamm thought Terrell's plans had been fouled, and he had had to leave the city by air, rather than train, then Coriolanus was finally forcing the issue. Hamm was planning to run down Terrell in Johannesburg.

Roy Decker's one-act play had served two purposes. It had given Coriolanus a direction to follow, and it had moved Hamm out of the action.

"Charter an airplane for me, Draper."

"Yes, sir. There's something else, sir."

"What's that?"

"Mr. Decker met with Hamm, just before he left the hotel."

The assistant DDO knew that. He had set it up. "Get me that aircraft."

Coriolanus replaced the phone in its cradle. Hamm had been stonewalling all along. He had known all along how to reach Terrell, but he was protecting his dear old buddy. Coriolanus did not think Hamm would risk losing the GABRIEL file, but Hamm might have some idea of talking Terrell into returning to Washington voluntarily in some kind of compromise deal.

Compromise with traitors was unacceptable to Coriolanus.

He would fry both Terrell and Hamm, slowly.

Coriolanus checked his map and found several likely spots where he could beat Hamm to the punch for a change.

Decker had a Rolodex file of frequently called

numbers on the desk, and Coriolanus flipped through it until he found de Vroot's. He did not like the idea, but he thought he had better have a local authority on tap. He was likely to incur the wrath of the Bloemfontein police force if he did not have somebody with clout along when he pulled Terrell off that train.

And he made a mental note to arrange a salary increase for Decker. Put a little pressure on the chief of station, Cape Town, and he performed.

While Hamm raced for Johannesburg, Coriolanus was free to do what he should have been doing from the beginning, recovering the GABRIEL file on his own.

Coriolanus felt very good about the whole thing. Some people in the White House were going to learn that the real expertise was headquartered at Langley, Virginia. Eugene Kuster and his people could go into some other kind of business. Real estate, maybe.

When de Vroot answered his home telephone, Coriolanus told him that he was certain de Vroot's earlier information about Bryce Calder was correct, and wondered if it would not be possible to pick up the man in Bloemfontein.

"Let me see if I can borrow a helicopter, Mr. Coriolanus. I'll call you back."

It was one-thirty in the morning when Jack Coriolanus and Peter de Vroot stood inside the Bloemfontein station and watched through the window overlooking the platform as the teams of policemen went through the passenger cars. An occasional hiss of compressed air could be heard through the window. The arc lamps along the platform provided an eerie half light that made the ribs of the railroad cars stand out in bas relief. The lights inside the coaches had been brought to full intensity, and disgruntled, sleepy passengers mouthed silent curses and peered out their windows.

Bloemfontein, the capital of Orange Free State, was a city of about two hundred thousand people, and because of its central location, it had always been a communications and transportation hub. The railroad yards were extensive, and de Vroot had them well covered with nearly a hundred men from police and army units.

Jim Draper, who was turning out to be a promising young agent, stood near at hand, ready for any task. Coriolanus had sent Roy Decker on to Johannesburg to pick up on Hamm.

"This won't take long," de Vroot promised. He smoothed the tips of his moustache with his thumb and forefinger.

"Oh?"

"We're looking for a white face."

"Yes, that's true."

"Then," de Vroot said, "I would like a little time with your man Calder."

"I suspect something can be arranged. I will need to talk to him first, however. I need to be certain that the weapons were all he removed from the arsenal. National security and all."

"Understandable, I would say."

After twenty minutes, two policemen approached the waiting room, leading a young lady carrying a baby. She walked tall, her back straight, and though her clothes were good, they were wrinkled badly. The older policeman opened the door for her and ushered her inside. The baby was crying.

"Mr. de Vroot, this is Mrs. Margaret Redding. She recognized the picture." The cop stepped back.

"What do you want with Mr. Simmons?" The lady addressed de Vroot, and she was on the up side of irate. The baby was crying, and Margaret Redding patted its back, cooing under her breath. It had no effect at all.

De Vroot offered her a winning smile. "Please excuse the delay, Mrs. Redding. It is insufferable, I know, but also unavoidable. First, we need to know if it is the right Simmons. Do you know the first name?"

"Albert," she said, succumbing to the smile.

"That will be the one. We need to talk to him."

"About what?"

"An emergency in the family."

She could understand family emergencies. "Oh, no! Not serious, I hope."

"Serious enough that Mr. Simmons should be traveling home immediately. Do you know which carriage he is in?"

Redding's face showed very real concern. "I'm afraid you've missed him. He got off the train sometime back."

"Do you know where that might have been, ma'am?" de Vroot asked.

"I was asleep at the time. But I missed him when I awakened."

Coriolanus spun toward Draper. "Call Johannesburg, locate Decker, and find out what time Hamm landed there."

Draper ran for the phones, but the concrete feeling in Coriolanus's stomach told him the answer. Hamm had not gone to Johannesburg.

The first time he had been in this part of the country, Terrell had been struck by its vastness. It was bigger than Texas, just miles and miles of miles. In 1967, he had never been to Texas, and he had no desire ever to go. At the time he had no desire to go to Vietnam, either, and the Peace Corps appeared to him an honorable alternative.

De Aar had looked the same to him now, except there were more cars, perhaps more color adorning the streets. Civilization brought with it an overlay of plastic and litter—soda cans, cardboard, and candy wrappers were cached in the alleyways. Advertisements glared from billboards and walls, some of them in English. He was advised to buy a Ford in Xhosa and spend his rand on Pepsi in Sesotho.

It was like placing a lacy doily over the worn spot on the couch, hiding the real South Africa. The poverty was just as appalling as it had ever been. Little boys, stomachs bloated, held out hands in supplication, their eyes big and hopeful.

It had been nearly dark when he had stepped down from his car and disappeared into the thin crowd around the depot at De Aar. A two-block walk found him a dealership that also rented cars, and some haggling over rand and the conversion price of American dollars had gotten him a Land Rover that was in fair shape. A few extra dollars and a promise to have it back within the week allowed him to sign the rental agreement with the name of Thompson, without producing documentation.

The roads were not in the best condition, and Terrell was not an exceptional driver. He drove carefully, alert for chuckholes or small animals that might dart into the glare of his headlights. The manual transmission was old, and the gears ground on every shift. His attention was focused on the road ahead, and he did not take time to think about what might be out in the brush and scrub on either side of him. For the most part, this was agricultural and stock-raising country, and infrequently he would spot the lighted windows of a farmhouse. The quarter-moon seemed much brighter here than it would have anywhere else in the world.

"How about that, moon? Didn't expect me back, did you?" he muttered to himself.

He had the windows open and the warm air was fragrant with the lives unseen in the darkness—feral and free. "Anyone out there?" he shouted to the night, raising his voice over the roar of the Land Rover's engine.

By two A.M., he had passed through Britstown and Camarvon and Sakrivier. When he saw the few lights of the next town several miles away, Terrell pulled off the road, banged over a quarter-mile of rough terrain, and parked in a copse of trees. He did not think it would be good to make his approach in the middle of the night. "There will be checkpoints," he told himself. "Early morning will be better, just before first light."

"They will stop you, Robert. You cannot return."

"You forget. I am Mzibele. I was given that name by Mbuoto himself. I know this land."

"You have been away many years, Robert. A quarter of a century. Think about it."

''It is still my land,'' he insisted, ''and the land of my fathers. I will not be denied my right.''

He could not be denied. Terrell knew that deep in his heart.

Turning off the ignition, he climbed out of the Land Rover and found a tree against which he urinated. Then he unclipped the two jerry cans from the rear rack and refilled the tank of the Rover.

He was hungry, but he had not picked up anything to eat. ''Rather shortsighted for a planner.''

''More shortsighted for a man who is supposed to know Africa, Robert. You do not have binoculars, a sleeping bag, or even a rifle.''

''I am not likely to run into a lion,'' he told himself. ''Especially not after what they have done here.''

''And that is a pity, Robert. It is beyond pity.''

He scrambled up a short slope on the other side of the copse and found a place to sit on a flat rock. Insects darted away from his intrusion, barely seen under the sliver of moonlight. Above him, the Southern Cross was a recognized focal point in a million stars. ''What was it Hamm told me about the stars?''

''That they were saviors. He told you how to recognize them, Robert.''

''But he spoke from a navigator's point of view. I have never needed them.''

''Until now, perhaps.''

''The Southern Cross is enough for me.''

It was strangely quiet there, more silence than he remembered. The chirping and slithering in the scrub around him was subdued. It was an induced silence, as if the animal and insect kingdoms were in some state of heightened awareness, waiting.

Despite that feeling of uneasiness, Terrell thought he could spend the rest of his years right there, dreamily and happily at peace with this world.

"The world will not let you rest for long, Robert."

"That is true. It falls to me."

He had to formulate the details of the plan that had come to him on the train. He would have to recover the software from Evensong, and he would need a computer, one of the big ones. He would need access to the microwave communications system.

"To anyone other than you, it would seem impossible, Robert."

"Nothing is impossible. Witness the masterful handling of GABRIEL by Dr. Lawrence Pelagio. God, Larry, despite your stubborn and tunnel-eyed determination, I miss you. We had good talks."

Pelagio had explained it to him in all its minutiae. The Soviet Union, for example, was quite deficient in her communications systems for personal and commerce utilization. Instead, she channeled her rubles and stolen technology into military uses, and that computer-controlled communications network for voice and data transfer was almost state-of-the-art. That was just what GABRIEL thrived on.

The basic premises for GABRIEL were: first, entry into the communications network via telephonic landline—which then led to microwave relay and satellite transmission facilities; second, unobstructed utilization of the network. *Unobstructed* was the key word, of course, and the bulk of GABRIEL's programming was dedicated to achieving that end.

Most confidential circuits in a communications network were protected by access codes. Highly classified circuits—those used by the military—were protected by multiple-access codes. In addition to security codes, some military transmissions had automatic frequency changes built into them, designed to confuse and to inhibit monitoring.

The theory, according to Pelagio, was that security codes were developed by men, and whatever men could do, the computer could do faster. GABRIEL, thanks to the Cray supercomputer, could contact a Soviet satellite and run random security access codes against the opposing computer's request for a code until it had the right one. GABRIEL did it in nanoseconds. No security system in any network, no matter how sophisticated, could resist GABRIEL.

"That is correct, isn't it, Larry?"

"He cannot talk to you, Robert."

"Ah, but he knew the power. No one can resist it. Every system is vulnerable—the Soviet, Chinese, British, French . . . and the American."

ELEVEN

"Commander Voros," DeMott said, "is scheduled to be released from active duty in October. When I talked to his wife, she told me that he had decided against a navy career because he had been offered an enticing position with the Central Intelligence Agency."

"We know who made the offer," Hamm said. "Gene do anything about Voros?"

"Not yet. He said he may want to use Voros as an unofficial conduit."

"It's a good thought," Hamm agreed.

"I can barely hear you." Her voice sounded weak and it crackled on the line.

"It's a temporary telephone system. The electromagnetic pulse effects of the blast fried most of the electronics in the area. I haven't been near the site, but there are nine aircraft grounded here because of damage to their radio and navigation systems. You get the Chukker file?''

''Yes. He's a real son-of-a-bitch, Steve. Forty-five, six-two, one hundred fifty pounds, dark hair. The picture I have shows he's grim-looking, very thin. There is a listing of places where he has been spotted—generally all over the world, and specifically in the Berlin area. It seems to be a home base. No specific crime or murder can be attributed to him, but he's suspected in . . . it must be over fifty cases. Most of them gruesome.''

''Education?''

''Moscow Institute and apparently all of the right FCD courses. The estimate is that he's very intelligent. He gets a lot of rein.''

''It's the same guy I was thinking of,'' Hamm told her. ''I've seen some of the remnants he's left behind.''

''You ready for a report of my activities now?''

''Yours? I haven't been keeping you busy enough?''

''There's a spare hour or two. I got Gene to push some buttons and get me into Bob's office.''

''And you found something.''

''Damned right,'' she said, ''but not what I was looking for. SPG had cleaned out anything sensitive, but I found a newspaper clipping and a set of SR-seventy-one reconnaissance photographs in a desk drawer.''

''All about Brandvlei,'' Hamm guessed.

''That's why you're there, isn't it?''

''I took a long shot. Tell me about the photos.''

Hamm listened while DeMott told him about the

eight twelve-by-fourteen photographs taken by a CIA Blackbird. They were on 2402-type film, which clearly highlighted details in blue and white against an orange background. Green circles were superimposed every two hundred yards, to provide range estimates.

Ground zero was eighteen hundred yards northeast of the edge of Brandvlei and about two miles from the airfield where Hamm was located. He had feigned engine trouble on the Lear in order to gain an emergency landing.

There was nothing left of what must have been an artillery battery at ground zero. Six miles to the north was a battalion-sized grouping of tents and vehicles. There were seven platoon- and company-strength groups spread about eight miles apart to the south of that encampment.

An air burst would have had wider effects, but the ground burst of a ten-kiloton yield—the CIA estimate—ground-launch vehicle had been contained to some degree. In the first three hundred yards, everything looked melted. Out to eight hundred yards, the vegetation was gone. Five armored personnel carriers at a thousand yards were now five steel skeletons. No one in the vehicles lived through it. At fifteen hundred yards to the west, four farm buildings stood, but the roofs were gone. The trees were denuded as far as Brandvlei, and the town itself, though still standing, was littered with glass, brick, overturned cars, and other debris.

Hamm could not believe they had been playing their war games that close to a population center.

"Current status?"

"Still quarantined. The report I've got says that

there are guard outposts about every mile around the zone. There are some roving patrols. Apparently, it's fairly clean within about a thousand yards of ground zero. Cleanup work is taking place over most of the area."

"How about to the east of me? Anything out there?"

"Let me see. No. Desert and scrub. It looks like most of the vegetation is burned off. Just a minute. Slightly to the east, and two miles to the north of the airfield, there is—was—something." Hamm waited while she perused the picture. "It must have been a village of some kind, Steve. It looks like there were thirty-two buildings. It's just foundations now."

A town disintegrated.

"That's probably it, then. Bob said his second Peace Corps assignment had been near Brandvlei."

Hamm considered his position. The security at the airfield was heavy, though he did not have a personal escort, probably because he was military. The general in charge had ordered him to stay in the canteen, the operations hut, or the hangar, where some poor mechanic was looking for his nonexistent fuel problem.

"How is Nancy doing?" Hamm asked.

"Not well, though her hopes are up a little."

"You didn't tell her Bob had been spotted?"

"Of course I did."

"Goddamn it, Diane!"

"Goddamn it, yourself!" DeMott yelled back. "He's her husband. She's entitled."

DeMott went silent, but did not apologize.

Hamm said, "Look, I'd better get going. . . ."

"Wait," she said, as if she did not want to lose contact with him. "Is it bad, where you're at?" DeMott asked.

"They want us to stay inside, as much as possible."

"Sound advice," she agreed.

Hamm had another thought. "What do your current photos show for Bob's village?"

"It's about seventeen hundred yards from ground zero. You wouldn't want to stay in the area for more than a couple of hours. You aren't thinking about going out there?"

"Not for more than a couple of hours," Hamm told her.

By the time they reached De Aar, in a convoy of four army vehicles, it was seven-thirty in the morning, and Peter de Vroot's cheeks were coated in reddish bristles of whiskers.

Jack Coriolanus levered himself out of the backseat of the utility vehicle and stretched sore muscles. He had slept fitfully for two hours, and he felt gritty. His mouth was dry and tasted rotten. His suit held compressed wrinkles. The dirt of Africa was ground into his skin and his shirt collar. His temper was shorter than normal.

De Vroot had alerted every police station on the railroad line between Cape Town and Bloemfontein, and they had received a continuous stream of negative radio reports throughout the night as they backtracked the route of the train. The police and army units canvassing the hamlets and towns could not find anyone who had seen Terrell.

Until this.

Coriolanus rotated his shoulders, working the

fatigue out of them as de Vroot clambered out of the truck. They stood in front of a gray, weather-beaten building with a false front. Across the top of the building, in faded red letters, was the sign: GORENVELD'S FINE MOTOR CARS. There was one two-year-old Buick inside, behind a window streaked with grime. There were four other automobiles in the small lot next to the building. The small sign stuck in the bottom corner of the front window read AUTOMOBILES FOR HIRE.

A lean man with a fat face leaned against the Buick inside the building, and de Vroot and Coriolanus went inside to meet him.

"Meneer Gorenveld?" de Vroot asked.

"The same."

"You're the one who saw Simmons?"

"I've been told as much. Only he called himself Thompson."

"Last night, it was? What time?"

"You going to damage my Land Rover?"

De Vroot paused, then asked again, "Do you remember the time, Meneer Gorenveld?"

"I want my Land Rover back in one piece."

"We'll do our utmost to see that that happens."

"Around six, little after. I wasn't paying attention."

"Do you recall in which direction he went when he left?"

"Didn't see it."

One of the policemen stepped inside the front door and called to Coriolanus, "Radio call for you, sir."

Coriolanus abandoned the interrogation and went outside to take a microphone hanging outside the window of the army truck. "Coriolanus, here."

"This is Decker. Over."

"Where you at?" Coriolanus did not bother with radio procedure.

"Johannesburg. According to the radio monitor tapes here, a Lear jet developed engine trouble and went down last night. Over."

Coriolanus did not care if Hamm plowed himself into the South African desert, except that the man was his link to Terrell. "How bad?"

"Emergency landing at Brandvlei military field was approved. I don't know the conditions. Over."

Shit! That meant the meet with Terrell was screwed up. If Hamm had intended to corner Terrell somewhere other than Johannesburg, it was all fucked up now. "Brandvlei? Where have I heard that name?"

"It's where the nuclear device went off. It's in quarantine at the moment. Over."

Well, that neutralized Hamm, anyway. Except that Coriolanus had no idea where Terrell was headed.

"One thing more, Mr. Coriolanus. Cape Town reports that Chukker is in the country. Over."

"Who the hell is Chukker?"

"On the air, sir? Over."

"On the goddamned air!" Coriolanus yelled into the mike.

"Alexi Naratsmov, KGB Department Twelve. Over."

More of the players were being identified. The Soviets wanted Terrell badly. "Current location?"

"In Jo-burg. Over."

"Get a tail on him. Out." Coriolanus dropped the microphone and stood for a moment, thinking about Brandvlei. When the connection finally unraveled in his mind, he ran back to the showroom. De Vroot looked up as he skidded on the dirty linoleum inside the doorway.

"How fast can we get to Brandvlei?" Coriolanus wanted to know.

The train had been late coming into Johannesburg. Alexi Naratsmov and one of the three agents he had commandeered from the Johannesburg contingent watched every face that exited from the arrival platform. Robert Terrell's was not among them.

The other two operatives, stationed at vantage points in the railroad yard, reported by portable radio that Terrell had not tried to slip away by another route. Only a black man, an apparent fugitive, was taken into custody by police.

Normally an even-tempered man, Naratsmov was becoming angry. Either someone was providing him with inaccurate information, or perhaps the information was incomplete. Naratsmov went to the public telephone, thumbed through the directory, and called the general aviation office at the main airport. He was searching for a friend who had not arrived as expected, he explained.

The lady checked her logbook, then told him, "I'm terribly sorry, sir, but I can find no entry for a private jet aircraft landing between six o'clock and midnight last night."

Alexi slammed the phone back on its hook. Now he had lost both Hamm and Coriolanus, his tenuous links to Terrell. They were all somewhere between Cape Town and Johannesburg. They had to be, if Terrell had been on the train, as Malengorov reported.

Turning to the agent standing beside him, Naratsmov said, "In psychoanalysis, where there is a problem, the analyst goes back into the patient's childhood."

"Comrade Colonel?" The man was extremely puzzled.

"I may have missed something. Take me back to the consulate. I need to use the communications room. And get someone out to the airport. We want to know what happened to Hamm's airplane."

Several hours passed before a KGB captain appeared in Alexi's borrowed office. Naratsmov pushed his hand through the forelock of black hair that hung over his forehead, then looked up from Terrell's file. "Tell me."

"An aircraft identified as Lear seven-nine made an emergency landing last night. At a military field near Brandvlei," the captain told Naratsmov.

"How close is it, and how would we get there?" Naratsmov asked. He had never been to South Africa before, and the geography was strange to him.

The captain smiled at him. "One of our cover companies has a helicopter available, and it has the range, but the area in question is under army control."

"Let us get under way, then," Naratsmov said, to the captain's consternation. Armies had never deterred him in the past.

TWELVE

A year ago, Mbuoto, who was nearly eighty years old, had sent him pictures of a valley green with crops and grass in November, of herds of cattle that numbered in the thousands. There were eland in the northern pastures, free to reach the salvation of stored water in the lake. The reservoir was more than eight miles long, and the trees that Robert had planted along its shores, working side by side with Mashona tribesmen, were fully leafed, providing shady refuges for migrating eland and buffalo. Water birds spotted the lake, swooping in graceful, frozen arcs. The visual senses were buffeted by the hundreds of colors of wild flowers spread like patchwork quilts along the rises and dips of the grazing land. It was not the drab, beige-toned picture of the African veld that most people visualized.

Terrell had parked the Land Rover on a slope slightly above where the reservoir he had helped build had once been. Below to the west was where the kraal of Mbuoto, Mashona chieftain, had once been.

"Mbuoto, my friend, where are you? Will you not come out to see me?"

"He is gone, Robert. And all he knew with him."

"It can't be. Think of the struggle."

"There will no longer be a struggle, Robert. Perhaps it is for the best."

"No! This . . . this is never the answer. I have killed my friend."

"Not you, Robert."

"Yes, me. And my ilk."

Now, there was no grass. There was red, packed earth, hardened to the consistency of iron by a relentless sun. The skeletal remains of five thousand cattle were like whitecaps on a vast red sea.

There was no lake. The earthen dam, broadened, strengthened, and heightened over a quarter-century, had a V-shaped cleft to the right of its center. He wondered if the water had boiled.

Certainly, the village below the reservoir had been destroyed before the water had ever reached it. The demarcations in the ground, where structures had once stood, were clearly visible. Terrell started the engine and drove down the slope, then parked clear of the village boundary.

It was very quiet. When the miniature sun erupted, the blast effects, the concussion, and the firestorm had eliminated all life.

He got out and stood for a moment, trying to recall the locations of the communal kitchen, the granary, the sanitary facilities he had built with his own hands. The kraal—the primary social unit among tribes of the Bantu—was always formed in a horseshoe shape, surrounding the cattle yard, with the first hut the residence of the first wife of the patriarch.

Terrell walked slowly through the debris. The flames had reached everywhere. Poles that had once supported thatched roofs were canted and fire-blackened. Corrugated tin that had adorned walls was bent and warped like crepe paper. Fabrics, pottery shards, silverware, furnishings, and cooking utensils were twisted and scorched. An old Citroën lay on its side, windowless; the wheels were hooped with the wires once enclosed in rubber. The army had been here, to clean up. The tire tracks of the trucks and personnel carriers crisscrossed the village, driving right through the places where people had lived.

The community water tank, hand-shaped from mud blocks, had been right here, the water piped down from the reservoir.

Here, to the east of the water tank, in a row of several huts, was where Mbuoto, proud Mashona chieftain, his three wives, his thirteen children, and his thirty-two grandchildren had lived. Terrell walked through the wreckage. An old porcelain bathtub, one of its feet missing, was upended in one corner. A propane-operated refrigerator lay on its side. Brittle pieces of bone were sprinkled about in the red earth and reflected the white light of the sun. The army had not recovered everything.

They would be back, with bulldozers, to sweep

away the residue of a human existence, a proud heritage, a struggle with nature that had been won.

Until the godplayers miscalculated.

Robert Terrell wept as he had been unable to do in three weeks. He had tried, from the moment he had read the press releases out of South Africa, from the time he had obtained the surveillance photographs.

He stood in the middle of a world he had helped to create and cried until his shoulders ached.

First, Hamm went back to the hangar where his Lear was being treated and made himself a nuisance to the two mechanics who were replacing the panels in the starboard wing and on the starboard engine pod. His constant questioning and inept advice quickly gave them a reason for wanting him out of their way.

"You sure you got it?" he asked.

"We flushed the line, mate. Should be all right now."

"I don't want to get her up and lose that engine again. Least of all on takeoff. You sure that panel's on there tight?"

"It's tight."

"Looks bent to me," Hamm told the chief mechanic, whose name tag red Wilcoxen.

"Mate, that's the way it's supposed to look."

"You sure?"

"You want me to take it up first, Yank? I'm qualified in twin jets, and I'm not afraid of it."

When he was sure the two men would be thrilled by his absence, he climbed aboard the Lear and removed the seat cushion from the seat next to the one disguising the Porta Potty. In addition to his extra set of papers, this seat hid a small arsenal. He retrieved a Browning automatic and a magazine loaded with nine-millimeter rounds, checked the action and the load, then slapped the magazine in place, locked the safety, and shoved the pistol into his belt, under his shirt. It was as hot as hell, so he shrugged out of his suit coat and left it lying on one of the seats. Pulling his tie free, he tossed it on top of the jacket. He wished he had shoes other than the thin-soled street shoes.

Climbing out of the aircraft, he said, "Maybe I'll take a walk."

"Good idea, mate," the chief mechanic told him and cast a look of relief toward his assistant.

There were only three hangars and an operations hut at the airfield, and they were crowded. Not many people wanted to venture outside. Most of the activity was based in the largest hangar and the operations office, where a brigadier general had set up his headquarters. Hamm found himself alone as he passed though the chain-link fence and walked along the asphalt road fronting the hangars. Within a block, he found a 1958 Chevy pickup angled into a low ditch. It was battered and bare-skinned where it had been blasted by wind-driven sand. The keys were in the ignition, and it started right away. It was of a vintage that had not suffered from high-tech electronic ignition.

He was not challenged as he backed it out of the shallow drainage ditch, then drove east on the asphalt. Hamm kept an eye on the runway and buildings as he passed, but no one appeared interested in him.

The inside of the cab was baking, and Hamm rolled down his window.

The pavement petered out within a quarter-mile, turning to dust and potholes, and he continued ahead on a dirt road that paralleled the runway. A mile later, he reached the boundary of the airfield and got out to pull back a gate composed of four strands of barbed wire stapled to three uprights. A C-130, with South African markings, took off from the base, passing over him as it climbed steeply toward the mid-morning sun. Off to his left, he saw a big, dual-rotor military helicopter working a search grid. On his right, outside the restricted area, he could see another helicopter. Its white skin suggested it was a civilian aircraft.

He drove east for another two miles, then left the meager dual ruts and headed north. Against the flat terrain, the shriveled trees and shrubs were eerie. This had been grazing and crop land, but now the cattle were lying on their sides, bloated by the heat into foul-smelling blimps. Hamm rolled up his window; the heat was better than the stink of rotting flesh.

The Chevy drove as if it lacked shock absorbers, jouncing and banging in rocky pockets, the wheels slipping in sandy stretches. It took him half an hour to cover the distance to the village. The farther north he drove, the more complete the devastation. Here, the slaughtered beasts did not have hide or meat on them, the bones grotesquely white.

Not exactly certain of the village's location or its current visibility to the eye at ground level, Hamm searched left and right as he drove. The blast effects were terrifying. Stunted trees were stripped to the nub, hardened bark whisked away in the firestorm. The ground was bare and red, and outcroppings showed ashen overlays.

Except for the clatter of unadjusted valves rising from under the hood, it was deathly silent. A landscape set in a vacuum.

A steeper hill appeared before him, and Hamm nosed toward the east, climbing it at an angle, the rear end of the truck sliding frequently. He shifted back and forth between first and second, unable to find a constant speed.

When he topped the hill and looked down on the remnants of the village and saw a Land Rover parked there, Hamm slammed on the brakes and cut the ignition.

He waited several moments, watching the figure beyond the Land Rover. The man was alone, pacing quickly back and forth.

Hamm got out of the Chevy and walked down the hill toward the village, keeping the Land Rover between himself and the man. When he was three hundred yards away, he could tell that it was Terrell.

He pulled his shirttail out and let it hang outside his pants so that he had quicker access to the Browning. He did not know how Terrell was going to react, but he knew he had to be cautious. GABRIEL was the first consideration, and he had to know where it was before he took any kind of action.

When Hamm reached the first row of what had once been dwellings, Terrell saw him. He stopped pacing and began prodding mounds of debris with a broken assegai, holding it by its charred shaft. The iron tip was a mottled blue. Terrell's eyes were reddened, and he moved as if he were in a half daze. Hamm turned his head slightly to hear better. It almost sounded as if Terrell were talking to himself, muttering queries and responses, but Hamm could not understand the words at that distance.

Bob was startled when he looked up and saw Hamm. He did not seem to care that it was Hamm. He halted his stumbling gait and drew the spear and a broken pottery shell tightly against his chest, as if he were afraid of losing them.

"Hello, Bob."

"What are you doing here?" Terrell's pockets were stuffed with items he had picked up. The left corner of his mouth trembled. Hamm could see the tear tracks on his dusty cheeks.

"That was supposed to be my question," Hamm said, slowing his pace.

Terrell did not say anything. He stood and looked at Hamm, but his eyes were focused somewhere way behind Hamm. In Vietnam, Hamm had seen shock victims with the same look.

He moved closer, dodging around a partially burned bureau of drawers that lay on its front, and halted ten feet from his friend.

"I came to see you. There's some things we need to talk about, Bob."

Abruptly, Terrell spun around, nearly tripping over his own feet, and waved the spear in an exaggerated motion. "These were my friends."

"Yeah, I know."

"They're dead now."

"I understand your grief, Bob."

"Do you?" Terrell's voice was squeaky. He kept turning in a circle, his eyes maddened, his motions with the assegai abrupt. "They haven't even buried them. Did you know a Mashona chief is buried with his possessions, with his beer pots?"

"No, I didn't know that."

"In the old days, he also got his servants buried with him."

"I didn't know that, either, Bob."

Hamm took a few more steps. He was not certain how he was going to deal with this. Terrell seemed to have accepted his presence, but Hamm was afraid that the man's mind was not going to accept rational suggestions.

On his next rotation, Terrell stopped to face Hamm, and his eyes were focused now. He pointed at the truck with the broken spear. "Who's with you? There's someone else there."

"All by my lonesome, Bob. I've got a Lear back at the field. I think we ought to go get on it and go home."

A single tear welled out of Terrell's right eye and trickled down his cheek. "Home. This was a home."

The man looked awful, Hamm thought. A zombie. Something vital had burned out within him. He took one more step. "Nancy would like to see you."

"I like Nancy."

"If we go get on my airplane, you can see her in a few hours."

Terrell's eyes narrowed in suspicion. "You got others back there. They'll get me."

"Not as far as I know, Bob."

"I don't want to talk to anyone."

"We'll give it some time."

Terrell turned around again, rotating three hundred sixty degrees.

Hamm did not know what else to say. He had never worked with anyone this close to the edge. He raised his right arm and put it around Terrell's shoulders, turning him back toward the Land Rover. The touch caused Bob to start. He leaned his head forward, staring into Hamm's eyes. He clutched his relics tightly. "I've got to bury these with Mbuoto."

"I'll help you. We'll find out what we need to do."

With soft pressure against Terrell's back, Hamm urged him into a slow shuffle, and they walked toward the Land Rover, skirting piles of partly recognizable domestic goods. A chair leg. Part of a table. A kerosene lantern, with the glass gone.

Hamm saw a foot. A baby's foot.

He slanted his body, hoping to block Bob's view. Terrell was staring off into the distance again, clutching the spear in his white-knuckled right hand.

Then they were out of the village ruins, picking up the pace a little. Under his arm, he felt Terrell's shoulders broaden and become stronger, the farther they got from the carnage.

He felt that if he could get Terrell away from the village, the man would come back from wherever it was he had gone. "One thing I have to ask you, Bob."

Terrell turned his head toward him. His face had a glow to it, a sheen of fresh sunburn over the tan, and yet it still appeared pale under the streaks running down his ash-covered cheeks. His eyes were magnified under the lenses of his glasses, and the corner of his mouth continued to twitch, not under his control.

"You have anything with you? A suitcase?"

"A what?"

"Luggage. We don't want to leave anything behind."

"I've got it." He held up the broken pot and the spear.

They reached the Land Rover. Hamm looked in the side window and saw the key plugged into the ignition.

There was a suitcase lying on the right seat. Gently, Hamm let go of Terrell and opened the door. "This all you have with you?"

Terrell nodded.

Hamm pulled the suitcase out. *Damn!* he thought. *It had better be here.* Placing it on the ground, he knelt and flipped one of the catches. "What does the file look like, Bob?"

"File?"

"The GABRIEL file. We've got to take it with us."

Hamm released the other catch.

Terrell dropped the pot, grabbed the haft of the assegai with both hands, and raised it high.

Out of the corner of his eye, Hamm saw the heavy iron point coming full circle. He raised his right hand in defense.

Too late.

A flash of white pain shot through his brain.

It lasted a microsecond, and was followed by blackness.

THIRTEEN

The sleek Lear jet, with a blue stripe and an HIC logo on its tail, had been standing outside the hangar on the tarmac, ready to go, when de Vroot and Coriolanus arrived aboard an army helicopter. The pilot put them down next to the Lear and the rotors slowed in a descending whine as the two men ducked out of the cabin.

Two mechanics lounged in the partially opened door of the hangar, one of them chewing on an unlit cigar. They stared at the arriving aircraft with only mild curiosity.

The NIS man led Coriolanus directly to the administration building, where they found a brigadier who was in charge of the "cleanup."

The brigadier, once he was introduced to Coriolanus, became quite reserved. He was not thrilled at having an American intelligence operative in his office, or anywhere in his neighborhood.

"Can't let you see the site, Mr. Coriolanus."

"Not our purpose, General," de Vroot answered. "We would like to talk to the man who flew that Lear jet in."

"Ah, Colonel Hamm. Yes, well, he should probably be in the canteen. I told him he had to leave as soon as his repairs were finished."

The canteen was in the same building. It was crowded with army personnel when Coriolanus and de Vroot looked in. The seating around the available tables was packed, and men leaned against the walls or stood in long lines at the vending machines.

No Hamm.

"You didn't expect to find him, did you?" Coriolanus asked.

"I cannot say as I did, no. Of course, I am still at a loss as to why we are looking for this Hamm."

"Because he may have an idea about Bryce Calder's whereabouts."

"And Brandvlei—why does that enter the picture?" de Vroot asked.

"Because Calder was once here, when he was in the Peace Corps," Coriolanus said.

"Here? Right in Brandvlei?"

Coriolanus tried to remember the entry in Terrell's file; he had most of it memorized. "Not exactly here. Some village in the vicinity."

"Perhaps the brigadier can spare us a map," de Vroot wondered aloud.

It took only a few moments over the map to find the village. The brigadier cautioned that it no longer existed. Coriolanus insisted on a quick fly-by.

The general pondered for a moment. "Why is this necessary, Meneer de Vroot?"

"The man we seek may be involved in selling illegal firearms."

The brigadier understood that readily enough. He nodded his approval.

Coriolanus and de Vroot ran back to their helicopter, calling for an immediate takeoff. A South African army colonel ran after them and piled into the rear cabin.

In the distance to Coriolanus's right, he saw two more helicopters. Pointing with his right forefinger, he asked de Vroot over the intercom, "Who are they?"

"Media," the colonel answered. He did not act happy about it, and Coriolanus understood his viewpoint.

On a dirt road east of the airfield, he saw an old, rusty pickup bouncing along, raising a trail of dust behind it. It did not seem worth commenting about.

Five minutes later, he saw the village, or what was left of it.

"That's it," de Vroot said, his voice clear in the earphones. The rackety flop-flop of the rotors and the whine of the turbine engine were diminished by the headset.

Thirty seconds later, Coriolanus spotted the vehicle. "Gorenveld will be happy to know his Land Rover is in one piece."

De Vroot and the colonel just looked at him.

Their pilot brought the chopper in low, making a wide circle around the truck. Everyone spotted the body at the same time.

"Put it down," de Vroot ordered.

The tail boom swung downward first. Then the helicopter settled onto its skids. Even as he was sliding out of his seat, Coriolanus recognized the broad back and strong shoulders of the figure on the ground. There was blood spread over the back of his head.

"Shit!" he said to his companions. "It's Hamm."

Robert Terrell saw the Lear jet sitting in front of the first hangar he came to, and he pulled over and parked the pickup next to the chain-link fence separating the apron from the road. Some kind of military cargo plane landed, racing down the runway with its engines screaming.

Over by the big hangar, the next one down, there was some activity. Trucks and personnel carriers were parked in rows, and a few men moved around them. Not much was going on here. He got out from behind the wheel and shrugged into his suit jacket, then picked the automatic pistol he had taken from Hamm off the seat and stuck it in his pocket. Leaning into the cab, he opened his suitcase, found a T-shirt, spat on it, and tried to wash away the dirt and ash on his face. He emptied the odd bits and pieces from his pockets into the suitcase. The assegai was on the floor, and it would not fit in the case, so he left it. Taking his bag, Terrell walked down to an opening in the fence, then started across the tarmac toward the hangar.

He was not certain what he was going to do. Everything seemed a little fuzzy to him. It was difficult to recall what he had been doing for the last day. He remembered the kraal of Mbuoto. He remembered the destruction and a feeling of utter helplessness. There was a strong sense of guilt. There was a numb and almost baffling sense of urgency pushing at him, but the reasons for it were not clear. He was near Brandvlei, and he must leave. No one must get in his way.

Terrell was aware that something had happened to him, fogging his mind momentarily.

"Hamm is here?"

"Confusing, isn't it, Robert? But yes, I'm sure he is."

"He's just like the others. He only wants the file."

"You always knew it could be that way, Robert. After all, he's one of *them*."

"Hey, mate! What're you doing in here?"

He looked up to see a man emerging from the hangar, about thirty feet away.

The man looked him over, checking his suitcase and his dirt-smeared suit. "You ain't supposed to be this side of the fence."

"I want to buy an airline ticket."

"This ain't a commercial field. You'd better scoot out of here, before the army lads see you."

His anxiety rose as he considered being trapped here. "Are you a pilot?"

The man's face relaxed and the unlit cigar in his mouth drooped. "I'm a pilot. Hey, you look kinda beat. You all right?"

"I'll pay you to fly me to Johannesburg."

The man looked skeptical. "How much?"

"How much do you want? A thousand American dollars?"

"I'd sure as hell like to help you out, but I ain't got a plane."

Terrell lifted his right hand and pointed at the Lear jet. ''How about that one?''

''Not mine.''

''You could borrow it. Two thousand dollars.''

The cigar shot to a jaunty angle as the man clenched his teeth, wariness flooding his eyes. ''You want to leave here pretty bad, do you? You got any I.D?''

Terrell bent over and set his suitcase on the concrete, then straightened up, reaching into his pocket. ''Certainly. Here you go.''

He produced the pistol, aiming it at the center of the man's chest. He did not know whether the safety was on. His hand was shaky, and the muzzle wavered widely.

''Hey! Look here—''

''Get in the airplane,'' Terrell ordered. He reached down and picked up his case in his left hand.

''Now, take it easy, mate. I—''

''I don't want to shoot you, but I will.'' He gestured toward the aircraft with the barrel of the pistol.

The man backed away, toward the jet. He had dropped his cigar, and he kept his eyes trained on Terrell's face. ''This is trouble neither of us needs, mate. Why don't we go over and see one of the bigwigs?''

''You want to die here and now, or come back later?'' Robert Terrell could not believe he said that.

The man turned, went around the nose of the plane, and pulled down the door of the jet, then scampered up the steps. ''Yeah, okay. But put that thing away, why don't you?''

Terrell followed him inside the airplane and held the gun as steady as he could, while he figured out how to close and lock the door. "Get in the seat."

His reluctant pilot lowered himself into the left seat, and Terrell took the right.

"Why don't we—"

Terrell held the gun up.

"Okay, okay."

The man went through some checklist, flipping switches, watching the power come up and the gauges spring to life. Terrell searched for a fuel gauge and found one that registered full. "Let's go."

"I've got to call the tower."

"Act like you're Colonel Steven Hamm."

"Hamm?" The pilot—it said Wilcoxen on his nameplate—was surprised. "You know the big Yank who flies this thing?"

"He won't be flying it anymore."

FOURTEEN

Colonel Winfield Storch's voice was squeaky on the temporary telephone system. It did not disguise the incredulity in his tone. He asked, "Just like that, they let him go?"

"You have to understand, Winnie," Jack Coriolanus told him. He spoke loudly to overcome both the telephone and a flight of two helicopters taking off. "The tower was not informed. They had orders to get Hamm and his airplane out as soon as the repairs were completed. Hell, they were happy to see it go."

"And you don't know where Terrell or the airplane is, naturally?"

Coriolanus did not like sarcasm, especially from a jerk like Storch, but he held his temper. He checked his watch. It was just after two. "They filed an oral flight plan for Johannesburg, but didn't show up there. They have about three hours on us."

"You keep saying 'they.' "

It was not a secure line, so Coriolanus used the code name. "Yardstick grabbed himself a pilot. Seems logical to me." *If not to you, asshole,* he thought.

"What about Hamm?"

"They sent him to the nurse's office for an aspirin and a Band-Aid."

There was a long pause while Storch pondered. Then, he said, "Tell me again what you're proposing."

"Hamm knew right where to go, and he knew the right time to go there. It's a goddamned burned-out village in the middle of a militarized zone, not an ideal place for a meeting."

"You're saying Hamm and Yardstick set it up, this meeting? That there's a conspiracy involved?"

From the man's tone, Coriolanus suspected that Storch liked the idea. "How do you read it?"

"I think you knew right where to go, too, based on Yardstick's Peace Corps background and the narrowing manhunt. It just took you longer to figure it out, and you got there late. I read it as Hamm outthinking you."

"Look, Hamm did not follow his orders. He didn't perform the task he was supposed to perform. He let the subject get the upper hand. And he lost a damned expensive airplane."

"Now, those are items I should discuss with the admiral," Storch said. "We'll get back to you. In the meantime, you keep Hamm in tow."

The CIA assistant slammed the phone back on its hook. Goddamned military. Here he was, trying to help out Dilman and Storch, and the bastards were feeding him orders. They did not like Hamm's part in this any more than Coriolanus did, but the tight-assed Defense Department wanted to keep the CIA out of it.

De Vroot entered the small office. The NIS director had taken the time to shave, and his gigantic moustache once again dominated his face.

"I've asked, through channels," Coriolanus said, "for the major airports in Africa to be notified of the stolen aircraft."

"It is unfortunate that we did not notice it was missing until Hamm regained consciousness," de Vroot said. "But you believe, now, that your fugitive arms dealer has left South Africa?"

It was clear in de Vroot's tone that the fugitive story had just about achieved maximum credibility. Coriolanus was no longer certain what he himself believed, but the events of the past few hours did not support the cover story of Bryce Calder's absconding from an Alabama arsenal with a load of weapons.

"It seems likely to me. The man just had a narrow escape."

"I will allow myself to feel relief, in that case," de Vroot said, "and escort you back to Cape Town."

It was obviously the time for diplomacy. "We do appreciate all you've done."

De Vroot shrugged. "It is only a matter of a few thousand man-hours from the army and police forces. And my valuable sleep, of course. No more than a million rand, perhaps two."

"I owe you a big favor."

"I will keep that in mind, you know." De Vroot smiled hugely.

"Let's spring Hamm, and get out of here."

In Johannesburg, Alexi Ivanovitch Naratsmov completed his report detailing what he had seen of the blast site. He gave it to the embassy's communications man. "Encode that, and send it immediately. It should assist the analysts with their evaluation of South Africa's nuclear capability."

"Right away, Comrade Colonel. Will there be anything else?"

"Let me know as soon as you hear anything at all about what happened at Brandvlei. I want to know where Hamm and Coriolanus go. And get Colonel Malengorov on the telephone."

The rotors of the helicopter that had landed at the village site had not allowed him to hear any of the men's shouts and yells. He had watched in helpless anger as they scurried out of the aircraft, racing around to look in the Land Rover and lift the body into the cabin of the helicopter.

He had recognized Coriolanus as one of the helicopter's passengers, but he did not get a good look at the body. It could have been Hamm, or Terrell, or someone else entirely.

Alexi had judged that from the speed with which they moved, the man on the ground had not been dead; they were rushing for medical treatment. That gave him some hope, and as soon as he had arrived back in Johannesburg, he had requested information from Cape Town.

When the telephone at his elbow rang, he picked it up. "Malengorov?"

"At your service, Comrade Naratsmov."

"Detail ten men to cover the Cape Town airport. I want to know if Blue Heron, Calypso, or Gray Tiger arrives there. If they do, the man who loses sight of them is to report directly to me. The railroad and bus terminals should also be watched."

Malengorov cleared his throat noisily. "Of course, Comrade Colonel."

Alexi had another thought. If Terrell were still alive, then Naratsmov had him geographically isolated. It was time to change tactics. He no longer needed Hamm, and it would be far better if the unpredictable ex-DIA man was unable to intervene. It was a task he would prefer for himself, but he asked, "Do you have a man reliable in special operations?"

Malengorov knew immediately the kind of special operation. "An Afrikaaner named Hendrickson."

"Without connection to you?" Alexi asked.

"Without connection to me."

"Good. If I am correct, Gray Tiger is seriously wounded. If he is brought to Cape Town, I do not want him to have a long recovery."

"We shall see that he does not suffer for long," Malengorov said.

"You got all that?" Hamm asked. He was sitting in a straight-backed chair at a tiny desk in the base clinic. It was stuck in the corner of a hangar, and it was small—just the office and two examination rooms.

His head hurt like hell, a throbbing, solid hammer pounding at the base of his skull. His head behind his right ear, and above his neck, had been shaved, and a white patch of bandage covered the stitches.

Diane DeMott read her notes back to him. "One, alert all our people to be watching for the airplane. Two, bring Kuster up to date. Three, call the numbers you gave me and bring those people up to date. You want me to read the phone numbers back to you?"

Hamm closed his address book. "No."

"Four, call the consulate in Cape Town and have them issue you a temporary passport."

He was lucky to have his wallet and his address book. Everything else had been on the Lear. "That's it. Thanks, Diane."

"You sure you're all right?"

"Headache. He got me with the flat of the blade. Took four stitches."

"I can't believe he attacked you," DeMott said. "That's not the Bob Terrell I know."

"He was acting pretty damned strange."

"And you don't know whether or not he had the file?"

"I was two latches short of getting into the suitcase. Which reminds me, Diane. We need to know what the damned file looks like."

"I'll check." DeMott paused while she wrote a note. "It changes things, kind of."

"Yeah," Hamm agreed. "We don't know what is primary—the file or the Brandvlei accident. Maybe Bob doesn't know, either."

The doctor, an army major, came back from wherever it was that he hid the medicinal goodies.

Hamm told DeMott, "I've got to go."

"Stay in touch with me, dammit!"

''I'd really like that,'' he said, and replaced the handset in its cradle.

The doctor shook two pills out of a vial and dumped them into Hamm's hand. ''Want a glass of water, Colonel?''

''I'll manage.'' Hamm swallowed the pills, then accepted the remainder of the vial and stuck it in his pocket. ''What do I owe you?''

''On the house. It's rare that I get to treat a spear wound. You're lucky it was a fellow countryman of yours handling the assegai. One of our boys would have been more accurate.''

Hamm noted the man's rank on his breast pocket tag. Vorhees. ''Happy to have provided the experience. Thanks, Major.''

He heard the tap of leather soles on linoleum, and Coriolanus appeared in the doorway, de Vroot behind him. ''Come on, Hamm. The only way you get out of here is to ride with us.''

The whine of the turbine did not bother him as much on the flight south as did the whopping of the rotors. Hamm sat in the back with his eyes closed, so he would not have to talk to Coriolanus, and waited for the pain pills to have some kind of effect. So far, they only made him dizzy.

Usually, Hamm was at home in the sky, but this flight lasted forever.

Roy Decker was waiting at the airport when de Vroot's borrowed helicopter landed at the military section of Malan Airport. Hamm's headache had diminished a little, but though his head buzzed, his thinking was clear enough to suggest he was headed in the wrong direction. There were not many places of interest south of Cape Town. Terrell would be headed north or east.

They made their good-byes to a de Vroot who was now a bit leery of the both of them, and as the three Americans walked through the terminal, dodging the large crowd of travelers, Decker said, "You look a little pale, Colonel. You going to be all right?"

Hamm remembered Decker's feeding him the misleading information in the Hilton lounge. "Well enough to repay my debts. I still owe you, right?"

It was Decker's turn to pale. He did not look so hot, either, Hamm thought. He turned abruptly away from the two of them and headed toward a public telephone.

"Hey!" Coriolanus yelled. "Where the hell do you think you're going?"

Hamm ignored him, dug his address book out of his pocket, and used his credit-card number to call Nairobi. He kept his back to the two CIA men waiting in the middle of the concourse while he dialed. A stream of passersby also served as a barrier.

"Messenger service." English, with a clipped Kenyan dialect.

"Dave around?"

"Outside, somewhere. I'll see if I can find him."

While he waited, Hamm turned and leaned against the wall, staring at Coriolanus and Decker. Coriolanus glared back at him. Decker looked down at his feet.

He looked at his watch: almost four o'clock. By now Bob would have had to put the Lear down somewhere; the fuel load would have been exhausted. Unless he'd found the HIC credit card in the chart case.

Coriolanus moved closer, shouldering his way through the mob, and Hamm turned his back on him once again.

"This is Messenger."

"Hamm."

"Hey, babe! I just talked to your girl friend. Does the bod match the voice?"

"Damned close," Hamm told him.

"You got a fuck-up, huh?"

"Now I need that transport."

"Where you at?"

"Cape Town."

"I can shake the one-thirty loose; be there in a few hours."

"Can you find something that'll do better than three-eighty? I'm chasing a Lear," Hamm said.

Coriolanus edged closer.

Dave Messenger thought for a moment, then said, "Guy over here, fellow charter service, he's got a Cessna jet, one of the trainers. That do it, if I can rent it?"

"That'll do it."

"Where do I meet you?"

Hamm turned around to look at Coriolanus as he said, "I've got an asshole listening in. I'll reach you."

"Gotcha. General Aviation? Somewhere south of the passenger terminal?"

"Why not?" Hamm hung up the phone.

"What the fuck you think you're doing?"

"Not often I get through this way, Jack. Have to check in with old buddies."

"You're going to go outside and get in that car with us."

"Lead the way, chief."

Coriolanus appeared relieved that he had not gotten an argument. They walked on to the front of the terminal, and Decker pushed open the glass door. A consulate sedan with a driver sat waiting, and they climbed in, Decker in front and Coriolanus and Hamm in the back. The car pulled smoothly into the traffic and headed in toward the city.

Coriolanus half turned on the seat to face Hamm. "Look, Hamm, I don't like this idea any more than you do, but it looks to me as if we'd do better working together. Christ, we're on the same side, man! Different agencies, but it's the same damned government."

"Problem is, Jack, I don't like your M.O. Haven't since 'Nam."

"Hell, I don't like yours, either. But who cares how we do it, as long as we get that file back?"

"I'll sleep on it, Jack."

Coriolanus nodded and his facial muscles relaxed.

At a quarter to five, they were inching along in downtown traffic when Hamm spotted a men's store on his side of the street. He began to think that once he was inside the consulate, Coriolanus might actually detain him physically. "Look out!" he yelled.

The driver slammed on his brakes, his head flopping back and forth. Hundreds of horns began to honk.

Hamm opened his door and got out. "Thanks for the ride."

Decker spun around in the front seat, and Coriolanus yelled, "Hamm! Get back in here!"

Hamm bent over to look back inside. The CIA assistant reached out, as if to grab his arm, but the motion halted in mid-grab.

"You have to go to the consulate for debriefing."

"I don't debrief with you."

"The hell you don't! Get in."

Hamm slammed the door and crossed the inside lane in front of a Volkswagen convertible driven by a striking redhead. She slowed to let him pass, and he waved at her. She smiled back.

The consulate driver was busily trying to get across the lane and into some parking spot as Hamm entered the men's store. A skinny and effeminate blond man was tallying up the day's receipts at the cash register. He looked up. "We were just about to close, sir."

Hamm crossed the thick carpet to a rack of suits and fingered the fabric of a tropical wool in light beige. "You still have a tailor on hand?"

The salesman paused in his counting. "Well, sir, yes, I think we do."

"Good. I'll take one of these. Where's the shirts?"

Hamm spent an hour being fitted, then sitting in a chair near the front door, reading a month-old *Gentlemen's Quarterly.* Concentrating on the printed page helped him forget the throbbing in his head. The salesman flipped the sign on the front door to read Closed before he went down the street to buy Hamm a canvas carry-all and an electric razor. He brought it back and took it to the rear fitting room to pack Hamm's purchases carefully in it—three shirts, underwear, ties, belts, a sport coat and slacks, a windbreaker, and one of the two pairs of shoes he had selected. When he was done, he left the bag in the back room, just as Hamm asked him to do. Hamm took the razor and shaved.

Coriolanus and Decker disappeared after three agents arrived to take their places. The agents stood around on the sidewalk, waiting for Hamm and watching through the big windows of the shop. It was starting to get dark, and the salesman turned on the lights. Hamm felt as if he were onstage, the audience gathered at the curb.

A Renault parked across the street contained two men. He figured them for NIS or KGB. The odds were more on KGB now, though. De Vroot was probably disgusted with the whole affair.

When the tailor called him, Hamm went back to the fitting room and tried on his new suit, dumping his old clothes in a wastebasket after cleaning out the pockets. "Very nice," he said.

The tailor stooped to look at the pants cuffs with a critical eye. "The right cuff could be evened a bit."

"It'll do as is." Hamm peeled off a U.S. fifty and gave it to the tailor. "That take care of your overtime?"

"Yes, sir. Thank you."

Hamm went out through the curtained doorway and checked himself in the triple mirror. He smoothed the coat cuffs, turned and looked over his shoulder to check the back. Shrugging out of the jacket, as if it needed more work, he carried it back through the curtain. The salesman followed.

When the curtain fell back in place, Hamm put the coat back on and picked up the canvas bag. He passed a fifty to the salesman, who beamed. "That a back door there?"

"Yes, sir. It gives onto the alley."

"I like back doors," Hamm said. "You two wouldn't mind hanging around back here for ten or fifteen minutes, would you?"

"Not at all, sir."

He shut off the back-room light, then slipped out into the darkened alley. At either end of the alley, he could see traffic flashing past, and against the intermittent lights the alley appeared empty. He decided to go to the right.

About sixty feet short of the street, a large mass moved out of the shadow of a doorway. Hamm judged him at six-six and maybe two-eighty. He could not see the face, but the head was huge.

Hamm slowed his pace, but continued forward. Ten feet away, he discerned a full beard.

The giant asked, "Meneer Hamm?"

"NIS?" Hamm asked.

"Ja."

When he was six feet away, he swung the canvas bag upward. Coming out of the blackness of the alley, the man did not see it until the last second.

He tried to dodge, but the bag caught him full in the face. It had no more than a startling effect, producing a grunt and a backward step.

Hamm sidestepped once to the right, and while the man was still off balance, Hamm lanced out with the tip of his new shoe. The kick caught the man squarely in the groin, and Hamm felt the shock as his toes mashed through flesh to the pelvic bone.

The giant doubled over, gushing breath and a croaky scream, clutching at his crotch.

Hamm went two more paces to the right, ready to dart past.

"Fucker!" Still bent over, the man lashed out with a heavy arm in a roundhouse swing that caught Hamm on the thigh. The blow sent him reeling into a fire-escape ladder. He grabbed the ladder to keep himself upright.

This son-of-a-bitch was strong. His leg sent white shrieks of pain to his brain. Hamm rolled back against a brick wall as the man, still hunched over, came at him.

A car rushed past the alley, and in the brief glare of light, he saw a left fist the size of a ham flashing forward. Hamm threw up his right arm to ward it off, but took a glancing blow on the shoulder. The shoulder went numb.

He would not last through many blows like that.

The right fist swung toward him.

Using his foot against the brick wall, Hamm ducked under the swing and kicked himself out away from the wall, toward the center of the alley.

He tripped over his canvas bag and went sprawling on his hands and knees.

Pivoting on his left hand, he spun himself around and rose in time to meet the giant coming toward him once again.

"Bastard! You fight fair!"

As the man lofted another roundhouse swing, Hamm went under it, locked his hands together, and brought both of them into a slamming blow against his right kidney.

"Unnh!"

He sprinted past, waited for the swearing man to turn again, then slipped a left jab past a slow defense, aiming for an eye.

He missed the eye, but found the nose and heard the splinter of bone.

As the man's hands went to his face, Hamm double-handed him in the kidney again, then hooked his toe behind the man's heel and whipped his leg out from under him.

The giant hit the concrete hard on his back.

Hamm waited until he tried to sit up, then kicked him in the cheek.

His adversary went over on his back, then rolled recklessly toward the side of the alley, smashing through loose tin cans.

Hamm bent over to pick up his carry-all and headed toward the street. He looked back to see the vague figure trying to rise to his knees.

FIFTEEN

The saloon was a neighborhood palace ten blocks from the men's shop. It had sawdust on the floor, dark ale on tap, and thick slabs of ham in its sandwiches. Once the after-work crowd departed for home and dinner, it had few patrons and an available telephone next to a table in a dark corner. A bartender with a Scottish brogue stayed behind the bar and did not try to clean anything. He made frequent trips to the far end of the bar, where he kept his own glass of something pale under the counter. Two regulars rolled dice from leather cups, their backsides sagging over familiar stools. Except for the two regulars arguing with each other in Afrikaans, it could have been New York or Detroit.

Hamm stayed there for two hours, rising from

his booth frequently to make calls. He chased a couple of his pain pills with ale. The back of his head was now a steady buzz, more irritating than painful. The outside of his left thigh ached a little, and he suspected it would sport a hefty bruise by morning.

By the time he had reached his sawdust sanctuary, he had decided that his assailant, though obviously an Afrikaner, was not in the employ of the National Intelligence Service. De Vroot and his people had nothing to gain by either detaining or eliminating him. Coriolanus? Possible, but improbable. But if the giant was working for Naratsmov, the KGB was close.

That was not a good sign.

Hamm checked his watch. He had time to kill before Messenger got in.

He called Sam Farley.

"Damn, Steve! It's about time you phoned in."

"My friend call you?"

"Yeah. Said you got bonked on the head bone. Bad?"

"I'll live. That was not the message she was supposed to give you."

"I know." Farley laughed. "But my old charm got in the way, and I finagled it out of her. We're getting married in the fall, by the way."

"Congratulations. But I thought you were retired?"

"I am. She loves older men."

"Uh-huh. She know about all of this?"

"Not yet. You want to be best man?"

"I'll plan on it," Hamm told him. "What do you have?"

"How do you lose an airplane?"

"Leave the keys in it."

"Every time. Anyway, your airplane was seen in Cameroon, at the Douala airport."

"Cameroon!" Terrell had never been to Cameroon. "When?"

"Sometime before five this afternoon. They had the tanks topped off without getting off the plane or going through customs, then took off again. Filed a flight plan for Rabat."

Bob Terrell had never been to Morocco, either. Maybe his hostage pilot, Wilcoxen, had. "You have good sources, Sam."

"Some are more reliable than others. This one's a hot lead, I think. There anything else I can do, Steve?"

"If you'd just keep your ears open, I'd appreciate it. Maybe have someone check on arrivals at Rabat, but I doubt my man's going there."

"The flight path is north, though."

"Algiers is a possible."

"I have a friend in Algiers."

"You have friends in Cairo or Tel Aviv?" Terrell liked both cities.

"Both. We'll get 'em covered."

"Thanks, Sam. We'll have dinner sometime," Hamm promised.

"It'll be expensive."

"My uncle's rich," Hamm said, then hung up.

He returned to his booth to give a newly arrived patron a chance at the phone and signaled the bartender for another stein of beer. The Scot stumbled twice en route to the table and his brogue now had a slur in it.

When the phone was free again, Hamm called the States, but Diane was at lunch. He left the payphone number with her secretary, cautioned her not to give it out, and told her he would be there for another half hour.

He called Messenger again, but the lady with the Swahili accent said he had taken off for South Africa. He sat down to finish his beer.

His headache was buzzing with slightly more intensity when the telephone rang. Sliding out of his booth, he picked the handset off the wall mount.

"Steve? You secure?"

"As secure as I'm likely to be," he told her.

"I left the building to find a public phone," she said.

"Far from Arlington Hall, I hope."

"Why?"

"The opposition regularly taps the telephone booths around the building. That's where all the interesting calls are made." That was a detail that most of the intelligence analysts did not have to deal with.

"I'll call you back."

Twelve minutes later, the phone rang again. "How are you feeling?" she asked.

"My concentration is divided. Half the time I'm thinking about this steam locomotive pounding the rails on the right side of my head. Any new word?"

"A bad one. I met with my friend from DOD Strategic Planning."

"And?"

"Steve, GABRIEL can bypass security and activate missiles." DeMott's tone carried a very real fear in it.

Hamm thought about that for a full minute.

"Steve?"

"I'm here. It gets around the two-key safety procedure?"

"As I understand it. And around any access codes in the communications link."

"No executive-branch involvement?"

"None."

"Son-of-a-bitch. I've got to think about this, Diane. Why would we want to launch the other side's birds? No wonder Bob's gone off the edge."

"I think he meant to destroy it, to keep it out of the wrong hands."

"Maybe. But he went looking for a computer in Caracas."

"The wrong computer," she countered.

"And maybe he found that out. You have the list of supercomputers with you?"

"I think so. Hang on."

While she searched her purse, Hamm found his address book and a blank page near the back. She read him the listings for Europe, Africa, and the Middle East. There were not many of the machines at large in the world just yet.

"Thanks."

"What are you going to do?"

"For the time being, I'm free of my intimate friends, so I think I'll go to Douala."

"Where in hell is that?"

"Try the west coast of Africa. My airplane went through there at five o'clock."

"Dammit! It hasn't hit our wires yet. You have good sources."

"I have good friends. And congratulations."

"For what?"

"Your impending marriage." Hamm hung up.

After throwing enough rand on the table to cover

his tab, he picked up his carry-all and left the comfort of the bar. He thought it likely that Coriolanus would have the taxi services covered by now, as well as the railroad station, the port, and both sides of the airport—commercial and general. He took a left at the corner of the block and headed back toward the center of the city. A group of teenagers, with their cars angled into the sidewalk, were sitting on the hoods and fenders, conversing about the things that interested teenagers. Hamm suspected the topics were not physics and foreign policy. Some activities in the free, or almost free, world were universal. The group went silent as he passed them.

Two blocks later, he found the right car. It was a Ford Anglia with tires that did not remember the concept of tread. On the bright side, they were all inflated. He checked the immediate area, found no one with an unusual interest in him, opened the driver's door, and got in. One of the steel coils in the passenger's seat protruded through the padding and torn upholstery. It took only a moment of manipulation behind the dash to cross the ignition wires, then short the starter circuit. He had to jump it four times, pumping the accelerator pedal furiously, before it started.

He pulled on the light switch and was rewarded with two headlights. The needle on the fuel gauge suggested the tank was empty, but if there was a gallon sloshing about, he figured he could get twelve miles out of it. Finding first gear with a slight clang, Hamm pulled away from the curb and headed for Bellville.

The old Anglia made it to Malan Airport, and he parked in a back parking lot, a block from the General Aviation section. Activity in General Aviation at that time of night was slow. Vehicle traffic was sparse and the parking lots were nearly empty. Hamm left the car and crossed the lot to the sidewalk, then stood alongside a newly planted tree for a while, scanning the street in front of the passenger and freight terminals. The streetlights cast a violet hue over the building facades.

Away from the terminals, to his right, the hangars and offices of private aviation companies stretched for several blocks. Some had reserved parking spaces in front of them, and the areas of separation between structures were protected by eight-foot-high chain-link fences. The recessed areas between hangars were dark, hidden from the streetlamps. Hamm watched those for a while.

A small red glow identified a cigarette smoker standing next to the wall of a hangar housing the Cape Helicopter Corporation. He was standing well back from the chain-link fence, on the other side of it, and Hamm could tell only that the face behind the glow belonged to a Caucasian wearing a white, wide-brimmed hat.

He stepped away from his tree and crossed the street to the sidewalk fronting the buildings, walking away from the terminals. When he reached Cape Helicopter's building, he slowed his pace. He stayed close to the fence as he passed it.

"Hey, Steve." The voice was a whisper.

"Thought you gave up smoking."

"I did," Messenger said, out of the dark, grinding the butt under his heel, "but you spooks look for those little signals, don't you?"

Hamm kept walking. "I guess we do. How do I get from where I am to where you are, without wrinkling my new suit?"

"Go on to the other side of the building. I popped the padlock."

He kept walking, crossing the front of Cape Helicopter's offices, and when he reached the next section of fencing, Hamm found a gate with the lock hanging free. He quickly opened it and slipped into the space between structures. It was littered with weeds and old cans. Messenger met him at the back corner of the hangar.

"Good to see you, buddy."

"You, too, Dave."

"How come we always meet like this—at night, in hostile territory?"

"Training," Hamm suggested.

Messenger led him across the tarmac to the airplane.

The Cessna was a low-wing jet designed primarily as a military trainer. Its Plexiglas canopy was pulled back, and Messenger climbed up onto the wing, then into the cockpit. Hamm followed him, tossing his bag into the small space behind the side-by-side seats. He got a leg over the coaming, sat on the back of the seat to pull his other leg in, then slid down into the seat. It was a tight fit for two big men.

Dave Messenger strapped himself in. "We don't offer G-suits to passengers, so I didn't wear one, either. Didn't want to offend you."

"I'll let it go, as long as you're not anticipating high-G antics."

"Only in a forward motion." Messenger went through his checklist, hitting the toggles. The engine whined to life.

Hamm clicked together the buckles of the restraint harness, adjusted the straps, then found a headset hung on a starboard hook and pulled it on.

Messenger removed his trademark Stetson cowboy hat. From inside his black shirt with white stitching, he pulled a plastic bag and slipped it over the hat, then carefully set the package on the floor behind his seat. He donned his headset.

Over the intercom, Hamm asked, "Same one?"

"Hell, yes. That's the hat you gave me in the hospital in Bangkok. Just had it cleaned."

"Survived well," Hamm noted.

"Better'n the rest of us. You have any idea where the fuck we're going?"

"Out of South Africa."

"Got a direction in mind?"

"Try north."

Messenger dialed in the Cape Town tower on the NavCom and said, "Anyone want to talk to Cessna one-one-eight?"

Hamm's pilot was well known in southern Africa. The ground-traffic controller came back with, "That you, Messenger?"

SIXTEEN

The U.S. consulate in Cape Town was darkened at midnight, except for the back corner on the second floor. Roy Decker's office and anterooms contained six Central Intelligence operatives manning telephones, staying in contact with their local sources. The black channels in the basement communications room were buzzing with telex and voice traffic in and out of Cape Town.

In the chief of station's office, Jack Coriolanus let Decker use his own desk. The special assistant to the DDO lay stretched out on a gold-tweed sofa, his shoes off, and his feet propped up on an arm of the couch.

''Jesus Christ! Decker, we were within two miles of him!'' Coriolanus said for the third time.

Jim Draper rapped on the doorframe, then brought a sheet of paper inside to hand to Decker. "Those are the phone numbers from the Hilton switchboard log, Mr. Decker. We've traced them all, but not one of them was obviously a cutout."

"Thanks, Jim." Decker took the listing and began to scan it.

Coriolanus sat up. "Let me see that."

The resident got up and came around the desk to pass him the typed list. There were fourteen names and one question mark on it. But Coriolanus recognized most of the others. "He made several calls to some of these numbers."

"Maybe they were out the first time he called?" Decker suggested.

"You know any of these names?" he asked.

"Couple of them."

"Fuckoffs and scatterbrains out of Southeast Asia. Any one of them could have been passing messages on to Terrell."

"You really think Hamm's in touch with him?" Decker asked.

Coriolanus went over the list again. "No. But this makes me think Hamm was scraping the barrel bottom, looking for information."

"Makes a good network though," Decker added.

Coriolanus and Decker both looked up as Draper came running back into the office, gripping a flimsy hard copy just ripped off a printer.

Draper handed Coriolanus the telex, and the assistant read through it quickly:

ENCRYPT: SECRET
0524/0036/CPT17899

TO: USCONS, CAPE TOWN
FROM: USCONS, DOUALA
SUBJ: YARDSTICK

LEAR AIRCRAFT IDENT HAMPSHIRE INSUR CO, N260179, ARR
DOUALA 1640 HRS PREV DATE, DPRT 1722 HRS PREV DATE,
DEST RABAT.

"Jesus Christ!" Coriolanus snapped, looking at his Rolex. "That's over seven hours ago. What are these assholes doing?"

Draper took the question seriously. "They've been checking arrival logs and fuel sales, Mr. Coriolanus. I don't know how—"

"Forget it." Coriolanus was certain he would not find commercial air accommodating. "Draper, go line up a charter."

"Yes, sir!" Draper left for a phone in the anteroom.

Leaning over to dig his shoes out from under the couch, Coriolanus sat down, slipped them on, and began to tie the laces. "So, you might as well come with me, Decker. Go get a toothbrush."

"All right! Thanks, Jack."

Coriolanus scowled at him. "It's no favor. You're on your ass in Africa. The people you hire dick around so much they can't even keep a tail on an over-the-hill asshole like Hamm. And once Hamm tells his buddies, your sources will be cut."

The lights of Cairo were spread all over the northern horizon. They seemed dimmer than the lights of most cities. Perhaps it was a deficiency in power production, or perhaps it was the time of the morning, close to two A.M. The Nile was a wide black swath cutting through the city, with a few dancing lights on it, the running lights of marine traffic.

"I'm going to have to call in, mate." The pilot appeared fatigued in the red glow from the instrument panel.

"All right. We're still Gulf Oil, remember."

"I remember."

They had identified themselves as a Gulf Oil business jet when they had been challenged by an air controller over Sudan. For most of the journey, Terrell had insisted on low altitudes that were hard on Wilcoxen's nerves, but which kept them off radar screens. Terrell knew that much from his work in military defense. At five hundred feet or lower, the Lear's return signal was lost in the ground clutter. It had worked well when they were flying up the western coast, staying well out to sea for much of the journey, though not so well as they crossed the continent on a diagonal toward the northeast. Midway across Chad's desert, two French Mirage fighters had suddenly appeared off each of the Lear's wingtips, very menacing with full loads of armament suspended on the wing racks. A disjointed radio conversation, relayed and interpreted through some ground radio installation, kept them from being blown out of the sky, and Terrell had finally acceded to Wilcoxen's request to gain altitude.

Terrell checked the fuel gauge. It was getting low again. He had begun to learn how to read the gauges after the South African tried to change course on him, when he had gone to the back to use the toilet.

"Lear seven-nine calling Cairo control. Over." Wilcoxen sounded tired in the headset.

"This is Cairo." A voice using stilted English came back over the overhead speakers. "Go ahead, seven-nine. Over."

"Cairo, seven-nine, VFR out of Riyadh, requesting permission to land. Over."

"Seven-nine, give me an I.D. Over."

The pilot leaned forward to flip a switch.

"What's that?" Terrell asked, suspicious.

"IFF. Sends a signal that identifies our blip on the screen, mate. Ain't gonna blow us up."

"We have you, seven-nine. Go to five thousand, heading zero-eight-five, repeat, zero-eight-five. You're fifth in line. The runway is one-eight, wind two-nine-five at four knots. Over."

"Cairo, seven-nine. Copy one-eight, wind two-nine-five at four knots. Negative on the hold pattern. Seven-nine is down to sixteen hundred pounds of fuel. Over."

Terrell glanced again at the fuel gauge, starting to worry. The air controller was not as flustered. "Cairo control to TWA one-five-six. Take one more circuit, please. I am going to land a Lear ahead of you. Seven-nine, go to two thousand, five hundred, heading zero-eight-five. You are second in line. Qantas QF-two-four, you are now . . ."

The jet rolled lightly to the right as the pilot picked up his new heading. Cairo dipped away on Terrell's left for a moment, and when it came back, it seemed closer.

"What happens when we get on the ground?" Wilcoxen asked.

"Just like Cameroon," Terrell said. Though he was fatigued, he had established a plan for the next few hours. Perhaps it was a result of clarifying an objective for himself. He had considered his tactics fully. "We refuel, then take off again."

"I don't know about you, mate, but I have about run my course. I only fly these things to check performance. I ain't a bloody airline pilot."

"The next leg will be a short one," Terrell promised.

"Where?"

"I'll tell you after we're airborne."

"I'll have to file a flight plan."

Terrell thought about that for a while, then said, "Tel Aviv."

"Then we part company, mate?"

"Then we go our separate ways."

His hostage allowed himself a look of relief, dropped his eyes to check the gun lying in Terrell's lap—his hands did not shake as much when he kept them pressed to his thighs—then shrugged and turned back to his controls. "I've got to take a pee pretty damned soon."

"When we get on the ground."

Hostage was not an alien word to Terrell, but having one of his own taxed his personal credibility. "I may have to give myself a title."

"Something memorable, Robert. Like the Contras have."

"I'm not a terrorist."

"You say something, mate?"

Terrell looked over at Wilcoxen, who was staring at him. His mumbling had not overcome the sound of the jet engines. "No. Just get us on the ground."

Fifteen minutes later, the twin rows of runway lights aligned themselves ahead of them, and the Lear lost altitude quickly. They shot over the five-mile markers, then the end markers, and the tires squealed as they touched down. Switching to a ground-controller frequency, the pilot followed directions and took a taxiway leading to a parking area. He asked for a fuel truck to meet them. A man in a yellow coverall pulled up in a Jeep, got out, and used a flashlight to direct them into a parking place.

The pilot shut down the engines, then quickly slipped out of his seat and headed to the toilet. Terrell heard the stream of urgent urination.

He riffled through the chart case, found the Hampshire Insurance credit card he had used in Douala, then levered himself out of his own seat. His muscles were so tight they were sore. The gun felt heavy in his hand. Terrell remembered the times he had ribbed Hamm about playing with guns; it seemed a long time ago, as if he looked back on it through heavy gauze curtains.

Terrell waited for the man to finish, then urged him back to the cockpit with a wave of the gun barrel.

"Damn, mate. I have to stretch my legs."

"After the fuel. Back in your seat." He stood to one side in the narrow cabin as Wilcoxen went past him.

Once the pilot was back in his place, Terrell closed the curtain to the cockpit, then lowered the stairway door. "I'll be talking to the men on the fuel truck," he called through the curtain. "Don't make any mistakes."

"I'll save those for the next leg, mate."

Before the fuel truck arrived, Terrell shoved the gun into his pocket, descended the stairway, and reached back into the cabin for his bag. He walked away from the airplane with a determined stride, found a trash barrel to dump the pistol in, and, twenty-two minutes later, had passed through customs on the Albert Simmons passport.

The airport looked like a half-deserted bazaar. Two old women in Arabic robes pushed brooms desultorily, missing half the dirt spread on the tile floor. Half a dozen vendors of vile concoctions approached him with pleas that he waved off. A blind man with no legs, scooting haphazardly on a castered board, chanted at him. Sinister faces followed him as he made his way across the plaza-like terminal. He checked the departing-flights monitor. Air France had the next flight out, bound for Paris.

The line in front of the Air France ticket counter was a short one. Albert Simmons bought his ticket with cash, then searched the concourse for a snack bar, but the offerings made him lose his appetite.

While he and Messenger were on the ground in Douala, refueling, Hamm called Sam Farley in Johannesburg. He had decided to follow in Terrell's tracks, not knowing whether the analyst would go north out of Cameroon or angle to the east.

"You're hitting thirty-three percent," Farley told him.

"Meaning?"

"Out of Algiers, Cairo, and Tel Aviv, Cairo's the one."

"No shit, Red Ryder?"

"No shit, Little Beaver. Your lost airplane found itself."

"Any other conditions you know about?" Hamm asked.

"My friend tells me that Egyptian authorities are huddled with someone from the airplane, but that's all he knows. The Lear is still there, by the way. Oops!"

"Oops?"

"I'm sitting here, Steve, in my rather comfortable retirement living room, drinking a retirement rum concoction, and I see a couple of nonretired gentlemen coming up my walk. They look suspiciously like friends of yours."

"I'll bet."

"You wouldn't want me to spill my guts, would you?"

"Not your fight, Sam. Do what you have to do."

"I'll hold off until they get to the toenails. I've an attachment to my toenails."

"Appreciate it, Sam," Hamm said, then hung up the phone. He bought two bottles of Coke and headed back to where Messenger waited by the plane, his Stetson, pushed back on his head, watching the men handling the fuel lines.

"Jesus! I don't even get a beer?"

"You're the pilot, remember?"

"Never stopped you in Thailand," Messenger reminded him.

Coriolanus and Decker were both asleep in the comfortable reclining seats of the chartered Citation business jet when the co-pilot came back and awakened Coriolanus.

The assistant to the DDO shook his head, then tried to sit up.

"Sorry to wake you, sir. I've got a message for you. They said it was urgent."

"Where in hell are we?" he asked, rubbing his face.

"Just crossed the northern border of Angola."

"What's the message?"

"A Mr. de Vroot called the consulate, and they forwarded the information. A Charles Wilcoxen called in to his superior at Brandvlei—"

"Who's Wilcoxen?"

"They said he was a mechanic."

"What else?"

"Something about his being released in Cairo. They said he had the Lear in his possession." The co-pilot looked puzzled.

Coriolanus was awake by then. "Change your course for Egypt."

"I'll tell the captain, sir."

SEVENTEEN

"Your report says nothing of Blue Heron," Colonel General Nikolai Andresev said.

Alexi Naratsmov drummed his fingers on the base of the blue telephone. It seemed incongruous to him that the secure communications center, on the top floor of the embassy, in the *rezidentia*, would have blue telephones. "It is simply information I thought useful to the analysts, Comrade General."

"And Blue Heron?" The general's voice was beginning to show impatience.

"I was not in a position to move on him. It was far more advantageous to remain patient." Alexi made an indirect reference to the general's current mood.

"What is the situation now?"

"Your agents in Cape Town performed at less than acceptable levels. The man detailed to neutralize Gray Tiger was himself neutralized. A sad performance, Comrade General." A member of Department Twelve, considered eccentric at best, could get away with such a statement made to the chairman of the FCD. He could assume that a number of First Chief Directorate operatives in Cape Town would be disciplined in one manner or another.

The general did not bother with a reply. Instead, he said, "Your mission has become more important yet, Alexi Ivanovitch."

When the general used Naratsmov's patronymic, the issues were important, indeed. "There is new information, Comrade General?"

"Cable traffic between Cape Town and Washington has intensified. Our sources, not yet confirmed, suggest that Blue Heron has in his possession a very important file."

"Does anyone know what is in this file?" Naratsmov asked.

"It is a plan of some kind, which defeats our defense mechanisms in a nuclear attack against the motherland. You must work at finding the subject. The Supreme Soviet relies on you."

"It would appear that two of the principals may be leaving the Southern Hemisphere. I myself am leaving for Tripoli"—Naratsmov checked his watch—"in an hour and a quarter. The location will be more central to my next move."

"Blue Heron has much of the world available to him," General Andresev observed.

"I am getting a feeling for the man's moves,"

Naratsmov said, though he hated to explain his own rationales since they were based on instinct, "and when I go through his dossier, I am able to see some possible destinations."

"The man's file tells you this?"

"History helps us to foretell the future, does it not, Comrade General?"

The Egyptian was a little man, barely reaching five-four, with dark skin, haunting black eyes, and a nature that suspected everyone. He held some kind of inspector's rank in the customs service, and his name was Sadawani. He was unaccustomed to being wrong. Begrudgingly, he told Hamm, "You were correct, Colonel. Your hijacker bought a ticket on an Air France flight."

"What name did he use, Inspector?"

"Simmons. Albert Simmons." The man had a competent command of English, and he smiled around the words. "You are familiar with the name, perhaps?"

"The ticket-counter people remembered him?"

"No. But he used American dollars to purchase the ticket."

"Could you tell me the destination, please?"

"He bought a ticket for Paris, but there are intermediate stops in Rome and Geneva. Naturally, he could leave the airplane in either of those two cities."

"Naturally."

Sadawani pushed a form across his small desk. "Sign this complaint, Colonel Hamm. I will notify the authorities in each of those cities, though the airliner has already passed through Rome and Geneva."

Hamm was not about to get Interpol, or any other police forces, involved. "I believe I'll hold off on that, for the time being."

The inspector's eyelids drooped, making his dark eyes even more cobra-like.

"I think what I'd better do," Hamm said, "is get my aircraft out of your way and go on to Paris."

"That will not be possible," Sadawani said.

"You did query Washington?"

"Oh, I am free to release the airplane to you, but there is the matter of your passport, or lack of one."

Hamm had not picked up a temporary passport at the Cape Town consulate. "I told you that it would be on the Lear. Apparently, it's been stolen."

"But you arrived in the country by a different airplane."

"I have not crossed through customs."

"There are irregularities involved," the man insisted.

Goddamned bureaucrats. They were the same everywhere. This shithead, however, would not likely respond like others had to a copy of his orders.

"Look, Inspector, if my plane was stolen, along with my passport, I can't get the passport, can I? And you're not going to let me leave without it. Correct?"

"I am sorry. . . ."

"Then I have no choice but to complain to my embassy that you are illegally detaining an American military officer. Before it's over, my President will be talking to your president and you'll be out of a job."

The man glared at Hamm for a full two minutes before saying, "I can see this is a special case, Colonel. I will allow you to leave."

Hamm got up and left the office, resisting an impulse to slam the door behind him. Outside the office, in the customs waiting area, Messenger was lounging on a wooden settee. Another man sat next to him, dressed in the wrinkled fatigue uniform of the South African army. The hubbub on the other side of the customs fence, primarily in Arabic, though other languages chimed in, could be described as a clamor. Burnooses were prominent in the crowd, but so were the tailored business suits of European travelers.

"Steve, I want you to meet my new buddy, Charlie Wilcoxen," Messenger said.

"We met before, when I was nagging him about fuel lines and the like."

Wilcoxen offered his hand. "Sorry about your airplane, mate."

Hamm shook hands. "I don't suppose you had a choice."

"He did have an automatic."

"I don't believe he would have used the gun," Hamm said, pressing his fingers lightly against the back of his head. The headache was still there, though he resisted taking any more pills.

"I am not a believer in taking chances," Wilcoxen said. "Gave it up when I got married."

"He tell you his name?"

"Just Robert."

"How did he act?"

The mechanic thought about it for a few seconds. "He was tired, same as me. Seemed a bit remote, I thought. Couple of times, he talked to himself. He was nervous. A tic in the mouth. His hands shook every once in a while. Made me shake, the way he held that gun. It wasn't cocked, but he never put the safety on the whole way."

Hamm nodded. He saw Inspector Sadawani standing in his office doorway, staring at them. The hooded eyes looked malevolent, and Hamm thought he might be pressing his luck. He turned to Messenger. "I think we're expected to leave Cairo, by the quickest route."

"Good advice, the way I'm thinking," Messenger said. He pulled down the brim of the Stetson, as if he were preparing for high noon.

"You got a way home, Charlie?" Hamm asked.

"Somebody's arranging a ticket for me, mate. I'll be doing all right, soon as I find me a seat to sleep in."

"Got any money?"

"A few rand."

Hamm withdrew the roll of bills from his pocket. It was beginning to get a little thinner. He peeled a few bills back until he found a fifty. "Get yourself some breakfast on the U.S."

"Appreciate it, mate."

Hamm and Messenger started toward the door leading out to where their aircraft were parked.

The sun was already high and hot, steaming the aroma of fuel and oil on the tarmac, as Hamm and Messenger walked toward the Lear. Screwing around with Sadawani, and confirming identities and ownerships through channels leading to Arlington Hall, had cost nearly three hours. As they pulled open the door to the airplane, a man approached briskly from one of the hangars. They waited for him.

"Your airplane, sir?"

"That's right."

He held up the fuel bill.

Hamm grinned at him. "I suppose you want me to pay that, huh?"

"Please, sir."

The card he normally used was gone, so Hamm found a personal card in his wallet; he was going to have a hell of an expense voucher to submit to Kuster. Pointing toward the Cessna trainer, a hundred yards away, he said, "Put the billing for that one on the same ticket."

"Yes, sir. I'll be right back with your receipt."

Hamm kept a few personal checks and several checks keyed to a DIA account in his wallet. He retrieved a DIA check. "Got a pen, Dave?"

Messenger unclipped a ball-point from his shirt pocket. "What the fuck are you doing?"

Hamm wrote quickly, filling in an amount of three thousand dollars, then handed the check to Messenger.

"Shit! You don't have to do that."

"I'm not paying for your time or your willingness to help, Dave, but I want to cover your rental on the trainer. Uncle's money."

Grinning, Messenger stuffed the check in his pocket and said, "As long as it's Uncle's, I'll have to grab it. I'll think of it as covering some of my overtime a few years back."

"Do that. And, thanks."

They took off from Cairo together, Messenger leading. At three thousand feet, the ex-mercenary waggled his wings at Hamm, then climbed away to the south.

Hamm followed an air controller's instructions

and settled in at eighteen thousand feet, trimmed out the controls, and set the autopilot.

He guessed he was heading for Paris, but he was damned if he knew why.

Albert Simmons had not boarded the Air France flight for Paris, and it might be a while before they realized it.

Instead, Terrell had used the Holding passport—his other forged one—to take a later flight to Marseilles. Whoever was behind him would assume that he would take the earliest possible flight. He thought he was learning to think like spies were supposed to think. In Marseilles, he had again purchased a ticket in Simmons's name, this one bound for Bordeaux. Both ends of the journey were within France, and did not require passport showings. He did not board that flight, either.

Taking a bus to Nice, then another Air France flight to Nancy, so he would not have to produce a passport, he had found himself almost as confused by his separate travels as his pursuers would have to be. He used the Holding passport once again for his Lufthansa flight to Berlin.

Robert Terrell knew some people in Berlin.

EIGHTEEN

It was nearly six by the time DeMott stopped by a deli for macaroni salad and pastrami and then parked in her slot in the open garage. She had just come from a meeting with Dr. Samuel Foster, and what she had learned scared her to death.

Entering her building, she pulled the mail out of her box without looking at it, let herself in through the glass door, and climbed the stairs to her second-floor unit.

Unlocking the two locks, she pushed the door open, tossed the mail on the foyer credenza, kicked her shoes toward the closet door, and went into the kitchen to set the plastic bag from the deli on the counter and to pour a small glass of chablis.

On the counter that divided the kitchen and dining area was an answering machine, and she rewound the tape, then hit the Replay button. Her sister wanted her to come for dinner on Sunday—the kids had not seen her in months. General Kuster told her to call him at home. The condo association, for which she was secretary, wanted to plan a summer party. Nancy Terrell had called.

And there was a formal message: "Miss DeMott, this is Colonel Winfield Storch. I have been unable to reach Colonel Hamm. You are to tell him that his evaluation and report are both due in two days. I will expect them to be on time."

DeMott wondered how Hamm was going to react to that. She would tell him if he called that night.

In the living room, she flopped on the big sectional sofa and leafed through her mail.

Bill, bill, bill, junk, junk, and another bill.

A small envelope with no return address. DeMott checked the stamp and the postmark. French stamp, Marseilles postmark.

Intrigued, she peeled the flap open and withdrew a single sheet of paper:

> Dear Diane,
>
> Please tell my wonderful wife that I am alive, that I am sane, and that I know what I am doing.
>
> What I do, I do for a broader cause, and it is up to me to do it. There is no other recourse.
>
> Thanks for being my mail girl.

It was printed roughly with ball-point ink, and there was no signature, but she did not need one.

* * *

Major Warren McAndrews, U.S. Air Force, was the duty officer, and he told Hamm, "Sorry, Colonel, General Kuster is not in the building."

"Where can I reach him, Major?"

"He is not available at the moment. I can take a message, and I have a note here that I am supposed to get your location."

All of which sounded phony to Hamm. Winnie Storch had his tentacles probing through DIA's corridors, no doubt. Probably all of the duty officers were under the informal instructions of the chairman of the Joint Chiefs to find Hamm's nest. "Yes, I'll leave a message."

"Go ahead, sir."

"I want you to personally tell the general his ass is red."

"Colonel, I can't—"

"It's a code, Major. You pass it on in those exact words." Hamm hung up before Major McAndrews could recover sufficiently to press him for an address.

In Paris, it was the Plaza-Athénée, the Crillon, or the George V. This time it was the Hotel George V.

If he left the hotel and walked north, he would intersect the Champs-Elysées. A three-block walk would put him at Place Charles de Gaulle, if he wanted to look at the Arc de Triomphe, which he did not.

Leaving by way of the main entrance, Hamm nodded to the doorman, paused to admire the architecture of the American Cathederal in Paris, then sauntered south. He was in no hurry; his promised call to Diane was three hours away. The

Crazy Horse looked tinny and vacant to him this early in the evening. A few American tourists hung around it, perhaps seeking more American tourists.

He dodged a slew of crazy taxi drivers crossing the Place de l'Alme and the Avenue de New York and found a place in the crowd strolling along the Seine. The Eiffel Tower climbed into a light haze on the other side of the river, but he had not come to see it, either.

Following the river's edge, Hamm continued to the southwest. There were a great number of women, commercial and private, to smile at, and Hamm did his best to provide equal treatment for both varieties. Many of the responding smiles were encouraging, though a few looked askance at the bandage still clamped to the back of his head. The fourteen hours of sleep he had gotten after arriving in Paris had reduced the headache to a minor irritation.

The Ministry of Commerce was almost directly opposite him, on the other side of the Seine, when he finally spotted Monty Palidin.

Montgomery Palidin, born in Bozeman, Montana, had grown up in London because his father was the outside end of a beef-export partnership. MI-6, the British equivalent to the CIA, had become interested in him when he was at King's College. They thought the lanky, red-haired American might be useful in special circumstances, and Monty thought that service to the Crown would be a lark. Both sides were eventually proven wrong. The peers who ruled the agency discovered in Palidin an affinity for intelligence work that made him serviceable in much more than special instances, and Monty evolved from a prankster to a sober and serious promoter of Queen and Country.

Because of his origins, Monty had been dubbed "Cowboy" when he worked out of the British embassy in Saigon, but he swore that the only cows he handled were on platters. He and Hamm had liased with each other on several occasions and developed a mutual respect.

Palidin's hair was almost pink now, the gray having gained prominence. He wore a vested gray suit, and, questionably for May, a blue Burberry. Waving at Hamm with one finger raised out of his fist, he pointed to the space beside him on the park bench.

"You're looking about the same, Hamm. Few extra pounds. How did you achieve the wound?"

Hamm sat down, grinning. "Got speared. Jesus! Monty, when you Brits go gray, you go gray."

Palidin had changed his citizenship when he was twenty-seven. "A result of the knockabout life."

"I was surprised to find you were still in the field. I talked to your mother and damned near had to promise marriage before I found out you were in Paris."

"Mother has a big mouth," Palidin said with humor. "And I'm still a field man because I prefer it that way."

And because he was born in the wrong country, Hamm thought. "Paris rife with intrigue?"

"Paris is rife with rumor. It is a good place to wile the time until pension. And you? You're not still snooping under people's posteriors?"

"At the moment, Monty, I'm in purgatory. The gods are trying to determine whether I go to heaven or hell."

"What's your prediction?" Palidin asked.

"I've always been closer to hell."

"What's your penance?"

Digging in his pocket, Hamm found a picture of Terrell. "I get to find this man."

"He's in Paris?" Palidin studied the picture like a man who knew how to look at pictures.

"It's an off chance. Somewhere in Europe, this side of the curtain."

"I like a broad scope, I do. What's the name?"

"Can you keep it to yourself?"

Palidin gave him a sneer.

"Terrell. Robert Terrell has a fake passport under the name Albert Simmons. Big shot in Defense planning. Took a powder a little over three weeks ago."

"Went over to the other side?"

"No. They're looking for him, too. I think the chief looker is Alexi Naratsmov."

"Nasty," Palidin said. "I can put out a few feelers for you."

"I'd appreciate it."

"I'll get back to you." Palidin rose from the bench and walked away to the south. He stopped to buy peanuts from a vendor and ate a few and tossed a few to the birds as he walked.

Hamm took his own time getting back to the hotel, and he had no trouble getting an early table in Les Princes. He was the only patron in the dining room. Someday, he thought, he might get back on an eating schedule that coincided with the time zone in which he was. He ordered *filet de boeuf à la ficelle* and let the waiter recommend a wine. He was not good on wines.

* * *

"I've got a red ass," General Kuster told her.

Was he putting her on? How was she supposed to respond to that? "I didn't know that."

Kuster laughed. "Neither did the major who delivered the message. The man was so embarrassed, he almost garbled it."

"I guess I don't understand," DeMott confessed.

"It was a message from Hamm. I get the impression I've got a few domestic spies in my shop, people intervening between me and Steve."

DeMott detected some bitterness in Kuster's telephone voice. "I still don't get it, General."

"Tell you when I see you."

"Yes. You left a message for me to call?"

"I want a progress report."

"I won't be talking to him for a couple of hours, yet."

"How did your meeting go this afternoon?"

She wondered how to respond. "Somewhat disturbing."

"Not good, then."

"Not good at all," she agreed.

"Anything else?" the general asked.

"From a message on my machine, I understand that Steve has to make a report of some kind in the next couple of days."

"To whom?"

To hell with the bug. "Colonel Storch."

"Steve works for me, but he didn't tell me about this. I'll have a word with the colonel. The information you got today—is it something Steve should have soon?"

"Yes, the sooner the better."

Eugene Kuster was silent for a moment, thinking. "What are you having for dinner?"

Startled by the change of topic, DeMott said, "Damn, I forgot. Macaroni salad and a pastrami sandwich."

"I hope you have rye bread," Kuster said. "I like my pastrami on rye. See you in about half an hour."

Just before eight o'clock, Washington time, Hamm left the lounge of the George V and walked down the avenue until he found a bistro with an open public telephone. He ordered a cognac from a waitress dressed in tight black satin, then walked over to the phone. He put in his call to Diane, but could not get an immediate line. He had to wait seven minutes before the operator called him back.

When Kuster answered the phone, it took Hamm a second to realize he had not used the wrong telephone number.

"Thought you were married, Gene."

"You taking an inordinate interest in my private life all of a sudden?"

"You know how close Claire and I are," Hamm said. Claire Kuster was one tough lady and the ideal military wife.

"Actually, there's been a change in plans," the general said.

"You want to find another phone?"

"Fuck whoever's listening. I got your message."

"Take you long?" Hamm asked.

"Longer than it should have. I'm getting old."

"So what changes do I prepare for?"

"We've got three things going," the general said,

''One, the company's all over me, with the director calling personally regarding your whereabouts.''

''Coriolanus is trying to key off of me.''

''Number two, we've had a contact. And number three, there's a puzzling development about the package.''

''What's that?''

''Nothing I'm going to tell you on this line, or any line. I've got an envoy en route to you.''

''There's no time.''

''Make time.''

BERLIN

NINETEEN

Herr Dokter Ernst Frohlberg spoke in heavily stressed English. The Germanic overtones laid over a clipped British form of the English language required weeks of acclimation for the listener. He spoke also in a basso profundo and laughed often and found humor in the most unlikely events.

Ernst Frohlberg was director-general of the Institute for Soviet Studies, a privately funded enterprise located in a ten-story, glass-and-steel structure on Kantstrasse, several blocks west of the Europa Center. The building was only three blocks from the small boardinghouse on Leibnizstrasse, where Robert Terrell had found a room. It had been an elegantly baroque hotel in the mid-thirties, and it was the same room he had rented for nearly three months when he and Pelagio were conducting their research in the early stages of GABRIEL. He had used the Simmons name. Five blocks away, on Krummestrasse, he had rented a shabbier room under the name of Geoffrey Holding. It was a place of refuge, if he needed it in a hurry.

On Thursday morning at ten o'clock, after his suit was returned to him from the dry cleaner, Terrell left the Leibnizstrasse boardinghouse and walked the tree-lined boulevard up to Kantstrasse and turned right. The traffic was heavy, bumper to bumper and door to door, and belligerent drivers communicated with one another using hand signals of frustration and aggression.

He turned in at the institute, passed through the glass door, and stopped at the reception counter. Terrell asked the security man to inform Herr Director Frohlberg he was here. After a brief phone call, he told Terrell to take the express elevator to the top floor.

The director-general's secretary, whom he remembered as Frieda, led him directly into the huge corner office. Through the full-length windows lining the two outside walls, in the near distance Terrell could see the woods of the Zoological Garden. To their left were the imposing buildings of the Technisch Universitat.

Frohlberg looked up from his morning newspaper, and the grim line of his mouth widened a half inch into what was his smile. "Robert! So good to see you! I could not believe my own ears yesterday when you called."

Terrell stepped forward to meet him as he came around the desk, and they shook hands. Frohlberg's grip was that of a constrained vise. Terrell hoped his nervousness did not show. He could feel the occasional flutter of his lower left lip.

"I was happy that you could see me on such short notice, Ernst."

"Nonsense. There is always time for friends. Come, let us sit." The director led him to a corner grouping of dark gray leather furniture and they sat across a low coffee table from each other. Frieda came in with a silver tray bearing coffee and cups, poured for them, then left.

The director leaned forward in his chair to study Terrell with an intense scrutiny. "Excuse my saying so, Robert, but you look tired."

Terrell nodded his head lightly. "It has been a long year. I'm looking forward to a vacation."

"Too often," Frohlberg said, "we ignore what our bodies tell us, preferring to follow what our heads say must be done. My own heart knocks at my head's door, but cannot get in. If I were to listen to it, I would retire." He laughed, a deep rumble of thunder.

"Retirement is an enticing thought," Terrell agreed. He let his coffee cup sit on the table, afraid that his hand might shake if he picked it up.

"I will have Frieda schedule a few days for me at some inn in the Black Forest where I can contemplate my rather disgusting navel. Perhaps you would join me?"

Terrell grinned. "I am afraid I have no interest in your navel, Ernst."

Frohlberg roared his appreciation.

"I am here to ask if I might peruse some of your archives."

"What section? You were interested in commercial and industrial areas before, I recall."

"Military, this time."

"Specifically?"

"Communications to start, I think."

"Historical or current?"

"I'm interested in the current levels of technology," Terrell said, though he was generally aware of most of the knowledge. He and Pelagio had already gathered the data for air- and land-based forces and utilized it in GABRIEL. "Particularly in naval areas."

The goals set out in the charter of the Institute for Soviet Studies promised that it was an organization seeking to understand Soviet culture and intellect. The ultimate and unstated goal, however, was to unify Germany, and toward that end, the institute collected a full range of information from public-domain works to highly classified materials. Much of their source material was obtained unknowingly from the intelligence agencies of the United States, Britain, France, and West Germany. And Ernst Frohlberg also had data-gatherers well placed in the services of the Soviet Union, East Germany, Poland, Czechoslovakia, and Hungary. The institute served as a library to many organizations, but restricted access to its unadvertised and classified documents. Few governments even knew about the sub-basement data-base files.

Frohlberg offered his ghoul's smile. "We do not have such information, naturally."

"Naturally."

"But you may see what there is to see. After lunch, perhaps?"

Terrell patted his stomach. "I had a late, and a heavy, German breakfast, Ernst. It would probably be better if I went right to work."

"There you go! Always work." The director shook his head sadly, again letting his eyes display a real concern over Terrell's appearance. Terrell's shaky condition appeared to unsettle Frohlberg to some degree. "Come. We will arrange your library card."

Frohlberg took him into the outer office, where Frieda typed out a special visitor's pass, with a security clearance number on it, and then helped him pin it on the lapel of his suit jacket, as if afraid that Terrell could not manage it himself. Terrell thanked her, then took the elevator to the lobby. A security escort was necessary for the trip to the sub-basement.

The subterranean room was starkly white, a tiled entrance area surrounded by cubicles containing computer terminals. Unseen behind a concrete wall was the separate computer facility that stored the classified materials. Frohlberg had once explained to Terrell and Pelagio that the computer was self-contained in the sub-basement, with no telephone line access and with its own backup electrical system. No computer hackers, and no unauthorized persons, would ever gain entrance to those files.

The guard left him with an attendant who checked the security number on his badge, then called upstairs for a separate confirmation. Once he had cleared those hurdles, Terrell was provided a cubicle, and the attendant typed in an access code on the terminal. The code was keyed to the security number on his lapel card, and he would only be able to scan those documents related to "Military, Communications."

Scan was the operative word; no written copies of information stored in the computer were allowed to leave the room without the personal permission of Herr Dokter Ernst Frohlberg. The only printer attached to the machine was located behind the attendant at the elevator access.

Once the attendant had backed out of the cubicle, closing the door behind him, Terrell nearly collapsed. His shoulders sagged, and his head fell forward onto his chest. He closed his eyes and took deep breaths. His arms felt as if they were coated with lead. His knees shook; each one rattled against the other.

Robert Terrell felt as if he were playing a role in a very strange play. And the character he portrayed was one with which he was not familiar. "It's just the pressure, Robert."

"There are too many out there who are looking for me."

"And we do not know what they look like, do we, Robert?"

"No. But it will be better when I am done here. I will sleep for a change."

After seven or eight minutes of forcing himself to relax, he looked up at the screen and placed his fingers on the keyboard. The monitor's green letters read: SECDATBA. It was the acronym for "Secure Data Base." The menu gave him a choice of French, German, or English languages for his communication with the computer, and he chose English.

The next screen told him he had access to classified data on Soviet military communications and asked him for a specific area of interest.

He selected "Naval."

And when the next screen came up, he selected "Submarine."

After his visit to Brandvlei, Terrell had decided it would be safer, and more humane, to blow up a submarine.

Tripoli was hot and dry, barren and monotonous in tones of beige. It was fortunate that the Mediterranean was visible from his window, or he would have drowned in an ecru sea of sand. The landscape was intended to heighten thirst, but Alexi Naratsmov could not even get a decent drink outside the Soviet embassy, and he did not stay long.

Before leaving Johannesburg, he had decided upon a new course of action. Following Steven Hamm through the secondhand reports of bumbling novice agents had not been fruitful. And it was not likely to be successful in the future, either.

He had wanted Hamm entirely out of the way, but Malengorov's supposedly talented Afrikaner had fumbled that assignment. As ever, it was one of the tasks he should have taken care of himself. Alexi would remain alert for Hamm, and then do what must be done. He couldn't continually be following the ex-DIA man.

He had learned that at Brandvlei, crouching behind a boulder while he watched the action take place around him, helpless to intervene.

No, he must be the first one to reach the target.

Therefore, he must project his mind ahead, attempting to think as Terrell was thinking. To project ahead, he could look back.

Terrell had gone to Mexico City. He had passed through Caracas, Venezuela, on his way to Cape Town. He had apparently been present at the village outside Brandvlei. All were places where Terrell had once resided, though sometimes briefly, according to his dossier.

It seemed to Naratsmov that the strategist had intended to go to the devastated village from the moment he left Washington. Perhaps there was an emotional attachment to the place where he had once worked while in the Peace Corps. A useless sentiment, he thought, but one that was apparently operative in the man.

Now, Terrell was headed north. There was a new, and an unknown, objective lodged in the man's mind, but if Alexi could rely on the man's history, he knew that his quarry would turn up in one of seven places. In Johannesburg, Naratsmov had sent explicit messages and accompanying photographs to KGB operatives he could trust in London, Brussels, Berlin, Bern, Paris, Cairo, and Tel Aviv.

He would no longer chase after Hamm, as Coriolanus appeared to be doing, but jump ahead, as the white knight to Hamm's black castle.

It came as no surprise to him, therefore, when, after only seventeen hours in Tripoli, he received a message from Pyotr Zhukov, the *rezident* in Berlin. One of his operatives had matched the photograph of Terrell to that of a passenger arriving on an evening Lufthansa flight.

Better yet, Zhukov had a Berlin address for the Berlin visitor.

TWENTY

The chief of station in Bern was named Frank Atwater. He was a congenial man, with an air of sophistication about him, and he had been with the agency for thirty-two years. Of average height and build, he was memorable for intense blue eyes and dark hair tinged at the temples with silver. His subordinates called him "Silvertip."

Jack Coriolanus and Roy Decker met with him at six-thirty in the evening. Coriolanus appreciated the spacious office, the walls finished in hand-carved cherry wood, with built-in bookcases that had arched tops near the high ceiling. The broadloom carpet was thick and spongy, a deep wine red that complemented the maroon leather furnishings.

"Come in, gentlemen," Atwater invited. He got up from his desk and went to the bar at the side of the office. A dozen lead-crystal glasses and a matching pitcher of water rested on the bartop, but the bottles were hidden within the cabinetry. Over the bar was an imposing landscape of the Swiss Alps in springtime. "What are you having, Jack?"

Coriolanus settled into the massive couch. "Bourbon, Frank. Don't bother playing with the water."

"Roy?"

"Same thing, I guess, but I'd add some water to it."

Atwater mixed their drinks and Decker picked them up, delivering the darker glass to Coriolanus. The chief of station mixed himself a shaker of martinis, standing with his back to the bar as he shook it. "Bad day at Black Rock, Jack?"

Coriolanus was tired. "Shit! I don't know where the hell they disappeared to. I've had your people combing this town from every gutter to every rooftop."

"It's a big place, with lots of nooks and crannies," Atwater said, pouring a stemmed glass full of his concoction, then adding an olive. He tasted it, frowned, then added a second olive. "What's Terrell's connection with Bern?"

"Something to do with economics. He met with some bankers, but the file is vague on the reasons why. My office in Washington is trying to pry the detail out of the SPG, but those assholes have gone tight on us since Congress landed on their case. At this point, I'd guess the KGB knows more about GABRIEL than the CIA does."

"You're positive he's in Bern?"

"Not absolutely, no. But it's one of the possibilities. Terrell's getting smart. He laid us a couple of false trails, one terminating in Paris, and one ending up in Bordeaux. The last positive location is Marseilles, and so far we haven't picked up anything out of there. That leaves Hamm as my contact, and that son-of-a-bitch has gone underground, too. The damned business jet of DIA's, which Hamm gets to play with, is sitting at the Bern airport. So we've had an eye on the plane since it arrived, but Hamm hasn't been back. And he hasn't checked into any hotel under his own name."

"Maybe Hamm's parked the airplane and left town," Decker offered. "That leaves us sitting here, watching the plane, and he's got all of Europe to himself. Hell, Paris is only five hundred miles away."

Coriolanus did not like the sound of it. The thought of Hamm's out-foxing him yet again rankled. "Not likely. That's not Hamm's style."

"He's got a lot at stake, Jack," Decker said.

"Roy's got a good point," Atwater told him.

"What pisses me off is that we're supposed to be on the same side. Fucking Hamm is spending more time dodging us than he is chasing Terrell."

"You want a suggestion from an old hand, Jack?" Atwater asked.

"Sure."

"I'm sitting over here at the side, remember. And I see you dogging Hamm's footsteps because he's a major link to Terrell."

"That's what I'm doing."

"If you think Hamm's close enough to Terrell, knows enough about him, that he'll lead you to the man, what do you think the opposition is also thinking?''

''Go on.''

''Knowing his public reputation, I don't think Hamm gives a damn about you, but he doesn't want to lead the opposition directly to Terrell. I'll bet you my next month's salary against yours that Colonel General Andresev has some of his FCD boys dogging your ass.''

Coriolanus got up and went to the bar to refill his glass. Turning back toward Decker, he asked, ''You told me that Chukker showed up in South Africa, Roy?''

''That's right. In Johannesburg.''

''Alexi Naratsmov, right?''

''Yes,'' Decker agreed. He swirled the melting ice cubes in his glass.

Coriolanus studied his alternatives for a moment. ''Roy, why don't you go down to the Communication Center and query Langley to see if there's been any recent movements noted for known KGB operatives? Let's concentrate on Naratsmov and any of his buddies in Department Twelve.''

Decker set his glass on the inlaid leather of the bar before he went out.

Atwater took a mild puff on his Havana. ''Didn't mean to take the reigns, Jack.''

''Hell, we're team players. What I need are guys like you closer to me. I'm surrounded by these half-witted, half-assed lawyers out of UCLA and Arizona, and none of them has any perspective. Why don't you come back to D.C?''

Atwater waved an arm expansively. ''And give up all this? Jack, where's *your* perspective?''

Coriolanus forced a smile. "I hate guys who only think about the perks and the pension."

Twenty minutes passed before Decker returned carrying a printout. "I got the last five days," he said. "There's been some movement of known operatives around the world, but the one we're interested in, Naratsmov, left Tripoli this morning."

"We're waiting, Decker."

"He was picked up arriving in Berlin at four this afternoon."

"Think Naratsmov knows something we don't?"

"I wouldn't doubt it a bit, Jack."

Two couples and a female extra were writhing about on the padded-velvet floor of the circular stage, their oiled flesh gleaming under the hot white spotlights. The action was sometimes confusing, with heavy breasts, shaven pudenda, buttocks, and massive erections the targets of undiscriminating hot red mouths and oily, slick hands.

Around the stage, in almost total darkness, postage-stamp-sized tables with white linen tablecloths and amber drinks rested on rising tiers six levels high. Bare-breasted waitresses, with their nipples painted with phosphorescent makeup, drifted through the rows, passing out more drinks to an enraptured audience.

Hamm divided his attention among the stage, the spectators, and the black curtain hanging over the entrance. When Diane slipped through the curtain, carrying a suitcase in one hand, the light of the foyer behind her, he could not see her face, but the body language told him her reaction to the stage show. Her back went rigid, and her shoulders went back in defiance.

She could not see him in the darkness, so he got up and climbed three rows to the top aisle and made his way to the entrance. He made his voice deep. "Help you, missy?"

Her attention jerked away from the stage, and she took a step back. "Steve?"

"It's almost our turn."

"I'm out of here!"

She backed through the curtain, with one more quick glance at the stage, and Hamm followed her.

The light in the foyer was tinted red, making her beige travel suit pink. Her face was also pink, he thought. Other than that, she looked awfully good to him. He grinned at her. "Don't you want to see the show?"

Her shoulders were still back, and she raised her chin to look at him. "This what spooks do on their day off?"

"What day off? It's a rendezvous spot. Didn't you see those people rendezvousing?"

"Is that the word for it? I'm way out of date."

Hamm reached down, took her suitcase from her, and put his hand in the small of her back, urging her toward the front door. The club was a half flight down from the sidewalk, and they climbed to the street, where Hamm was able to flag a cab. He opened the door for her, and once they were seated, he told the driver, *"George Cinq, s'il vous plaît."*

"That's as polite as I've ever heard you," DeMott said.

"It's the only French I know."

Her jawline was still tense. "I'll bet you and Gene Kuster get a laugh out of this when you're old and gray. He just gave me an address."

"It was the only address he had, given the code."

"You two must have been real cute in your youth."

"I thought I was still pretty cute."

"You thought wrong." She crossed her arms under her breasts and sat quietly for the rest of the trip.

Hamm sat sideways in the backseat, scanning his trail. He did not see anyone following them. DeMott's job as an intelligence analyst—or even as his assistant—might rate a phone tap, but not manpower chasing after her.

Hamm had the cabbie let them out before they reached the hotel, on the rue de Marbeuf, and they walked the rest of the way. He watched the pedestrians and the onlookers carefully, but did not note any suspicious behavior. Inside the hotel, he led her directly to the elevator and up to his room.

Unlocking the door, Hamm let her enter first.

"Aren't you going to feed me? The food on the Concorde was too rich for my taste."

"We'll order something sent up. I haven't been hitting the public spots when there's a crowd around."

"So I noticed," DeMott said, then looked around the sumptuous room. The brocaded wallpaper and damask drapes were highlighted in gold. The fruitwood furnishings were highly polished. On the table in one corner were a basket of fruit, a bottle of champagne in an ice bucket, and a mini-liquor store. "You're living the life to which you've grown accustomed, I see."

Hamm remembered some hotels they had

shared. He shrugged. "I haven't changed much, Diane."

"Uh-uh." She went to the phone, picked it up, and dialed room service from the card lying on the dresser. Ordering a small filet, a salad, and coffee, she looked over at him. He nodded. "Do that twice, please," she said.

Hamm threw her suitcase on a velvet-covered ottoman and went over to the table to mix a Scotch-and-water. "You want one?'

"You're in France, and you're not drinking the champagne?"

"Saved it for you."

He spent some time getting the cork out, while she wandered around the room and looked out the window. He poured the bubbly into a stemmed flute and handed it to her.

"Gene shouldn't have sent you. You're a hell of an analyst, Diane, but you don't have any field experience."

His attitude had rubbed off on her, and she was not in the best of moods. "I've been doing some damned good investigation, Hamm."

He took the chair across the table from her and rested his elbows on the waxed surface of the table. "I don't want you in harm's way, though."

"I'll worry about me. You worry about you. How's your head?"

"I know it's there." He took a long pull at his drink. "What have you got for me?"

She recapped her interview with Foster. "Minor point first. GABRIEL, in hardcopy, is in one or more vinyl binders, if Bob still has them. The software is on a reel of tape, one of the big ones, like fifteen or sixteen inches in diameter."

"Goes in a suitcase, then," Hamm said, "but not necessarily through customs without a lot of questions."

"I suppose. Then, the other thing I learned is that GABRIEL is designed to detonate missiles in their silos. Anyone's missiles. First strike is totally unnecessary."

"You must have charmed the old boy out of his pants to get that."

"I think he might have had that in mind. What do you make of it, Steve?" She leaned forward, intent on his answer, and her concentration seemed to dissolve some of her resentment.

"I agree with your assessment," he said. "I first thought that GABRIEL, as a communications intervention device, was a good intelligence-gathering tool. But now, if it has evolved into something that could get around the fail-safe mechanisms and blow them in their silos, we are in real trouble. No wonder the President and the Pentagon were in an uproar. From what I've learned about this systems designer, Pelagio, he was a real right-winger. I thought he was giving the generals something to hold in their back pockets, if politics got in the way of military strategy."

"Boggles the mind," DeMott said.

"You know, though, as much as I might bitch about the system—"

"And so openly."

"I still think the safeguards are key. The military reports to a civilian administration. I don't like Dilman, and I don't like a number of other high-echelon commanders, but I don't really believe that their philosophies would go so far as to launch a first strike without the commander in chief's stamp of approval. That doesn't make me like them, though."

"I'm glad to see that you've come to grips with your emotions." She held up her glass.

Hamm reached across the table for the bottle and refilled her glass. "Now that you're telling me what GABRIEL was designed to do, it doesn't read. Sure, it'd be a hell of a gimmick, if it worked, but for what reason?" Hamm switched positions, leaning back in his chair.

"I had a few hours to think about it, eating peanuts on the plane," she said. "If it makes first strike obsolete, it could effectively neutralize all nuclear war plans."

"But wouldn't Bob have liked that aspect? The more I think about him, and the way he talked, he would have appreciated some idea that neutralized strategic weapons systems."

"It would be one-sided. An impotent Supreme Soviet, but an overpowered U.S. Defense Department. Still, I suppose he might have thought along those lines, shutting down Moscow. Maybe even shutting down the American system."

Hamm thought for a moment. "Even then, we're talking about some one thousand U.S. ICBM's, and nearly fourteen hundred Soviet ICBMs that fall under the control of GABRIEL."

"Enough to do the job," she agreed.

"What else do you have?"

While she got up to rummage in her purse, Hamm found the Chivas Regal bottle and tilted it over his glass. He dipped into the champagne bucket for half-melted ice cubes. DeMott came back and handed him a piece of paper. "That came in my mail."

Hamm read it. He did not think the tone was good.

"I sense a crusade under way," Diane said. "Something's gotten to Bob—likely something in GABRIEL. . . ."

"Or the accident at Brandvlei," he suggested. "I'm beginning to think the explosion in South Africa was what set him off."

"Maybe. Or a combination of the two. The village is obliterated and makes him think about what he's been doing. He thinks he's the only one who can do something about it."

"In a way, he *has* done something," Hamm said. "GABRIEL is compromised. We can't use it, and the Russkies can't use it. We're scared to death about what he might do with it. Even releasing the details to the international media would have far-reaching consequences on public faith. The Soviets probably don't know exactly what he has, but they want it, anyway. What's the latest on Naratsmov?"

"When I left, he was in Tripoli."

"Good place for him. I hope he gets sunburned. Anything else I should know?"

She did not look up. "You're in the wrong luxury hotel. You should be at the Bristol-H. Kempinski or the Brussels-Sheraton."

"Why?"

"Bob and Larry Pelagio were in Paris and Bern for different projects—something about economics and Interpol data bases. They did their GABRIEL research in Berlin and Brussels."

Hamm got up and went to the dresser for the phone. "You know specifics?"

"In Berlin, it dealt with communications. In

Brussels, it had to do with NATO information on missile sites and the like.''

Hamm held his anger in check. This was information he should have had from the beginning. Goddamned Dilman and Foster. He dialed the desk and asked the clerk to find him a flight to Berlin.

When he hung up and went to the closet for his suitcase, DeMott asked, ''Why Berlin?''

''Missiles. Besides, it takes me longer to get there, and I'm running out of time. Couldn't have done it without you, kid. I'll call you back at the office as soon as I can.''

''But, I haven't eaten,'' she complained, as she watched Hamm pack.

''Get something at the airport.''

TWENTY-ONE

Pyotr Zhukov, the *rezident* in Berlin, had provided Alexi Naratsmov with a rented Mercedes 300 sedan. It was parked in line with a dozen other cars on Leibnizstrasse, across the street and a half block up from the entrance to the boardinghouse where Robert Terrell had registered as Albert Simmons.

It had been raining off and on since five o'clock, and beads of moisture dotted the polished black paint of the hood, reflecting the light of lampposts along the street. As darkness descended over the street, the shadows became blacker and deeper, absorbing the yellow rays from the windows of apartments overlooking the street. It was the Berlin Naratsmov knew so well. Here, he could not stray from his course, as he had in South Africa.

By ten o'clock, Naratsmov had been waiting in the car for more than four hours. Some passersby, going in one direction, then returning, offered sidelong glances, then picked up their paces. It was not something in which they wished to become involved.

He had arrived at an overcast Tegel Airport just after four in the afternoon, traveling under an assumed name on diplomatic status. He did not assume that the ruse fooled anyone; his face was too well known in Berlin, and one of the British, American, or French spotters at the customs entry would have reported his arrival. He rented a locker for his suitcase, then walked briskly toward the taxi stand at the front entrance.

A British agent from MI-6, whom he knew as Ogilvy, left the terminal behind him, but Naratsmov managed to elude him within forty minutes by taking a taxi to Friedrichstrasse and joining the flow of people returning to East Berlin through Checkpoint Charlie. Instead of crossing to the east, however, he dodged his way out of the crowd, and there was no pursuit in sight when he met Zhukov's courier in Volkspark Hasenheide as the darkened sky began to release large drops of rain. Opening the passenger door of the sedan, Naratsmov slipped into the front seat.

The courier was no one he had seen before, and he did not ask for a name. Reaching inside his jacket, he produced the equipment Naratsmov had requested, a Stechkin nine-millimeter automatic, and handed it to him. He checked the magazine quickly, then the action, working a shell into the breech and setting the safety. He slipped it inside his belt, on his left side. The courier then gave him two small leather cases, and Naratsmov opened the first to find the locksmith's tools he had demanded. The second contained two syringes and four small vials of liquid.

And now he had waited four fruitless hours. He had gotten out of the car twice, when the rain slackened, once to take a walk around the block. On the second foray, up the alley behind Frau Koln's boardinghouse, he had discovered that the two rooms on the second floor at the back were unlit. He used his lock picks to let himself in through the brown steel door, and climbed the stairs to investigate Terrell's room. He found the man's suitcase partially unpacked, toilet articles surrounding the washbasin. Two dirty shirts were hung over the back of a chair. Terrell was actually living there, he decided, and debated whether to wait for him in the room or out in the car. He elected the automobile, since Terrell might not return alone, and he could not see the street from the room. Alexi let himself out quietly and returned to the car.

A gnawing hunger in the pit of his stomach was becoming more noticeable when Terrell appeared. He was alone. He was not wearing a raincoat, nor carrying an umbrella. He hurried along the now nearly deserted street toward the Mercedes, his shoulders hunched, his hands stuck in his pockets, walking close to the building fronts abutting the sidewalk. Naratsmov had never seen the man before, but the recognition was instant and total when Terrell passed under a cast-iron streetlight. The thick lenses of his glasses were beaded with raindrops.

Naratsmov slid down in the seat, making himself

as inconspicuous as possible in the darkness of the car.

Terrell passed by without glancing toward him.

Naratsmov counted to five, then eased upward in the seat, to where he could use the rearview mirror. Terrell turned off the sidewalk between two parked automobiles, paused to allow a truck to pass, then trotted across the street. He scampered up the six steps fronting Frau Koln's Rooms, shaking his shoulders and peeling off his wet suit coat.

He looked like a man eager to be out of the rain, ready to closet himself in his warm room and take a hot bath. Had he eaten dinner yet? He would have missed Frau Koln's dinner hour.

He did not look like a man who possessed the super secrets of a superpower.

But that was for General Andresev to decide. Alexi Naratsmov accepted that much on faith.

He waited fifteen minutes, then started the car and drove around the block to park on Mommsenstrasse, under a leafy elm near the entrance to the alley. After once again checking the Stechkin, Naratsmov pulled the key from the ignition and got out of the car. The rain had picked up again, and like Terrell, he was not prepared for it. He hurried up the alley to mid-block and was soaked by the time he reached the back of the building. The windows in Room 205 were now lit.

He went directly to the steel door with a small window in its center. The window had steel mesh embedded in the glass. Beside the door was a small sign, in German, warning trash collectors not to block the exit.

The KGB agent peered through the window. The stairwell was vacant; a door toward the front and a door to one side marked Storage were both closed. One overhead, forty-watt bulb provided weak illumination.

He looked up and down the alley. Trash bins and stacked boxes made it narrower than it actually was and cast alien shadows against the streetlamps at either end. No living thing moved. He heard a window being slammed down farther up the alley. Retrieving the case of lock picks from his jacket pocket, he opened it, selected the pick he wanted, and bent to the lock, working by feel and sound in the night.

It took two minutes, a minute less than the first time he had opened it.

Stepping inside, he eased the door shut, then immediately climbed the concrete stairs, taking a turn at one mid-level landing.

On the second-floor landing, he reached up to unscrew the weak light bulb, then opened the door to the short hallway, leading from front to back. Immediately to his right was Room 205.

Waiting patiently for another ten minutes, Naratsmov adjusted himself to the silence. It was not late enough for all of the residents to have returned for the night. He would have to be quick.

He kept the knob turned, and the latch back, as he closed the stairwell door behind him, releasing the knob slowly. Moving to the paneled door to 205, Naratsmov pressed his ear lightly against the stained oak and listened.

He could hear nothing through the thick slab of the panel.

It took him less than a minute this time, fishing for the tumblers in the cylinder, before the lock clicked open. He turned the handle, pushed open the door, and eased himself inside Room 205. Terrell was not in the room, but the door to the bathroom was nearly shut, with a sliver of light showing through the gap.

He took care to close the hall door quietly on his way out.

Jack Coriolanus and Roy Decker had arrived at Tegel in their chartered Cessna Citation at nine-forty-five, but it was close to eleven by the time they had obtained Terrell's address. The CIA operation in Berlin had turned out in force to canvass the hotels and boardinghouses for registrations in the name of Terrell and Albert Simmons.

On their way to Leibnizstrasse, Decker said, "I can't believe it was this easy to find him."

"The fucker's crazy," Coriolanus agreed. "Out of his goddamned mind. He's starting to slip."

"Why would he use a name we could trace?"

"Could be he wants to attract the KGB's attention. This is a damned good town for crossing over to the other side."

"On the other hand, he and Pelagio were here for nearly four months," Decker countered. "Maybe he's doing some follow-up on the file?"

"What the hell for?" Coriolanus asked.

"I don't know. If I knew what GABRIEL was, or did, I could take a guess at it." Decker sounded peeved that he had not been given details.

Coriolanus did not like divulging his own ignorance of GABRIEL's specifics. "I wouldn't count on Terrell being here to work."

Their driver drove the Kurfurstendamm at a fast clip, switching lanes frequently in the heavy traffic of the thoroughfare. Two more cars with CIA operatives trailed behind.

"Terrell and Pelagio were in Berlin over a year and a half ago. Early in the project," Coriolanus said, as if that explained something. He wondered how much Hamm had been told about GABRIEL.

The driver took a hard right in the mild maze at the junction of Kurfurstendamm, the Konstanzerstrasse, and Leibnizstrasse, causing Coriolanus to slide across the seat toward Decker. He grabbed the door handle and pulled himself back. Two blocks later, the driver double-parked across the street from Frau Koln's Rooms. The other two cars pulled up behind them seconds later.

The rain was pouring down now. Coriolanus got out and went back to meet the others. "Two of you hustle around to the back and see if there's another door. Check for fire escapes. Remember, we want him alive. We have to know if he's talked to anyone. And keep an eye out for Naratsmov. We know he's here ahead of us."

With Decker and five more agents trailing behind, Coriolanus crossed the street at a run and quick-stepped the granite risers at the front of the old hotel. In Berlin, boardinghouses normally locked their front doors each night, but the proprietress had been called earlier and was waiting for them, standing in the foyer behind the glass door. She unlocked it as soon as she saw Coriolanus.

She was probably in her seventies, heavy and stooped, dressed in a faded blue robe. Tufts of her white hair peeked from under a bandanna tied under the loose skin of her chin. She backed into the tiny lobby ahead of him.

"Herr Meeker?" she asked him, expecting the

man who had called her earlier. Her rheumy old eyes filled with suspicion.

"No. I'm Coriolanus. What room is he in?"

"It is Room Two-oh-five," the old woman answered hesitantly.

He did not answer her, but headed for the stairway off the left side of the lobby, taking the steps two at a time.

TWENTY-TWO

Hamm did not reach Berlin until after midnight.

The rainstorm stacked up air traffic, and his British Airways flight, every seat filled, even at that time of night, was kept in a holding pattern for more than thirty minutes.

He missed having the Lear at hand, but hoped that it was keeping Naratsmov at bay.

Customs was stacked up because of all of the passengers deplaning from the delayed flights. Hamm stood in line for forty minutes, watched the raindrops sluicing down the big glass windows, and silently railed at the uniformed men who had decided that the middle of the night was the time to check every bag thoroughly. If it were U.S. Customs, he might have said something regrettable, which would no doubt have made the morning news.

When he reached the head of the line, he unzipped his canvas carry-all and pushed it toward the inspector, a jowly fat man who appeared as if he enjoyed more than his share of sauerbraten.

"American?"

"Yes." He handed over his passport.

"Welcome to Berlin, Herr . . . Whalen?"

"That's right. Dean Whalen." He had been traveling on the Whalen passport since Bern.

The fat hands darted in and out of his carry-all, stopping only to examine the electric razor. "Business trip, Herr Whalen?"

"Yes."

"What business?"

Hamm told him he was engaged in the export of beef, trying on Monty Palidin's history, and he was finally passed through. He stopped at the exchange office and traded dollars for deutsche marks.

He looked for a phone, to call Palidin and to check with some Berlin contacts, but he spotted a quicker source.

In his mid-forties, with a ruddy complexion and ears that jutted out from under long blond hair, the man grinned his recognition.

"Hello, Chet."

Chester Ogilvy was MI-6, a long-termer, and also a veteran of Southeast Asia. "Thought you might appear, sooner or later. Infrequently, the grapes on the vine are real, rather than rumored. Fancy a cup of tea?"

"You have the tea. I'll try coffee."

They found a restaurant featuring instant, poly-packed German meals on the main concourse, took chairs at a small table, and ordered tea and coffee from a grumpy fräulein who obviously thought the tip would prove to be minuscule.

"You've heard from Monty?" Hamm asked.

Ogilvy's eyes tended to roam the crowd passing by on the other side of their window, while his fingers toyed with a toothpick. "That I did. Talked to him just after having seen your Alexi Ivanovitch pass through here."

"Appear to be in any rush?"

"No. Took his sweet time losing me. Appeared to cross over at Checkpoint Charlie, but I couldn't swear to that."

"You see the other man I'm looking for?"

"Terrell? No. And put away the dirty look. I'm not spreading the name about. Is he the same man Jackie Coriolanus has an interest in?"

"You see Coriolanus?" Hamm was beginning to think that some momentous piece of evidence had passed under his nose, apparent to anyone but himself.

"Didn't surprise me. We *Berliners* are accustomed to covert faces. He got in around nine-thirty."

"Any ideas about where Naratsmov would go to ground?"

"Berlin is a bit of a home base for him, though he stays away from Soviet officialdom. There's a *haufbrau* on Uhlandstrasse, called the Friesenhof, where he likes to recreate. He's not a fancier of ultraposh. From time to time, he can be located at the Remter on Marburger Strasse. That's when he doesn't object to being located, mind. Otherwise, he knows Berlin like an alleycat knows his favorite fence.'' Ogilvy's eyes continued to roam the tide of airline passengers.

Hamm asked, ''Monty say anything more?''

''Afraid not. We'll keep our eyes open. I say, you happen to know that chap?''

Hamm turned slightly to see a gray-suited man, obviously American, and possibly an ex-linebacker, leaning against a pillar at the side of a ramp leading to the Lufthansa concourse. ''No. CIA?''

''Certainly. Name's Cameron. I forget the first name. He's been part of Berlin station for six or seven months. I estimate him as a veteran of some year or two's experience. I believe he'd like to meet you, much as he appears more interested in the parade of bosoms.''

''I'll introduce myself. Cheers.'' Hamm downed the last of his coffee.

Ogilvy rose from his chair. ''This doesn't work out for you, give me a call.'' He walked off, back toward customs, whistling softly through his teeth. Hamm did not know the song.

Dropping marks on the table, Hamm stood, looped his bag over his shoulder, and headed straight for the men's room next door to the restaurant. He pushed through the two self-closing doors and found himself in a lavatory area, a row of sinks along the opposite wall. Two men stood at urinals in a back room, three pairs of shoe toes peered from under stall doors, and two men stood at sinks, chatting in Danish to each other.

Hamm turned around to face the door and leaned his left shoulder against the tiled wall. He dug a copy of his orders out of his wallet, unfolded it, and reversed the creases. His copies were becoming somewhat dog-eared, reminding him that Terrell had been a free spirit for entirely too long.

When Cameron came through the door, he was startled to discover himself face to face with Hamm.

"Hello, sailor."

Hamm startled him. His mouth parted slightly.

"What have you got for me?"

"Got? I haven't got anything." The big shoulders tensed, and his arms curled slightly. He was ready to sack the quarterback, intercept the pass.

The two Danes brushed past them on their way out.

"You're supposed to give me our man's location." Hamm posed the question, even though he doubted that the agency had located Terrell.

"Bullshit!"

"What did Coriolanus tell you?" Hamm felt as if he had been outflanked by two enemies, the KGB and the CIA. He needed a shortcut, and here was one right in front of him.

"Coriolanus?"

"Quit fucking around. You don't have enough time in to get away with it."

The man's eyes slid sideways as he thought that one over. Finally, he decided to give a little. "If you show up, I'm supposed to take you into the office."

"Coriolanus must have thought you were big enough to accomplish that," Hamm said.

That raised the dander, along with the linebacker shoulders. "Look, Colonel, I don't know what the hell's going on. I only know what I'm supposed to do. We can walk out of here, or we—"

Hamm handed him the orders.

"What am I supposed to do with this?"

"Read it, if you can."

He read it twice before the eyebrow rose.

"Coriolanus show you written orders?"

The big head shook negatively.

"That's because he doesn't have them. Now, where are we, Cameron? Working for an agency hack, or for the President?"

"Look, Colonel, I'd better call in—"

"I don't have time. You call in after I take off. Where'd Coriolanus go?"

"I can't tell. . . ."

"Goddamn it, Cameron! You bucking for some time on the Director's carpet?"

"Well, shit, sir, I mean. . . ."

"Get out of the way."

The man stood to one side as Hamm reached for the door handle. At the last minute, he opted to avoid a reprimand he did not understand. "It's a boardinghouse on Leibnizstrasse. Frau Kohl's Rooms."

"He take people with him?"

"Seven or eight of them."

Shit! Hamm thought. Coriolanus was playing Elliot Ness. "What are you carrying?"

"Carrying? Oh." The man touched his side. "Colt forty-five."

"You're not one to mess around with dainty firearms, are you? Let me have it."

"You can't take my gun." The shoulders squared off.

Hamm's hand darted out, whipped the young man's coat open, and lifted the big automatic out of a shoulder rig. "I'll mail it back to you."

He shoved the pistol under his belt, in the small of his back.

Hamm took the first cab in line, a chocolate Mercedes, and told the driver, "Frau Kohl's Rooms."

"I do not know where that is." He had an Italian accent.

"I don't, either. Find Leibnizstrasse, and we'll flip a coin for right or left." Hamm dumped a thick sheaf of marks on the front seat.

The driver took one look at the currency, and the cab shot out of the taxi line. They were immediately picked up by two civilian cars, both dark, one a Volvo and one an Audi.

Hamm looked back, then said, "I don't like shadows."

The driver looked down on the seat beside him, raised his head to look at Hamm in the rearview mirror, then said, "Shadows do not last long at this time of night, *signore*."

The Volvo was not a problem, but the Audi hung on for twenty-five minutes. Hamm decided that if he ever ran a car in the Grand Prix de Monaco, he already had his driver. Toward the end, the Mercedes was hitting speeds of one hundred twenty kilometers per hour on Berlin's back streets, taking corners in controlled four-wheel drifts.

When he got out in front of the boardinghouse, he was riding an adrenaline high after the chase. It was almost two o'clock, and it was chilly. His new beige suit did not fit the mood of middle-of-the-night Berlin. As the cab pulled away, Hamm climbed the six steps to the glass door, found it locked, and pressed the button alongside the door.

He waited ten minutes before an old lady appeared. She peered through the door at him for several seconds before unlocking it and pulling it open three inches. There were large bags under her eyes.

Hamm used his rusty German to say, "Frau Koln, I must ask a question."

"In the middle of the night?" She was irritated, at best, and she went on to compare him to some variety of sausage. Hamm missed most of the rapid-fire exchange and considered himself fortunate.

He produced the picture of Terrell. "Have you seen this man?"

She needed only one glance. "Herr Simmons? Yes. He has a room here."

"He is here?"

"He has a room. He is not in it. The other men could not find him, either."

"The other men? Where are they now?"

"They have left."

So they missed him. Hamm thought for a minute, while the drizzle settled in his muscles. "I would like a room, Frau Koln."

Hamm had been up by six, aroused by the half-dreamed conclusion that Bob Terrell had selected an out-of-the-way rooming house because he had used it two years ago, when he and Pelagio were in Berlin.

He shaved, then painfully pulled the bandage off the back of his head. It was difficult to tell how the stitches looked, but he decided to live with it.

Skipping the breakfast available in Frau Koln's dining room, he descended to the street. There were spots of blue in the gunmetal sky, but not very many of them. The trees and shrubs spotted along the street looked fresh after the night's rain. Red and yellow and purple flowers in boxes hung under window sashes were pinpoints of brightness in what promised to be another drab day.

Starting to the south along Leibnizstrasse, Hamm began his search by walking clockwise around an ever-expanding circle of blocks. Most Germans were early risers. He nodded to butchers and produce vendors and gas-station attendants unshuttering and sweeping out their respective establishments.

He walked briskly, and his eyes took in everything, each little sign in a second-floor window advertising dental or chiropractic services, every notary, travel agency, or boutique. What he was looking for might not be obvious. Where would a war planner do research? Usually in a governmental setting, or a university campus.

GABRIEL was unique, however, and the research involved might not have fallen into the usual pattern.

He hoped Diane had gotten a seat on the Concorde out of Paris. He had not given her any other option but to return to Washington, though she had wanted to stay in Europe to help.

He was walking along Kantstrasse when he spotted it. The gold Gothic letters against a black background were large and bold: INSTITUTE FOR SOVIET STUDIES.

That had to be it.

He checked the door, found it locked, and read the small plastic sign inside the glass: BY APPOINTMENT ONLY. LOBBY OPEN AT NINE O'CLOCK." A security guard and a receptionist stood behind a counter, and Hamm banged on the door until they looked up. The guard shook his head negatively. Hamm wrote down the telephone number, then continued down the street until he found a restaurant to have breakfast.

At nine o'clock, he called the institute and asked for a manager.

"Were you interested in conducting research, Herr Hamm?" The young lady wanted to be helpful.

"No." He tried to think of a subtle but influential way to get an immediate appointment. "I have some official questions on behalf of the U.S. government to pose to the manager. A matter of ten minutes, perhaps."

"One moment, sir."

He waited for more than one moment. When she came back on the line, she said, "Director-General Frohlberg can give you ten minutes, Herr Hamm. Is nine-thirty convenient?"

"That'll be fine."

Hamm walked back to the institute and found the door unlocked. He entered and crossed the broad lobby to the blond-wood counter. The receptionist took his name, surprisingly asking for both his home and his local addresses. "Please have a seat, Herr Hamm. I will call you when Dokter Frohlberg is free."

Lowering himself onto one of the rigid sofas, Hamm picked up a brochure from the table alongside it. It described the institute's collection of research materials and its avowed mission to broaden understanding in the cultural and traditional mores of the Soviet nation.

An open collection of materials such as described in the pamphlet might have been expensive, and might require security, but it did not require security guards who were armed. There was one guard behind the counter, with the receptionist, one standing beside the last elevator in the bank of five, and one roaming aimlessly about the lobby. The three of them were uniformed in gray twill and outfitted with revolvers and portable radios. Typical of Berlin, he thought. Games within games.

When his name was called, Hamm took the first elevator to the top floor, exiting to a paneled room with more uncomfortable sofas and one desk with a nameplate reading FRIEDA LISL ZEIGER.

She stood as he entered. "Herr Hamm?"

"Colonel Hamm, actually, Frau Zieger."

"Yes, sir. You may go right in."

Hamm passed through the door she opened for him into a large and airy office.

Ernst Frohlberg stood up behind his desk and offered his hand. Hamm shook it while introducing himself, finding the director's grip firm and almost overly hard. He looked to be a sober and serious individual.

"You would not mind, Colonel, if I asked for identification?"

"Not at all." Hamm produced his I.D. card and DIA identification.

"Please, have a chair." Frohlberg reseated himself while closely studying the credentials. Finally, he handed them back. "How may we assist you, Colonel? It is not often that the American Defense Intelligence Agency visits us."

"But they do, from time to time?"

Frohlberg waved a beefy hand. "Occasionally,

information we have on file proves useful. It is there for anyone to see.''

''I'm interested in the use of your files made by Robert Terrell.'' Hamm watched for the response to the name.

''Terrell?'' The deep bass was level and clipped, and the broad face remained almost impassive. Frohlberg's mouth, which was a severe line in his face, narrowed imperceptibly, and his eyes took on a hooded look. ''I would have to check our visitor logs to be certain of the name.''

''Check for Lawrence Pelagio, too, then. It would have been for four months, two years ago.''

Hamm waited, but Frohlberg made no move toward his intercom to have his secretary check on the dates and names. ''What is your interest, Colonel?''

''My agency is backtracking Terrell, since Pelagio died.''

There was no response to that tidbit. This man did not accept bait at face value.

''You might also check for me, if you would, the date of Terrell's last visit to the institute.''

The director again made a small wave with his hand. ''We do not normally give out the names of researchers who utilize the collections, Colonel. It is an institute policy, you understand?''

''Is that for all research personnel, or just the ones using the confidential files?'' Hamm voiced his supposition.

''Confidential?''

''Surely there must be a great many of them.''

''It is also our policy,'' the director said, without responding to Hamm's observation, ''to be helpful, wherever we can be, to the governments of friendly nations. If you would leave your telephone number with Frieda, Colonel, I will have one of our staff check the records and call you back with the information. Naturally, we must also verify your credentials."

Hamm stood up. "Naturally. And it might be quicker to start with the White House. Thank you for your time, and your assistance, Herr Frohlberg."

By the time he reached the street again, Hamm was convinced that Bob Terrell was inside the building. He was positive that Terrell had been there the day before.

If Terrell were in the building, and learned that Hamm was waiting for him, he would not be leaving by the front entrance.

Hamm started around the block, looking for an alley.

Behind the high-rise building that housed the institute, a hundred meters south, was a three-story parking garage. The second level of the open-sided structure offered an excellent view of the service entrance and loading dock at the back of the institute.

Alexi Naratsmov had been waiting there since nine-thirty, sitting in the rented Mercedes. He watched delivery vans come and go, unloading boxes of beef and onions for the restaurant, picking up parcels from a dress shop. None stopped at the back of the institute. Two cooks emerged from the back of the restaurant, carrying steaming mugs. They lit cigarettes and leaned against the wall, talking to each other.

The first and second levels of the garage were

full, and a few cars passed behind him, climbing up to the top floor. A woman in high heels made her way gingerly down the incline, passing out of sight toward the first level.

Terrell had outwitted him the night before. Frau Koln's was a front that the strategist had prepared effectively, leaving the shaving gear and dirty clothes in evidence. There would be a safe house elsewhere, where Terrell had slipped off to, after turning on the lights in Room 205.

Naratsmov's morning hours had been devoted to finding either Terrell's refuge or the reason he was in the area. He drove a search grid of twenty square blocks before he decided that the Institute for Soviet Studies was the logical choice.

He had been parked on Kantstrasse, up from the entrance, when Terrell arrived at eight-thirty. Naratsmov was out of the car, and partway down the block in seconds, but too late to reach Terrell before he turned into the building, someone unlocking the door for him.

Prepared to wait all day, he had returned to the car, and fifteen minutes later he saw Hamm come around the corner, check the door, then continue up the street. The DIA agent went into a restaurant just before reaching Naratsmov's parking place.

Hamm's appearance complicated things. It could mean Coriolanus was close behind.

Half an hour later, Hamm emerged from the restaurant and went back to the institute. This time, he went inside.

Alexi started the car and drove around the block once, then again when he decided on the parking garage as his vantage spot.

It was not likely that Terrell would exit the building from the front. And it was not likely that he would be in the company of Hamm. If they did appear together, then he could solve two problems at once.

What *was* likely was that he would not now have to wait all day. Terrell would bolt out the back, right into his arms.

Naratsmov checked his Stechkin automatic, then opened the thicker of his two leather cases and prepared a syringe. He left the key in the ignition when he got out of the car and took the back stairs down to ground level.

TWENTY-THREE

"You've looked at a hundred flow charts, Robert. Maybe more."

"And there are more to go."

"The submarines are out, Robert. They are too frequently out of contact."

"But they are so much safer."

Robert Terrell debated with himself as the charts on the screen changed to his touch of the keys. In almost eleven hours of search, he had been able to trace communications links from the Kremlin to various headquarters and divisional commands within the Red Banner Fleet. After the first few hours, he had abandoned his trace of voice circuits, focusing instead on telex message and data-transmission channels. With surface ships, he had discovered almost continuous contact between vessels and satellites, but the subsurface fleet had erratic communications with its command structure.

The cubicle door opened abruptly, breaking Terrell's concentration on the terminal screen. He looked up.

Ernst Frohlberg slipped inside and closed the door. It was a small room and the director's bulk instantly made it smaller.

"Robert, there may be a problem."

"Problem?"

"Robert, are you all right? You don't look well."

"Just tired, Ernst."

Frohlberg shook his head from side to side, again with that sad expression. "Do you know a Steven Hamm?"

"Hamm. Yes, I know Hamm. He's in the army."

"He was just in to see me."

"Is that right?" Terrell turned in the little swivel chair to face the director. He clasped his hands in his lap to stop them from shaking. "What did he want, Ernst?"

"Information about you, and about the institute. I am concerned, Robert. Do you have troubles of which I am unaware?"

"Did you tell him I was here?"

Frohlberg frowned. "I said nothing."

"Perhaps it would be better if I left, Ernst."

"If there is trouble, I might be able to help." Frohlberg's offer carried a trace of insincerity. His life was the institute, and he did not want to jeopardize it.

"No. It is best that I leave."

"Your Steven Hamm may be waiting."

"By the back way, if that is all right with you?"

"Come."

Terrell shut down the terminal and followed the director to the elevator. They took it to the first basement level, and Terrell stepped out.

"Follow the corridor to the end. The stairway will take you up to a door."

"Thank you, Ernst. I appreciate all that you've done."

"Please be careful, Robert. I want to see you again."

"Of course, and soon."

Terrell smiled, but his mind was on another matter: if not a submarine, perhaps a missile frigate. Two of them, well out to sea, would be enough to make the point.

He followed the hallway, which was unfinished—plain white drywall with tape over the joints between panels and open doorways. Stacks of books, supplies, and mechanical equipment could be seen through the portals. At the end of the hall, he climbed the steps to ground level and pushed open the steel door.

For some reason, he had expected a bright sun to assault his eyes, accustomed to the semi-dark of the terminal room. Instead, it appeared to be late afternoon. The cloud cover hung low, and it had started to drizzle. Terrell drew his coat tight and buttoned it, then stepped outside.

There was a loading dock to his right. On his left stood a man he had never seen before. He was a tall man with chopped, dark hair, a banglet hanging over his forehead.

"Mr. Terrell, I have been looking for you," he said quietly.

"Who are you?"

"I am your escort." The man grinned, waving his hand to the left. "Come. We must go this way."

"I'm not going anywhere with you." Terrell started forward, to make his way around the dock.

The man pulled open the left flap of his coat, then retrieved a blue automatic pistol. "I will insist. Or you may die here, in a Berlin alley. Is that what you desire?"

Russian. He was a Russian. KGB. *Oh, Jesus!* Terrell thought. *This can't happen!* He was not finished with what he had to do.

The agent looked up and down the alley, then motioned with the gun. "Now, Mr. Terrell."

He looked about frantically, searching for an escape route. All he saw was a very clean alley. Two men were smoking in back of a building to the south, but they threw their cigarette butts in long arcs toward the center of the lane, then disappeared through a door.

The Russian jabbed Terrell in the kidney with the gun barrel.

Terrell moved unwillingly in the indicated direction. His legs made the required motions, but his mind freewheeled. Under the layer of fright, he tried to sort out his options. Surely, at any moment, there would come a chance for him to run. The man would drop the gun. He would trip over something. He would look away.

He stumbled twice on broken asphalt crossing the alley. Ice chilled his spine.

The man stabbed him in the back twice with the muzzle of the gun. The small jolts felt like lightning strikes. He wanted to scream. He wondered what it felt like to die.

He was walking in syrup, the end of the alley miles away.

"Here. Turn here."

The man jabbed him again hard, and the pain shot up into his shoulder. Terrell turned into an open stairway. He looked around. It was a garage. Concrete steps and concrete pilasters. Flashes of colored metal. The world in his vision was picking up speed, while his feet could not keep up with it. He tripped on the first step and fell down, banging his knee on the sharp edge of cement.

The gun barrel hit him again, a sharp blow in the kidney. He needed to urinate. "Up the stairs! No noise."

Almost on hands and knees, Terrell negotiated the steps, becoming bewildered when he had to make a turn at the landing.

He was going to die. All along, he had known the Soviets were looking for him. It had never crossed his mind that they would actually find him.

The bare concrete of the garage made him think of prisons. They would put him in a prison. He would die in a prison.

Interrogation. They would shoot him full of drugs.

The man shoved him up against a black car. "Stand there."

Terrell felt a sting in the back of his right arm. They would interrogate him, hurt him.

And get nothing. His mind was full of concepts, but not details. Suddenly, through the blanket of fear, triumph arose.

He felt dizzy, a blackness trying to swarm over him, as he spun around to face the KGB agent, falling back against the car. He grabbed at a door handle to keep from falling down. "I don't have it, you know."

The man was putting a syringe into a leather case, the case held awkwardly in his gun hand. His eyes narrowed. "You do not have what?"

"The tape. You don't have anything without the—" Terrell collapsed to the cement floor.

Steve Hamm had posted himself at the end of the service alley, next to the entrance to a parking garage, where he could watch the rear wall of the institute. It was only a short run to the corner of the block to check the front entrance if he needed to do so.

When Naratsmov appeared, supporting Terrell, Hamm backed around the corner. It was the first time he had seen the agent in the flesh, but he did not doubt his identification.

Hamm turned and ran up the ramp into the garage. He waited behind an Audi on the second level, crouched below the roofline. Pulling the heavy .45 from his belt, he flipped off the safety and rammed the slide back, cocking it.

Hamm bent lower and went around the Audi, then around the silver nose of a Honda. One blue Renault was between them.

As Naratsmov opened the rear door of the Mercedes, Hamm rose and laid his arms across the top of the car, resting his gun in his left hand. "These slugs are hollow-point. Your head will explode like a melon."

Naratsmov froze in place.

"Turn around, Alexi, old buddy. Do it slowly."

The Russian did as he was ordered. His left hand, out of sight below the car's top, still held his weapon. His eyes went directly to Hamm's, passing over the sights of the Colt. The muzzle was very close, but there was no sign of fear on his face or in his eyes.

"Lose the gun."

His arm moved, as if to toss the weapon, and he dropped straight down.

Out of Hamm's view. Hamm clambered onto the Renault's top, slithering across to the other side.

As he peered over the side, Naratsmov fired. The slug slammed the car's drip rail and ricocheted into the concrete roof overhead, splintering into a hundred pieces. The sound of the shot echoed on metal and cement.

Naratsmov moved under the Mercedes.

Hamm got his foot under him, then leaped to the roof of the Mercedes and went flat. He called out, "I like your dedication, Naratsmov."

The Russian did not answer. Hamm heard the rustle of fabric on concrete.

"I'm not going to wait you out, Alexi. I'm going to put a few rounds in the gas tank and see if we can't get a bonfire started."

"Your friend will perish."

The son-of-a-bitch could talk. "Part of the job. You know that."

Naratsmov tossed the automatic.

Hamm heard it clatter on the concrete, sliding out from under the trunk.

"Okay. You next."

The man slid out from under the car on the passenger's side. Hamm trained the Colt on him, sat up, and slid down onto the trunk. He pushed himself off the car and picked up the automatic, never letting the muzzle waver from Naratsmov's head. "What did you give him?"

Naratsmov's eyes flicked away from Hamm's eyes to the Colt. Hamm tightened his trigger finger until the knuckle was white.

"Do not become nervous, Colonel Hamm. It was merely a tranquilizer."

"I have several options available, Alexi. Killing you is maybe third on the list. First would be depriving you of knees. Do I make myself clear?"

"Very clear."

"Open the front door carefully. You're going to be driving."

He sat up, then stood up. With his left hand, Naratsmov opened the car door.

"Get in."

The Russian slid in sideways, then sat down on the seat and drew his legs in.

Hamm looked in on Terrell. Naratsmov had laid him out across the backseat, his left arm dangling to the floor.

Shutting the back door, Hamm motioned with the automatic, and Naratsmov slid across the seat, behind the wheel. Hamm got in and shut the door. He noted that the key was already in the ignition.

"Shed the tie."

Naratsmov loosened the knot, then pulled off his tie. Hamm used it to bind the assassin's wrists together. The KGB agent flexed his wrists, testing the strength of the fabric.

"Start the car, and get it out of here."

Awkwardly reaching around the steering wheel, Naratsmov started the engine, then shifted to reverse. He backed it out of the stall, shifted to drive, and drove slowly down the ramp. "He doesn't have the tape with him, Colonel. Perhaps we should try his room.''

Hamm kept the .45 in his right hand, as far away as possible from a quick move by Naratsmov. How much did the Soviets know about the computer tape? he wondered. Or maybe the Russian was fishing? ''Just drive. You've probably been through his room already.''

The Mercedes nosed out into the street and the drizzle immediately coated the windshield. Naratsmov found the wiper switch and turned it on. ''The tape was not at the boardinghouse, no. But there must be another room.''

If it had been at Frau Koln's, Coriolanus would have found it. But Naratsmov could be right; there might be another room, somewhere, Hamm reminded himself. ''How long is he going to be out?''

''Forty-five minutes. Perhaps an hour.''

''Find a place to park.''

And Hamm's first priority, according to the President of the United States, was GABRIEL. He had to wait until Terrell came around and try to get the information out of him.

Naratsmov did not drive far. He parked on a side street off Paulstrasse, shut off the engine, and rested his bound hands on the top of the steering wheel. To the south, the woods of the Tiergarten were wrapped in the foggy rain. Two blocks away, Hamm could see a bridge that spanned the Spree River.

Dark cars sped by, spraying water to either side.

Naratsmov was studying Hamm, his stare bold and calculating.

''Forget it, Alexi. I've expanded my alternatives. One that's particularly attractive is turning you over to Coriolanus. You can be his guest for four or five years, and even if you never say a word, when he turns you loose, what are your masters going to think?''

The Russian's face remained impassive, but his mind had to be working.

''You think your usefulness will be at an end? What do they do with Department Twelve snitches, Alexi? I mean, what do they do after you've been on the table for a few hours, spilling blood and various pieces of your anatomy?''

Still, Naratsmov did not react. His hands, resting on the wheel, were steady.

''Or, here's another thought, Alexi. You go get in the trunk and wait quietly, until you're pretty sure I'm a long ways away.''

The Russian revolved his shoulders, as if they were fatigued. ''You would just leave me there? In the baggage compartment?''

''You have to promise to count to two thousand, once you feel the car stop moving.''

Naratsmov studied him for a moment. ''We are of the same mold, Colonel Hamm.''

''Not quite, I hope. Anyway, it's your choice.''

''I let you walk away, and you let me walk away.''

''That's the deal.''

Naratsmov reached both hands for the door handle.

Hamm kept the Colt trained on him, hidden by his own body, as he slid out after the agent. Two cars swished by on the wet street.

The trunk of the Mercedes was unlocked. It locked when a key was used to lock the doors. Hamm lifted the lid, waited until there was a lull in the traffic, then said, "Okay, Alexi. It's been nice meeting you."

Naratsmov sat on the lip of the compartment, then lowered himself inside. Hamm slammed the lid down, then went back to get behind the wheel, and started the engine.

His routes out of Berlin were limited. A high-speed run on the autobahn to Brunswick was a possibility, but one fraught with checkpoints. And the Lear, sitting in Bern, was effectively grounded by watchful eyes. Hamm went through the list in his head, considering just whom he might want to involve.

After an hour's drive around Berlin, with frequent checks in the rearview mirror, which he tilted toward Terrell's inert form, he began to see movement. Hamm did not know what drug Naratsmov had used. What he wanted was for Terrell to be mildly mobile, but groggy.

Another ten minutes passed before Terrell groaned, then vomited on the floor. He retched dryly several times, then tried to sit up. He almost made it.

Hamm drove along Huttenstrasse until he spotted the man he was looking for: on the down-and-out, dressed in worn clothes, walking in the light rain looking for the fortune that would buy him a stein of lager. He pulled to the curb, left the car running while he got out and approached the derelict. They were out of earshot of the car. Naratsmov would not hear. "Can you drive?" he asked in his rusty German.

"Drive, *mein herr*? I am among the best of drivers."

"Good. My friend is sick, and the car must be

delivered to the Mercedes dealer on Kurfurstendamm. I will give you two hundred marks to take it there, park it, and lock the doors. Leave the key under the floor mat."

"Two hundred marks?" Beneath the stubble that covered his face, a rosy glow surfaced. "Certainly, *mein herr*!"

Hamm led him back to the car, got him settled behind the wheel, and eased a sick and spittle-mouthed Terrell from the backseat. Terrell squinted weakly through his thick lenses. "Steve?"

"It's me, buddy." He slipped an arm around Terrell's waist, pulled one of the man's arms around his neck, and half lifted him onto the curb.

The Mercedes pulled away very tentatively, as one of the "best" drivers tried to figure out the controls.

With Terrell lurching along by his side, Hamm walked a block through the rain, until he found a neighborhood *haufbrau*. Inside, there were three customers sitting at a planked table, and a buxom blonde of fifty years encased in an oversized, tight peasant blouse. Hamm made his way to the back of the room, where he could shove one of the backless benches against the cedar-planked wall. He lowered Terrell onto the bench. Hamm pulled him forward to rest his head on his arms on the table.

"God, I feel awful, Steve. I think I'm going to get sick."

The blonde came over, her face creased in concern, and six or seven inches of cleavage showed between her tightly bound breasts. She spoke in German. "Is he sick?"

"Not feeling well," Hamm agreed. "Could we have two coffees, black, and some aspirin?"

“I don’t want him to die here,” she threatened.

“He will not die.”

Not until Hamm knew where GABRIEL was, at least.

TWENTY-FOUR

It was nearly three o'clock, Berlin time, before Coriolanus had the information he'd requested from Washington about Terrell's time in Berlin. Pelagio and Terrell had done their research at the Institute for Soviet Studies.

It was nearly four o'clock by the time he and Decker returned to their hotel, frustrated by a stubborn German named Frohlberg. He knew Terrell, but would not say when he had last seen him. No, he was not free to discuss Terrell's research, even if he knew what it was. Frohlberg felt that the CIA, if it was not now privy to the data, was not to receive it from Herr Dokter Ernst Frohlberg.

The only thing Coriolanus did learn pissed him off. Hamm had shown up at the institute six hours earlier. The son-of-a-bitch was always a few hours ahead of him.

With Coriolanus's luck, Dokter Frohlberg had probably told Hamm everything he had in his little mind.

Terrell drank lots of water and cup after cup of coffee. The drug had dehydrated him. He recovered slowly from its effects, but by eleven o'clock he was able to keep down sausage and eggs. The overbuilt waitress was as relieved as Hamm was. Terrell was able to walk to the men's room without assistance, though Hamm stuck close to him. He was not going to let him out of his sight from now on.

Terrell seemed lucid part of the time. He did not want to talk about South Africa, Germany, or the KGB agent who had picked him up. For the most part, he stared at the initials carved into the plank top of the table and drank from the coffee mug in front of him. At odd moments, he would get nervous. He fidgeted; his hand shook; he got that faraway look in his eyes.

He made Hamm nervous.

"Bob, I need to know where the tape is."

"Tape?" Terrell's eyes hooded over, and he appeared to shrink back against the wall.

"You know what I'm talking about. It's important."

"No tape. There's no tape here."

Shit! The longer he waited, the worse the odds became. Hamm had hoped to arrange a flight out of Berlin on a British plane, but he could not leave Terrell at risk for much longer.

At eleven-thirty, when Palidin had not yet

checked back, and when Terrell still refused to talk about the tape, Hamm called the Berlin Brigade.

The United States had three infantry units and an armored unit headquartered in Berlin. Hamm thought he would be in better shape if he stuck with the military, if the commander was someone he had not antagonized somewhere along the line. He certainly was not going to walk into the Berlin CIA chief of station's office with Terrell. His job was to find GABRIEL, and he was not going to let Coriolanus bungle it. Hamm could administer the drugs to Terrell as well as anyone, but the priority now was to get Bob Terrell into secure surroundings. Then he could put him under and start asking the right questions.

Finally, he was patched through to a Colonel James Calumet, who was adjutant to the brigade commander. Calumet sounded leery on the phone. "What can I do for you, Colonel Hamm?"

"I'm operating under Special Order Number two-zero-nine-six-five-one, the Pentagon, Colonel. Would you like me to hold while you check on that?"

"Might be a good idea," the adjutant said. "I'll get right back to you. . . ."

It took him almost fifteen minutes to verify the order, but when he came back, he was very cooperative. "I've got the gist of it, Hamm. What do you need?"

Hamm told him, then gave him the address of the *haufbrau*.

Forty minutes after Hamm hung up, he and Terrell were walking in the rain along Spandauer Damm when a gray van slowed, then pulled to the curb. The driver leaned across and rolled down the passenger's window and called to Hamm, "Charlottenburg this way?"

It was to the south. Hamm called back, "No. East."

The side door popped open and slid back, and Hamm bustled Terrell into the back of the van. Besides the driver, there was a short, fair-haired kid in his early twenties. He slammed the door shut, then sat on top of several mail sacks stacked at the rear doors and grinned foolishly at them. The driver and his assistant were clad in air-force enlisted uniforms.

Terrell eyed them cautiously. "What are you doing, Steve?"

"Leaving Berlin."

"I've got to pick up my suitcase."

The van took off. Hamm watched his friend closely. "How important is your suitcase?"

"Well, it's got some things I picked up in . . . in South Africa. Mementos, really. And . . . and my passport."

And a computer tape? "But you've got another passport, don't you, Bob?"

Terrell patted his chest, then pulled out a blue American passport. "Not in my name."

"That's okay," Hamm said. "Neither is mine. We'll have your luggage picked up later."

Terrell lapsed into silence, then a few minutes later asked, "Where are we going?"

"How's home sound to you?"

"That's good. That's on the way."

Hamm was glad to hear that, and wondered where it would lead him. He did not press for more, but watched the streets slide by through the windshield. The right-side windshield wiper left smudgy streaks.

The airfield was a military one, near Tempelhof. It was small and would not handle the larger jet aircraft; it was old and patched; black asphalt repairs were spotted along the length of the runways. The courier van was passed through the gate without an inspection of the interior.

The van was passed through a chain-link fence directly onto the parking apron, and it pulled up alongside a C-130 Hercules decorated in U.S. Air Force markings. Hamm and Terrell got out and stood under the wing, out of the rain, while the kid tossed the mailbags to a crew chief standing in the fuselage doorway.

An army sedan drove through the gate in the chain link, parked next to the van, and three men got out. Two of them carried small valises. The tallest of the three, wearing an overseas cap and a raincoat with silver eagles on the shoulder epaulets, approached them. "Colonel Hamm?"

"That's me."

"I'm Jim Calumet."

They shook hands, and Hamm said, "I appreciate your help, Colonel."

"Not first class, I'm afraid. It's the milk run into Fort Devon, Massachusetts, but it gets you headed in the right direction. There will be stops in London, Reykjavík, and Halifax." Calumet took a quick look at Terrell, but said nothing.

Terrell's head was on the move, watching the activity along the tarmac with some trepidation. He obviously did not like having the three new men so close to him. He took a step closer to Hamm.

Calumet introduced the two men with him.

"Meet Staff Sergeant Doyle Quigley and Sergeant Ken Meter. They're from our military police department and will accompany you."

"I don't know that that's necessary," Hamm said. He did not like last-minute additions to his plans.

The adjutant showed him a pained expression. "A recommendation of the chairman of the Joint Chiefs."

"One of those recommendations, huh?" It was probably Storch's idea.

Calumet shrugged. "I'm always happy to go along with the Pentagon."

"Me, too."

It was apparent that Storch, or someone, had provided Calumet with a capsule biography of Hamm. He merely let his eyes go wide in wonder.

Standing beside him, Terrell looked over the M.P.'s and asked, "Am I under arrest?"

Hamm beat anyone else to an explanation. "It's a matter of protection, Bob. We don't want any more KGB stunts."

"You had one of those?" Calumet asked.

"A bit of a skirmish. It's taken care of."

"Well, then, Colonel, have a good flight."

Hamm looked up at the C-130's wing. It was streaked with oil. "Yeah, we'll do that."

Calumet got back in his car, and it backed away, then sped off into the rain.

A few minutes later, the crew chief looked at Hamm, then stabbed a thumb toward the inside of the plane. Terrell and Hamm climbed the short metal ladder and found themselves inside the stripped fuselage. The two M.P.'s clambered in behind them, toting their AWOL bags. There were no creature comforts. Bare aluminum skin showed between the fuselage ribs and wiring conduit ran along the overhead. Crates and boxes were lashed to the steel-mesh floor. Along the right side, canvas sling seats supported on aluminum tubing had been lowered, and the two of them strapped in with wide web belting. The M.P.'s lowered a similar seat on the left side and dug around for seat belts.

There were no windows, either, and the heating was minimal. Military air transport was not new to Hamm, but Terrell looked anxious.

"Keep in mind, Bob," Hamm said, "that the taxpayers think we're living it up."

Terrell gave him a grim smile. "They don't see the airplanes you fly. What was that one we used in the Africa days?"

"A King Air."

"Yeah. Those were pretty good days, weren't they, Steve?"

"The old days always are," Hamm told him.

The crew chief pulled the door in and dogged it in place. He plugged his headset into a jack, spoke to the pilot, then dropped into a seat next to the M.P.'s.

The engines sputtered to life, port first, then starboard. With no insulation wrapping the fuselage, the din was on the lower side of bearable. Twenty minutes later, the nose rotated, and the aircraft rose into the sky.

Hamm was relieved to be out of Berlin, relieved to have Terrell at his side, and uncertain just how he was going to pry GABRIEL out of Terrell's hands. He hated using the drugs developed in CIA and DIA laboratories, but suspected that that was going to be the only way. Bob Terrell could be damned stubborn.

For his part, Robert Terrell stared at the left fuselage wall as if it had portholes. Through his thick lenses, he was looking a long way away, seeing something that Hamm could not fathom.

TWENTY-FIVE

Alexi Naratsmov had recovered the knife sheathed against his inner left wrist within a minute of entering the Mercedes's trunk. A minute after that, his hands were free of the knotted tie and were exploring the mechanical intricacies of the trunk lid's lock mechanism. He had to work by touch in the blackness.

He believed along with Houdini that locks were meant to keep people out, not in. After a few more minutes, he found the outlines of the electric solenoid, explored it, and knew where to press in order to release himself.

Then it was a matter of waiting until the car stopped and Hamm and Terrell exited. He would not, of course, wait as long as Hamm intended for him to wait, just long enough to ensure his safety.

It was a long wait. The car drove about with seeming aimlessness. It stopped many times, but the engine continued to run. Once, two doors slammed. Perhaps Terrell had moved to the front seat. Naratsmov worried a little about the air in the confined space, and he hoped there were no exhaust leaks. Carbon monoxide was odorless.

The Mercedes bounced through a dip, drew to a halt, and the engine was turned off. He did not count to two thousand, but to fifteen, then pressed the solenoid plunger of the electric lock.

The lid popped up several millimeters.

There was no alarm, no deafening roar of Hamm's army automatic.

He pushed the lid up a bit more and raised his head to peer out of the crack.

The car was parked in a lot full of other cars, most of them Mercedeses. Several people wandered about in raincoats, carrying umbrellas, looking at the cars. An old man in shabby clothes hurried along the sidewalk.

Pushing the lid to its limit, Naratsmov quickly rolled out of his prison, slammed the lid down, checked to find the doors locked and the key missing, and walked away. A couple examining a BMW ten meters away stared at him with open mouths.

He did not bother searching the area for Hamm and Terrell. As soon as he had freed himself it became apparent to him what Hamm's tactic was. The DIA agent and the quarry would be on their way out of Berlin by now.

It took him twenty minutes to flag a taxi. "Where to, *mein herr*?"

"Drive around."

"Drive around?"

"Do it."

The taxi continued east, the Brandenburg Gate drawing closer, while Naratsmov warmed himself in the backseat and considered his moves. He needed to know where Hamm was going. Would he take Terrell back to the United States before the intense interrogation was initiated? Terrell had appeared run-down, perhaps physically ill. They would feed him, build him up for the ordeal.

He must choose a course of action, and he opted for a return to America.

By mid-afternoon, Jack Coriolanus was extremely frustrated. He did not like being frustrated.

He had Decker out with the field men, covering the exits to the city. He had alerts out all over Europe, couched in terms that would keep the manhunt out of the public eye. The director would fry him if Terrell, and his knowledge, became center ring for the media or for a court system.

He and the Berlin chief of station, Bert Cummings, sat in an office next to the Communication Center, close to radio and telex traffic.

"You think the fucking generals at Brigade or Military Liaison are screwing us?"

The overhead fluorescent lighting tinted Cummings's face with a greenish hue. "We, and they, tend to be protective of our sources and our information, but I doubt they'd hide something like this."

"I think they would put a big blanket over Hamm. He's one of them."

"Not likely, Jack."

"Shit! This isn't that big a town. How can we lose three people?" The dragnet had pictures of Terrell, Hamm, and Naratsmov.

"I hate to mention it, but the east side of the wall is a hop and a skip for Naratsmov. He could already be over there, with his shoes off and his feet up, and a bottle of warm vodka on the table."

"Yeah, you told me. And Terrell's in the next room with his feet up, too, and his balls spiked to the table. Spare me the word pictures, Cummings. Naratsmov hasn't got him yet."

"You're pretty damned certain of yourself, aren't you, Jack?"

"If Terrell was on the east side of the wall, Hamm would have surfaced."

"Or gone over himself, to try and get him back—or kill him."

The communications officer stuck his head in the room. "Call for you, Mr. Coriolanus."

The special assistant hopped out of his chair and followed the man into the communications room. He was pointed in the direction of a cubicle containing a secure phone, and he went in, shut the door, and sat in the small chair. The phone rang and he picked it up. "Coriolanus."

"Winfield Storch."

"What do you want, Winnie?"

"Hamm's coming in. He's got Terrell."

"When?"

"I don't know when they'll get here. They flew out of Tempelhof early this afternoon."

"Has he got the package?"

"That is unknown."

Coriolanus did not bother with niceties. He hung

up and stepped out of the booth. When the communications officer looked up, he said, "Track Decker down and tell him to meet me at Tegel. Then call Paris and get us two seats on the Concorde."

QUÉBEC

TWENTY-SIX

It was eight-thirty in the evening in Halifax, Nova Scotia.

When the wheels touched concrete with a screech of burning rubber, Hamm sat up. For most of the trip, he had stretched out on the canvas sling seat, his suit coat tossed on a stack of crates, and slept. Bob Terrell had slept, too, a man exhausted by his journey. During the stop in Reykjavík, they had deplaned for half an hour to eat, with the M.P. sergeants, Quigley and Meter, close at hand. The sun had been bright and warm in Iceland.

Several times, Hamm had probed Terrell gently, trying to find a flap he could open, to get at the hidden recesses. But Bob Terrell was not talking, unless it was about the "good days in Africa."

When he was awake, Terrell had frequently lapsed into long silences when his facial muscles would slacken, like a man in a coma, and his eyes appeared to cloud over.

Hamm did not know how to deal with his friend. He was afraid of pushing him over some mental abyss, into a place where he would never get the information he needed about GABRIEL's hiding place. And yet, he was also pressed by time.

The pilot parked his C-130 in line with two sister ships in an area leased by the American military for the maintenance and refueling of aircraft. The co-pilot stuck his head through the companionway high over the cargo deck and called down to them, "You have about an hour, gentlemen. We'll be off again at nine-thirty."

Hamm rubbed his stubbly cheeks, unhooked his belt, and stood up. "You want something to eat, Bob?"

Terrell yawned widely and rose from his uncomfortable bed. His response was listless. "I'm not hungry."

"Coffee, then?"

"Sure."

Hamm and Terrell found their suit jackets and pulled them on. Hamm skipped his tie, but Terrell took time to button his collar and tighten his tie in place. Then they descended from the aircraft. Meter and Quigley trailed behind as they crossed the tarmac to the cafeteria. The tang of salt air, mixed with kerosene and oil, helped revive Hamm.

Inside the cafeteria, after Hamm surveyed the few customers, they went through the short line for two coffees and a couple of doughnuts for Hamm.

They sat at a small table by the window, and the two M.P.'s sat down at a table fifteen feet away.

Hamm bit a chunk out of a doughnut while Terrell used his spoon to toy with the small crevices in the chipped Formica top of the table. When he looked up at Hamm, his eyes through the slab-like lenses were as focused and as intense as Hamm remembered from earlier days. "I didn't do it for myself, Steve."

"Never thought you did," he replied cautiously.

"Appreciate your help, though."

"You know me, buddy. Anytime."

"I couldn't believe what they had done to my friends at Brandvlei. It was—"

"It was bad."

"Worse than bad, and you know what? It was only a ten-kiloton warhead. Tiny. Minuscule. A damned firecracker compared to what we have in our inventories." Terrell swigged from his coffee mug.

Hamm sipped his own coffee. If Terrell was going to become talkative, he did not want to disrupt the process.

"Some goddamned corporal who didn't know what he was doing blew away a little chunk of humanity," Terrell said.

"It might have been electromagnetic interference, from what I heard."

"Whatever. It doesn't matter how it happened. It happened, and no one cares."

"Some do," Hamm said. "I do."

"Yeah. You were there. Imagine that, Steve. Imagine Brandvlei a hundred times over. Hell, a thousand times over. Lifeless sand extending to the horizons."

"I don't like the picture."

Terrell nodded and tilted his mug.

He was quiet for a while. Hamm watched the planes taxiing on the apron, not wanting to break the spell, afraid he might crack a fragile shell that encased Terrell.

"One man can do that with GABRIEL."

"Can he?"

Terrell turned his head to look out the window. After a moment, he turned back. "I'm not stupid, Steve. You're here with me because of GABRIEL, and you know all about it."

"I know very little about it, Bob."

"We never talked about our jobs, did we?"

"No."

"What's your job now? It's not with the inspector general anymore, is it?"

"Temporary duty."

"To find GABRIEL."

"Some people are concerned, Bob. You can understand that."

"Yes. I'm concerned. I like my world as it is."

Hamm smiled. "No, you don't. You always wanted it better than it is."

Terrell snorted a laugh. "True. Maybe there's a chance, now."

"With GABRIEL?"

"With GABRIEL," Terrell agreed.

Hamm pushed the rest of his doughnut dinner aside. He was no longer hungry.

"GABRIEL is a nuclear weapons system," Terrell blurted suddenly.

"I know that much, Bob."

"It started out better."

"Yes. As an intelligence-gathering tool."

"But Larry wanted more. He had friends in the Pentagon, big chiefs with hot trigger fingers."

"I didn't know that."

"See the owl?" Terrell was pointing off to the right.

Hamm saw the big spread of wings just as it glided to a landing on the peak of a hangar. "Wise bird."

"Popular misconception. Same misconception as their ability to see at night. They're stupid birds."

Come on back, my friend, Hamm's mind urged.

"A new source of intelligence wasn't good enough. Larry wanted a maximum-killing machine."

"And he got it?"

"Oh, yes, he got it. It killed him, too."

"Heart attack, the doctors said."

Terrell shrugged. "He had the attack while I was there in the lab. We were arguing. I wanted to bury GABRIEL, confuse the programming, do anything to make it useless. Larry didn't, of course. Jesus! Steve, he died right in front of me! His face was blue. He was gagging. He was begging me, Steve!"

"Nothing you could do," Hamm consoled.

"There was a lot I could do. Call a doctor, for one. I didn't. I watched him die. Goddamn. I killed him."

"I think that's debatable."

"Not in my case. I let him die because I could then destroy the tapes."

"And you did that?"

"Except for the one I've got."

"Well secured, I hope."

Terrell grinned at him, his eyes bright under the lenses. "Damned right."

Hamm thought he might tighten the faucet, so he said, "I could never figure out why we'd want to launch Soviet birds."

Terrell's head jerked back to him. "Launch? You mean launch missiles?"

"Well, yeah."

Shaking his head negatively, Terrell said, "GABRIEL can't launch missiles."

"Somebody gave me the wrong data, I guess."

"Too many sub-systems involved. Fuel, telemetrics, inertial navigation, on-board computers, weather corrections."

"Now I'm lost, Bob."

"GABRIEL sets off the warheads right in the silo."

Hamm was silent. Diane was right.

"Sure. It's like we've already delivered fourteen hundred missiles into Soviet territory. Gives us an immediate increase in the balance of nuclear warheads of four hundred units. Hell, it gives us twenty-four hundred ICBMs, Steve, with most of them already on target. They're our warheads with GABRIEL. No flight time involved, and no warning to the Soviets. There is no such thing as a Soviet first strike. They push the button, and we detonate them right there. Shit! Steve, the U.S. doesn't even need a nuclear strike force. We've got them all covered—China, France, Pakistan."

"Jesus Christ, Bob! That's a hell of a poker hand to hold. We could just let the first secretary know about this, and order him to dismantle Soviet armies and navies?"

"Admiral Dilman liked that aspect."

"He would," Hamm said. What Dilman did not like was the ability of GABRIEL to do the same for U.S. warheads, if the Kremlin held the software.

"You didn't know that part?" Terrell asked.

"No," Hamm lied.

"That's why I've got GABRIEL, and no one else has it."

"You can't handle that all by yourself."

"I won't let Dilman and his people have it," Terrell said, and his eyes slipped their focus once again. He turned to look through the window, but Hamm did not think he was interested in airplanes.

"Bob . . . ?"

There was no response.

Hamm checked his watch. Half an hour to takeoff. He looked over to where the M.P.'s had taken a table. He signaled Quigley, and the staff sergeant rose and came to the table. Hamm stood up. "You want to sit here a minute? I'm going to the head."

"Yes, sir." Quigley took Hamm's chair, and Hamm walked across the room and down a short corridor, following the signs.

His mind was struggling with the overload of new data. GABRIEL upset balances that had been more or less in place since the aftermath of World War II.

And Bob Terrell thought he could control it. Jesus! If Naratsmov had known what he was so close to, he would have taken greater chances to get it.

Worse, GABRIEL was still on the loose. Hamm started thinking about a telephone. He would have to make arrangements to get from Fort Devon to Washington. He needed to have Kuster find him a safe house where he could work with Terrell. He needed a doctor on hand, with the latest series of drugs. He needed . . .

Hamm pushed open the door to the men's room, saw Meter stepping away from the urinal, zipping up his uniform trousers. Meter said, "Hello, sir."

"Hello, Sergeant."

Hamm stepped up to the urinal and flipped back the skirts of his suit jacket. The right side was heavy with the Colt automatic in the pocket.

The left side was surprisingly light.

Hamm hesitated, patted the left pocket.

The Stechkin he had taken off Naratsmov was gone.

Spinning, Hamm pulled open the door and ran down the hallway. Sergeant Meter ran after him.

When he reached the dining room, he was already too late.

The table at the window was vacant, and Doyle Quigley and Bob Terrell were nowhere in sight.

TWENTY-SEVEN

The morning fog had burned off, leaving damp spots on the pavement that were quickly drying in the new sun. Stream rose from the sidewalks and the cast-iron manhole covers in the street. It promised to be a better day than London had seen in several weeks.

Alexi Naratsmov did not care. He stared from the window in his third-floor guest room of the embassy, but he stared at nothing in particular. The window sash was raised a few centimeters and he could hear the cooing of pigeons clinging to the gutter on the roof above.

Dmitri Talensk, the KGB political officer attached to the embassy, stood beside him at the window. Naratsmov detested Talensk, as he detested all political officers. Talensk told him, "They tell me that the American CIA is out in force. There are at least six watchers surrounding the embassy."

Naratsmov knew they were watching for him. They had been present from the time he had arrived at Heathrow. He was not bothered by it. He was in residence here only until his flight to Washington was ready to depart.

He turned from the window to glare at the political officer. "Are you going to get to the point, Comrade Major Talensk?"

The political specialist shrugged. "I have spoken to General Petropol."

Petropol was the chief political officer assigned to the First Chief Directorate, supposedly subordinate to Andresev, but representing the interests of the Communist Party. It was he who determined whether ideology was served by the activities of the FCD. Often, it was he who determined what the ideology of the moment was. Within limits, of course.

Talensk wanted to keep the suspense going. "And he has spoken to Colonel General Andresev."

This little game did not interest Naratsmov. He took an abrupt step toward Talensk and let the malevolence of his eyes shine. "Do I have to twist your balls to retrieve your message?"

Startled, Talensk backed quickly away. "The generals have agreed that the matter of Blue Heron has dragged on for much too long. You have let the Americans recapture the strategist."

"You are to take over, then?" Alexi asked, and took one more step toward the man.

Alarmed, the political officer reached back for the doorknob. "Oh, no! No, what they have decided is that you will be allowed the last chance you requested." He smiled. "You have forty-eight hours, and . . ."

"And?"

"And I am to accompany you."

"Very well. You know it will be dangerous."

"Danger does not bother me, Comrade Colonel. And what danger could exist in Nova Scotia, anyway?"

"Nova Scotia? What are you babbling about?"

Talensk enjoyed the power of information. He dribbled it out, slowly. "You did not know, Comrade Colonel? The strategist seems to have slipped away from his captors. The Americans are in a frenzy, according to the cable."

Now, there was yet another reason for Alexi to hate political officers. "When did this take place?"

"About nine o'clock, in Nova Scotia."

"I will change my flight plans."

"Already accomplished," the efficient man told him. "We leave in two hours."

Terrell was free again. The odor of reprieve was in the air. Once more, Naratsmov had time on his side.

"These matters, when they culminate, are always dangerous, Comrade Major," Alexi said gravely. "Judging by your lack of experience, I suppose you will die."

Dmitri Talensk paled visibly, then turned and exited.

Alexi Naratsmov turned back to the window to stare at the embassy grounds three stories below, idly watching a man mowing the lawn while riding on an American-built John Deere tractor.

When he arrived in Washington on Saturday, Jack Coriolanus had gone directly to his office. He spent much of the day catching up on the massive accumulation of paperwork sitting on his secretary's desk.

He waited for Hamm to show up with Terrell. There was no force on God's green earth that would keep him from taking part in Terrell's debriefing.

He met with the DDO for two hours. One of the minor topics they had talked about was Roy Decker's reassignment.

After a quick meeting with the director, at which the two of them brought him up to date, and the director promised to put the heat on the director of DIA to force a joint debriefing, Coriolanus checked his decoded communications. Naratsmov had been seen at Heathrow Airport, outside London. Currently, he was holed up in the Soviet embassy.

He hit the button on his intercom. "Get a cable off to London. I want somebody—everybody, if necessary—on Naratsmov. If he moves, I want to know about it A.S.A.P."

All Coriolanus needed was for Naratsmov to reach Terrell before the debriefing. One bullet could eradicate thousands of man-hours of work. "Where's Decker?"

His secretary said, "Down at Administration. He said he had to arrange shipment of his personal items from Cape Town."

"Fuck that. Get him up here."

As soon as Decker appeared, Coriolanus said,

"We're going to Arlington Hall," and led him to the elevator.

"What about?" Decker asked.

"I'm not letting Hamm debrief Terrell alone."

"You sure somebody's going to be there, this time of night?"

"If they aren't, the duty officer can call them in."

They were on the main floor, headed for the parking lot, when Coriolanus was paged. He went to a phone hanging on the wall and picked up. "Coriolanus."

"Just a moment, sir."

A couple of clicks transferred him to Communications. "Mr. Coriolanus, we have word from Halifax that Yardstick has just escaped custody."

"When?"

"That's all I have right now, sir."

Coriolanus slapped the phone back on its hook.

"Something wrong?" Decker asked.

"That fucking Hamm is trying to pull a fast one on us. Come on, we'll put a stop to this shit. You drive."

The summer heat had arrived early in Washington this year. It felt like August, with humidity stretching to match the temperature, which was seventy-six degrees at nine o'clock at night. Coriolanus's armpits were soaked, and a patch of moisture glued his shirt to his spine, in the few minutes' walk from where they had parked the car to the entrance to the DIA's headquarters.

DeMott's office was frigid. The building engineers had not yet found the air-conditioning balance they were looking for. Coriolanus strode right past the secretary, Decker in his wake, and pushed open the door to her office. It was crammed with cardboard boxes almost reaching the ceiling on one wall.

DeMott looked up from a file she was reading, then closed the file. "Well, Mr. Coriolanus."

She was wearing a white dress that set off the tan of her face. She was also wearing an amber sweater against the chill; her breasts kept it nicely taut.

He did not bother introducing Decker. "You're working late."

"Some of us do."

"Where's Hamm?"

"I was going to ask you that." She smiled at him, and her teeth also contrasted nicely with the tan. Underneath it all, though, he detected an agitation she was trying to hide.

He tried to warm to her. "I'm worried about him, Diane."

"Come on, now, Jack. Don't patronize me."

"He and Terrell disappeared on us again. I'm afraid Naratsmov may have gotten to them."

"You know as well as I do that Naratsmov is in London."

"Something happened to them. He hasn't called in?"

"Your stooges would have reported that, wouldn't they?"

Coriolanus was not going to discuss his sources in the building. He changed topics. "You got a briefing on GABRIEL from Foster. What did you think?"

"I think you'd better talk to someone else about it," she said.

"Diane, baby, we're on the same side here."

"That's true. And the side has several levels."

"And I know them all."

One corner of her mouth rose in skepticism. "Can I go back to work?"

He backed out of the office, forcing Decker out behind him. "Let me know if Hamm calls you."

"You'll know the minute the phone rings, I'm sure."

"When he calls, you tell him to get his ass back to Washington. With Terrell. If he gets cute, he's going to regret it."

"I'm sure he'll appreciate your concern, Jack."

He turned, passed through the outer office, and backed into the corridor. He nearly banged into a pile of boxes leaning against the wall.

Decker hurried to keep up with him. "Nice-looking woman."

"She's a bitch."

"Oh." Decker mulled that over a moment, then asked, "Where to, now?"

"Now, we go lean on Storch."

TWENTY-EIGHT

It was nine-twenty by the time they found Staff Sergeant Doyle Quigley. He was out cold in an employees-only rest room, and he had a hell of a gash in his temple, with bright crimson blood covering the side of his face. The Stechkin lay on the floor beside him. Hamm bent over him long enough to find a pulse.

"He's alive. Meter, you get a medic and stay with him. Take this." Hamm passed him the Colt .45. He would not get through customs with it.

"Sir!" Meter grabbed the automatic and ran back toward the military offices.

Hamm ran for the customs checkout, found an officer who told him that Terrell had already passed through, and managed to get past the desk quickly with his sense of urgency. He ran across to the commercial terminal, drawing the haughty stares of a number of travelers.

Inside the terminal, it took him fifteen minutes to locate the car-rental booths and check them for last-minute rentals. All the young ladies were reluctant to provide information to him, and Hamm became a bit brusque with them.

Neither Robert Terrell nor Geoffrey Holding had rented a car. The Holding passport was the only one Terrell still had, but he might still have his own driver's license.

A check with the man directing taxi traffic in front of the terminal only confirmed that fifteen or twenty taxis had departed in the last half hour.

Shit! Every minute counted, and Hamm was quicky losing minutes. He went back to the military operations office, found that the paramedics were tending to Quigley and that Sergeant Meter had called Washington with the news. "Those were my orders, Colonel Hamm. There's a message for you to call Colonel Storch."

To hell with Storch, he thought. He went back to the cafeteria, found a phone, and started calling the downtown agencies of the car-rental companies. No one would give him information over the phone, and he quit trying after the third call.

He waved Meter over to him. "If Quigley's fit to go on, you take him on to Fort Devon with you. I'm staying here."

"But, sir, Terrell's our responsi——"

"That's an order, Sergeant."

"Yes, sir."

Hamm went back to the main terminal and found

a girl at a desk under the Hertz sign. "You have anything with a V-eight in it?"

"There's a Mustang convertible, sir. It's red, with—"

"Write it up."

He drove into Dartmouth, headed for the closest car-rental agency, which was another Hertz franchise.

The girl behind the counter smiled brightly. "How can I help you, sir?"

"I seem to have missed two friends of mine at the airport. We're going fishing together. Could you tell me if either Bob Terrell or Geoff Holding rented a car?" The twenty-dollar bill he laid on the counter bought an examination of the records.

"I'm sorry, sir. I don't have either name listed."

It was nearly midnight, and Terrell had a three-hour lead on him. After crossing into Halifax on the toll bridge over The Narrows, Hamm tried the Avis counter in the Halifax Hotel, and he discovered that Geoffrey Holding had rented a blue Oldsmobile.

He thanked the lady and went into the lobby in search of the telephone bank.

Now what?

He had verified that Terrell had a car and was loose in Nova Scotia. But where in the hell would he go? In any other case, Hamm might have enlisted the help of the Royal Canadian Mounted Police in locating the car. With what he knew about GABRIEL now, though, he was not going to chance it. The KGB would have alerted all of their assets in the area. A call to the RCMP for help would only help the KGB. Hamm could be certain that Naratsmov had already learned of Terrell's escape. The man might already be en route.

Terrell's frame of mind was shaky, Hamm had observed. Would he go home to Arlington Heights? The Boston area?

One thing he needed was a big computer. Boston had supercomputers available at Harvard and M.I.T., if he remembered correctly, and Boston was a familiar place for him. Terrell's parents lived in there.

He went back to the phones, digging his credit card out of his wallet. He called information in Boston and got the telephone numbers of the seven people named Terrell.

The fourth call was the right one.

"Mr. Delbert Terrell?"

"That's me. Who are you? You know what time it is?"

"I apologize for the hour. My name is Steve Hamm. I'm a friend of Bob's."

"Robert's mentioned you a number of times. You haven't seen him, have you?" Mr. Terrell asked cautiously.

Nancy, as well as the FBI, would have talked to the Terrells. In fact, when he thought about it, the Bureau would probably have a tap on the line. "Between the two of us, Mr. Terrell?"

"Maybe among the three or four of us," the elder Terrell said.

He was not a stupid man, Hamm thought. To hell with the FBI. "I've seen him."

There was a catch in the old man's breath. "What shape is he in?"

"Physically, fine. I think he's a little confused mentally."

''He's not done what they're suggesting?''

''What are they suggesting?''

''That Robert is going to the Russians.''

''I don't believe that is his intent, Mr. Terrell. In fact, I know for certain that it is not.''

A sigh of relief on the line. ''Where is he now?''

''I need to ask you a question, and to do it, I have to ask you to go to a public phone.''

''Take me five, six minutes.''

Hamm gave him the number of the phone he was using, then hung up and waited. It was closer to eleven minutes before it rang.

''You know where he is, Colonel? You're calling from a Canadian number.''

''I'm trying to narrow it down. I've lost track of him in Halifax. What can you tell me about that?''

''Halifax? I don't know about Halifax. We have a cabin in Québec. . . .''

There was nothing in Terrell's dossier about Canada. ''Did Bob often go to this cabin, Mr. Terrell?''

''Not in years.'' Delbert Terrell paused, then continued. ''Look, I can reserve a seat on the next—''

''It would be better if you let me check it out first, Mr. Terrell. Where's this cabin located?''

The old man recited a list of directions, and Hamm memorized them. He promised to call when he knew more, then hung up and went into the hotel's souvenir shop and bought a map. He marked out the quickest route, assuming Terrell would follow it. He bought several cans of Seven-Up and half a dozen candy bars, then went back out to the Mustang.

* * *

At nine o'clock on Sunday morning, Robert Terrell pulled off the asphalt of Québec's Highway 155 onto the narrow graveled road leading to Lac Edouard. The period from two to four A.M. had been the roughest for him. He kept nodding off, and several times between Rivière du Loup—where he had crossed the St. Lawrence by ferry—and Chicoutimi, he had jerked to wide-eyed alertness when the Oldsmobile had drifted onto the shoulder. Gravel pinging under the fenders had startled him into wakefulness. Once, he had veered into the oncoming lane and nearly sideswiped a semi. That near miss had forced him to pull over and walk around for a while. What if he went and killed himself before he'd accomplished his goal? The world would perish in a set of fiery mushrooms because he was a poor driver.

After Chambord, on Lac St. Jean, when he turned southwest, he had begun to feel very good, almost excited, about what was to come.

The car entered a tunnel in the trees that blocked out the morning light. The forest on either side of the road was nearly black, and the occasional overhang of boughs obscured the sun. It had been too many years since he had been on this road, but not much seemed to have changed. Many of the side roads that led to vacation cabins had different names on the routered boards tacked to trees and posts, but some of them were still the same.

From the highway to the village of Lac Edouard was almost fifteen miles, and just before he reached the lakeshore, Terrell slowed to twenty miles per hour, looking for his road.

A new growth of seedlings almost obliterated the entrance. The ancient spruce that had held the two signs—EVENSONG and TED'S HAVEN—was gone, as were the signs themselves. There were tire tracks evident on the twin ruts that wound up the slope to the north, so he assumed that someone was using Ted's Haven, or its equivalent in a new name.

The Oldsmobile was low-slung, and the weeded hump between the ruts grabbed at the oil pan and transmission as the car struggled up the hill. The going was easier after he topped the hill and followed the snaking route around upthrust boulders and frequent stands of pine. Needled branches reached out to scratch the car's paint as he went by. When he made hasty glances out the passenger's window, he could see the icy blue water of Lac Edouard on his right, down the craggy slope.

He passed the cabin that had been built by Ted and Doris Chatham. The Chathams and the elder Terrells, Boston neighbors, had bought their forty-acre lots at the same time. Ted Chatham and Delbert Terrell had taken a long time getting their cabins erected; long hours of fishing intervened. There was a new sign: HALFWAY THERE. There was a silver Jeep Cherokee parked alongside the house.

"Nothing remains the same, Robert."

"No. The good things die, and the new things are always in bad taste."

"Come, Robert. You must not be pessimistic."

"You're right. It's a brand-new, fresh day. Smell that air. Taste the pine and the water."

A half mile later, he topped another rise and took a familiar, abrupt turn to the right. Evensong lay directly in his path. It was a square building, with a steeply sloped, cedar-shingled roof. It was built of roughhewn logs, dappled gray mortar filling the chinks between logs. Inside, there were two small bedrooms and a tiny bath, in addition to the large great room that included a kitchen at one end and a stone fireplace at the other. The front, with a covered porch, overlooked the lake.

Terrell nosed the Oldsmobile up against the back wall, then got out. He stood beside the car for a few minutes, rotating his shoulders, working the twelve hours on the highway out of them. Halifax was a long way back.

Walking around the north side, he noted that the wooden shutters over windows all seemed to be in place. The path alongside the cabin, once beaten into concrete hardness, was now overgrown with grass and weeds. He waded through them, going slightly downhill until he reached three wooden steps that took him up onto the veranda. The roof-line covered it, but the sun shone through in three slim rays where shingles and tar paper had torn away. He could see the reflection of the morning sun on the lake now. It was serene and comforting. Off to the east, beyond the forested ridge rising beyond the lake, the pinkness of day was creeping upward.

Terrell felt his way along the front wall, his hand touching familiar outlines. The solid slab door was firmly locked in place. He moved on to the first of the three big front windows. Its shutters were gripped tightly by the galvanized hooks that were set from the inside. The right-side shutter on the second window swung free. He found that the window had been broken, the sash raised.

He climbed through, stepping on splintered glass. There was little light escaping through the shutters. Moving back toward the door, he stumbled into the big recliner in which his father had fallen asleep many nights. Terrell worked his way around it, found the light switch, and flipped it. Nothing.

"They wouldn't leave the electricity on, Robert."

"No, you're right."

"Wasn't there a kerosene lantern in the closet?"

"Two bits it's gone," Terrell bet himself.

It was. He walked across to the fireplace, and there he found several old pieces of logs. It took him nearly ten minutes to get a fire going. In the growing light of yellow and blue flames, he looked around. The place was a shambles. Whoever had broken in had wrecked anything decorative. Paintings, vases, china, and lamps were broken and the pieces scattered over the hardwood floor. A quick search through table drawers and kitchen cabinets confirmed that the portable and the utile—silverware, radios, lanterns, cookware, and the like—had been pilfered. There were no canned goods left. Broken beer bottles, smashed beer cans, and food wrappings littered the floor. Birds and squirrels had been inside, leaving their traces.

"There is no respect for anyone anymore."

"Nor their property, Robert."

A sudden thought hit him. "I hope Steve understands."

"There's an important task to be done. He was an impediment. You know that, Robert."

"He was helpful. Talking to him was almost like old times. It seems like a year since I've been able to talk to anyone."

"You know they're using him to get to you, to get to GABRIEL, Robert."

"Like me, Steve doesn't have many choices."

Terrell went to his father's old recliner, batted the dust and dirt off it, and settled back into it. He tried to sleep, but his mind was too active.

It was not a peaceful interlude.

The fire ebbed as midday approached, and the interior of the cabin warmed. The light broke piecemeal through the gaps in the shutters and through the single window that was open. A large square of light crept slowly down the opposite wall, then across the floor, approaching the window. It was mesmerizing, watching the square, and he lost track of time.

When he finally emerged from his coma-like state, his watch read twelve o'clock. He got up to raise the windows across the front and unlatch the shutters. Unlocking the door, he went out and fastened the shutters back against the outside wall.

"I need to get someone up here to clean, and I'd better find some glass and repair the window, don't you think?"

"Robert, you're just here to get the mail."

"Well, that's right." Terrell forgot to close the door. He stepped down from the porch and went around the cabin to climb into the car. It started right away, and he reversed it back to the road.

He drove slowly and carefully back down the road. The green hues of spring looked particularly fresh. Out on the lake, near the southern shore, two boats rested, their fishermen casting lines.

"Maybe I ought to go fishing. I haven't touched a pole in twenty years."

"Afterward, Robert. Perhaps there will be time, afterward."

The village of Lac Edouard was the same: a tiny cluster of old buildings, the primary one being the general store with its post office and single red gas pump out in front. He parked at the pump and waited until a tall man came out. He was thin, with dark features.

"Fill it up?"

"Please. Is Madame Gurnette here?"

The man unhooked the nozzle from the pump and bent to open the gas tank. "She died in '84. I'm her son, Phillip."

Nothing stayed the same, he thought. "I'm sorry to hear that. I've been away too long."

Inserting the nozzle into the receptacle, Phillip asked, "You've a cabin around here?"

"Evensong. My folks' place, actually."

The man had his nose wrinkled in suspicion as he stared at Terrell. He glanced down at Terrell's hand on the steering wheel. Terrell was gripping the wheel so tightly that his knuckles were white.

"It's been broken into," Phillip said.

"I know. I've got some work to do."

"There's a package inside. Must be for you."

"Yes. I'd intended to spend a few weeks working where it's quiet."

After the tank was filled, Terrell followed Phillip inside the jam-packed store. Fishing gear was displayed along one wall. Canned and boxed food filled shelving that left very narrow aisles. The old glass-fronted candy counter had disappeared. He bought several sacks of supplies, aware of Phillip's interest in his hands, the shudder of his lower lip, the thickness of the wad of bills in his wallet. Finally, he accepted the fat package wrapped in plain brown paper with Venezuelan postage marks.

Once again, he had GABRIEL in his hands.

* * *

It was almost two o'clock on Sunday morning by the time Hamm had waded through downtown Halifax, located Bicentennial Drive, then found his way onto Highway 102. At three-thirty, he was in Moncton, New Brunswick.

The sun began to peek above the horizon as he drove east toward the coast, then picked up Highway 11 northward. Occasionally, he got a glimpse of the Gulf of St. Lawrence on his right. Towering fir and pine filled the hills around him, and the early morning went by quickly as he passed through quaint townships with names like St. Margaret's and Black River. The short distance between towns, in fact, broke up the high-speed driving.

In Chatham, before he crossed the tendril of Miramichi Bay, he stopped for gas, a six-pack of Molson, a sack of potato chips, and two hamburgers. After crossing the bay, he took the forty-five-mile stretch of Highway 8, which cut across the peninsula to Bathurst, rather than follow the coastline around it.

After Bathurst, he began to open up the Mustang. Hamm knew Terrell was not a good driver. He would drive carefully, and Hamm hoped to close the time gap.

At eight A.M. he picked up a speeding ticket on the stretch of road south of Causapscal, Quebec. He accepted it, stuck it in the glove compartment, and got back on the road, rolling the speedometer up to seventy again, almost before the trooper was back in his car.

It was nearly two o'clock by the time he reached the side road that led up to Evensong. He went by it first, then had to back up. The description Delbert Terrell had given him had suffered from time.

There was no sign, but there was the huge granite boulder that looked like half a globe.

Hamm rolled down the window and let in the fresh air as he followed the dual track up through the forest. When he reached the top of the incline, he could see the lake. The afternoon sun put shimmers of light on its rippled surface.

The first cabin he came to had a Jeep out front and a name different from what Terrell had told him. He went on by and noted the tire tracks in the ruts. They were fresh, and there were several sets. Hamm stopped long enough to open the door and lean out to study the traces. They were all of the same tire tread, both coming and going.

He could not tell whether the car had passed in one direction more often than in the other direction. Hamm decided he was not much of an Indian scout.

A few minutes later he dodged an outcropping, then turned hard to the right.

There was the cabin, but no Olds.

Parking in the small clearing, Hamm shut down the engine and got out. It was eerily quiet, with just a sibilant whisper of the breeze in the pines. He looked around and decided that this was a place where he would like to spend some time, if he ever had time. The placid lake looked cool and inviting. The lack of people was even more inviting.

Maybe Delbert Terrell would consider selling it.

Noting where the weeds and grass had been crushed downward, Hamm walked around the north side of the cabin, then climbed to the porch. The windows were all shuttered, but when he tried the door it opened readily. He stepped inside.

The place had been ransacked. The floor under

one window was littered with glass. He wandered around, noting the fresh shoe marks in the dust of the floor and where the fabric of the recliner chair had been brushed off. Bob Terrell had spent some time here, though not much.

Closing the door firmly behind him, Hamm went back to the Mustang and drove back down to the gravel road. He turned toward the lake and drove until he could drive no more. Parking alongside the store, he levered himself out of the low seat and went inside.

"Can I help you?" The man was tall and thin, with the hint of French heritage in his features.

"I hope so." Hamm looked around the crowded room. There were shelves all the way up to a ten-foot ceiling, and some of the tools and implements appeared as if they had been stored in the same spot for decades. A patina of dust covered the higher shelves, though the lower ones had been cleaned. One wall held a large display of fishing gear, and a locked glass case contained several rifles, shotguns, and hand guns.

The proprietor eyed Hamm's rumpled suit. It was not the norm of the Canadian woods. Hamm picked out a pair of Levi's, a flannel shirt, and hiking shoes. If Terrell had gone deeper into the forest, he had better be more prepared.

Prepared for anything.

He walked over to the gun case.

"Looking for a gun?" the man asked.

He was afraid he might need one, and he regretted the need to abandon CIA Agent Cameron's Colt in Halifax. On the top shelf under the glass counter was another Colt, this one a .357 Magnum. Just what a hunter needed, Hamm thought.

"Let me take a look at the Python."

The store owner unlocked the case and pulled out the Colt. Hamm went over it quickly with a professional eye, working the cylinder and trigger mechanism. "Got a box of shells?"

"Sure do."

"Good. I'll take it."

"Yes, sir. Let's get the paperwork taken care of."

Hamm pulled his wallet out of his hip pocket. He leafed throught the bills and found five hundreds. Fanning the bills like a card hand and holding them out, he said. "This ought to be enough paperwork."

"Uh . . . I'm afraid there's more to it than that."

"You handle the rest of it any way you like."

The man eyed the bills, then reached for them, folded them quickly, as if they were hot, and stuffed them into his pocket. "I guess I can do that."

Hamm moved over to the wooden counter, his eyes searching. He found what he was looking for: a set of pigeonholes below countertop level. The sign outside said this was a post office, too.

"Now," Hamm said, "I'm here to meet a friend of mine. Bob Terrell. He hasn't been in, has he?"

The man's eyes lit up as if he had received a reprieve. This was a friend of a local owner, rather than some hood buying heavy firepower. "He was in earlier this morning. I'd guess he's gone on up to the cabin."

"How would I get there?"

Hamm listened patiently while the instructions were delivered to him.

"Thanks."

"You guys have some work ahead of you."

"That's what I understand." Hamm supposed he was talking about the break-in. "I wonder if I should take something up there with me."

"He stocked up pretty good."

"He get the package?"

"Package? Oh, the one in the mail. Yeah, he took it with him."

Terrell had GABRIEL, Hamm thought. It was a deadly combination.

He thanked the owner once more, then went back to the Mustang. Cranking the engine over, Hamm reversed away from the building, spun the wheels, and dropped the shift into first. He gunned up the hill, heading back to Highway 155. Twenty-five minutes later, he slid onto the asphalt and headed south with the speedometer needle bouncing at one hundred miles per hour.

He rolled into Grande-Mère at four o'clock, having passed the Grand Maurice National Park without noticing it. His mind had been busy with Terrell's motives and options. While the car was being filled, he called Diane DeMott.

"Where the hell have you been?"

"You been looking for me?"

"For Christ's sake, Steve! I've been here all night and all day, waiting for you to call in. Coriolanus is raising hell. Storch just called for the fifth or sixth time. General Kuster wouldn't mind a report, either."

Hamm did not have time for any of them. "Go find a phone."

She gave him a number she had recorded earlier, then hung up.

* * *

After allowing Diane fifteen minutes, Hamm dialed and she answered immediately.

"Steve, what's going on?"

"You don't know?"

"I know Bob got away, that an M.P. was hurt. Where in hell are you?"

"Québec. Look, give me the list of supercomputers again."

"Québec! Where in Québec?"

"The computers, dammit!"

"All of them?"

"No. For the northeast U.S. and Canada."

"Where's Bob?"

"Somewhere close. Come on, the list."

She read him the list of cities, and Hamm noted them in his address book.

"Okay, start with the universities, and find out if anyone, under any name, has recently requested time on their machines."

"Jesus, Steve! Do you really think he's going through with this?"

"I know he's got the tape with him now, and I think he has blackmail in mind."

TWENTY-NINE

The Cray supercomputer was a cylindrical mass in the center of the renovated room, standing tall enough almost to touch the raised ceiling. The floor was raised also to accommodate the mass of wire bundles, keeping them out of sight. It was a large room, air-conditioned and humidity-controlled. Terrell knew that the computer generated so much heat that a web of tubing carried a coolant through the core of superconductors. Two technicians were in the room with the computer, manning a master console, and keeping tabs on a variety of monitoring devices he did not understand.

Terrell also knew that the Cray supercomputer was a symmetrical work of polished art as far as engineers were concerned, and it was a source of undisguised pride to its owners. A sightseeing tour was almost obligatory for visitors.

Robert Terrell did not care about the machine, but he took the tour and listened to the excited young tour guide because it was expected. The computer was on the other side of a long glass window in the corridor in which he stood. The young lady, dressed in a lab coat, told him about processing speeds and heat and power. Terrell did not listen. He had other things on his mind.

For one, he memorized the floor plan. Larkness Research Unlimited was located in a restored three-story building of granite blocks and narrow windows. The exterior had been sandblasted and the windows replaced with bronze-tinted, sealed units. The interior had been gutted and rebuilt to the specifications of Harvey Larkness. The first floor contained the offices, terminal rooms, and research labs of the company itself. The second floor contained more labs and a half dozen rental offices. The third floor, divided by the central hallway, housed the computer and its peripheral devices in separate rooms along one side of the corridor. Each of those rooms was secured by steel doors requiring the entering of a five-digit code into a panel next to the door in order to release the electric locks. On the other side of the hall were large offices for programmers, operators, and technicians; storage rooms; and repair facilities. The third floor itself was protected at the elevator entrance by armed security guards and an enclosed reception area.

Terrell understood the security. Harvey Larkness and his board of directors and investors wanted to protect their twenty-five-million-dollar investment.

They also wanted a return on that investment and so leased time on the machine. In fact, as with many of the big computers around the North American continent, users were not lining up at the door, as had been expected, and hourly rates had been lowered in order to attract new users. Once they had been fully mesmerized by the power and the speed, the rates would rise again.

Terrell had had to use his true name because his academic credentials were required in order to obtain access. Larkness Research Unlimited might want an endless supply of new customers, but it also wanted users who knew what they were doing. There might have been forty or fifty businesses and research centers with direct land-line links to the Cray, for all Terrell knew. The computer was large enough to handle all their needs. For special, short-term projects, there were the rooms on the second floor. The rate was thirty-six hundred dollars an hour, but it was charged only for actual time on the machine. After spending the night in a motel room, Terrell's first chore on Monday morning had been to find a bank and obtain cash for a four-thousand-dollar cashier's check. He presented it to Larkness at their ten o'clock meeting.

Harvey had then turned him over to the young lady for the expected tour.

"If you'll step this way, Dr. Terrell?"

He followed her along the hall and peered through another window.

"This is the data-storage room," she said.

Banks of disk drives and reel-to-reel tape machines were lined up in rows. From time to time, a red diode would light up on a drive, and the reels would rotate. The computer knew which drive to go to, to retrieve data.

On to the next room, filled with a wide variety of printers. "The hardcopy, if it is necessary, is printed out here," she said. "There is a separate miniature elevator that delivers printouts to the first floor for pickup."

"Efficient," he said, not caring. His hardcopy proof would come in another form.

The last room on that side was the power room, filled with equipment that filtered the electrical requirements of the Cray, avoiding surges and power spikes. There was also a bank of batteries and an emergency generator that kicked in automatically, should power from the outside world be interrupted. Power interruptions meant lost data, perhaps years of work destroyed. Here, Terrell listened closely. The emergency power arrangements meant that no one from outside the building could shut him down, once he had assumed control of the machine.

At last, she took him down to the second floor and showed him into an office. It was well equipped, perhaps to help justify the hourly cost of time on the computer. There was a window to the hallway, and the door alongside it was lockable. There was a big, L-shaped desk in one corner, and the computer terminal sat on the L. The monitor was not visible from the hall window. Centered in the outside wall was a bronze-tinted window. A small couch was pushed up against one wall, next to a narrow door leading to a bathroom, and a corner counter-cabinet held a small sink and a coffeepot. It was ideal, as far as Terrell was concerned.

"You did say that your media was tape, Dr. Terrell?"

"Yes."

"Good. We've got you in the right room." With a wave of her hand, she indicated the tape drive standing next to the terminal. "If there's anything at all that you need, or that we can help you with, just ring two-one-one."

"I'm sure I'll be fine. Thank you."

As soon as she stepped out, Terrell locked the door behind her and drew the drape over the window to the corridor. He had two thick briefcases, purchased that morning after he had bought a business suit.

Laying the briefcases on the couch, he opened each of them. They were packed with the supplies he had purchased in Lac Edouard, intending to spend several days at the cabin. Only after he had returned to the cabin had he decided that it was pointless to delay further. Before he could dally any longer, he had closed up the cabin, then driven to Trois-Rivières to abandon the Oldsmobile on a side street and rent a Mercury from Avis.

Terrell stacked crackers, bread, peanut butter, some cans of beans and soup on the corner counter, then started a pot of coffee. He laid two yellow, lined tablets and four ball-point pens on the desk. He took off his coat and tie and tossed them on the couch. He did everything but look at the terminal.

He was putting it off.

He opened a box of Wheat Thins and grabbed a handful.

Chewing, he asked himself, "You know what they say, Robert?"

"What's that?"

"No time like the present."

"We don't need clichés."

"No, Robert, we need to talk to some people in Washington and Moscow."

"Washington will not be a problem. When I give my name, they'll have the President on the line in nothing flat. The Kremlin will resist, of course. The General Secretary will be unavailable."

"Even the President may not believe you have the power, Robert."

"Yes. There will be skepticism until after the demonstrations."

"It will have to be Kimball and Novaya Lyalya, Robert."

"Yes."

North of Kimball, Nebraska, on the southern edge of the sandhills, there was a missile silo serviced by crews out of Warren Air Force Base in Cheyenne, Wyoming. There would be a crew of perhaps eight or ten men. The silo had originally been constructed for the Minuteman, but now housed an M-X with eight Multiple Independently Retargeted Vehicles. The eight Mark 4 MIRVs would each yield a one-hundred-kiloton thermonuclear blast. Kimball, Scottsbluff, Sidney, and Cheyenne would all feel the effects. Even Denver would go to a radiation alert.

Better than a major city, Terrell had decided.

Novaya Lyalya was located in the Central Ural Mountains, near where the U.S.S.R. conducted many of its space programs and missile tests. The silo-emplaced Intercontinental Ballistic Missile was one of 360 deployed SS-19s, and the warhead was also a multiple one, with six 550-kiloton retargeted vehicles. Terrell estimated the range of destruction might extend to Perm and Sverdlovsk, but there were a lot of small towns that would also be vaporized.

The fact that the blasts would take place within hardened silos would help to limit the destruction, he hoped. Beyond that, the radiation dispersal was up to the wind, and he could not control the wind.

"It is time, Robert," his other self prompted.

"Yes, yes." Terrell went to the briefcase and lifted out the tape.

Then he carried it over to the tape drive, recalling the many times Larry Pelagio had shown him how to mount the reel and thread the tape. He was a trifle clumsy and it took him fifteen minutes to get it threaded correctly.

When it was done, he turned on the terminal.

Sunday night's telephone calls on Communication's secure line had been fruitless. While the supercomputers might be at work, no one in the front office was. Diane DeMott called General Kuster to report her conversation with Hamm, then went home.

On Monday morning, she tried once more, again using the secure telephone line down in the basement communications room. There were only twelve supercomputers available in the area of interest, and after her first calls, DeMott had learned that only seven of them leased time to outsiders. At nine in the morning, none of them could report a Robert Terrell leasing time.

At ten-fifteen, after talking to a distraught Nancy Terrell for half an hour, she started making the rounds again. On the second call, she found him.

"Larkness Research Unlimited," the female voice told her.

"Yes. I'd like to speak to Dr. Robert Terrell, please. This is his office calling."

"One moment, please." There was a short pause. "Dr. Terrell is in two-one-seven, but he has left instructions not to be disturbed."

"It's very important," DeMott insisted.

"I'm sorry, miss. The note is explicit. Under no circumstances is he to be interrupted. I can take a message."

"No. I'll wait." DeMott hung up, then took the elevator back up to her floor.

In her office, she sat at her desk, despondent. Now, what? Bob Terrell had access to a computer. What he did in the next hours could prove cataclysmic. She did not know where Hamm was.

If she told Coriolanus, he would go in with guns blazing. He would kill Bob Terrell, and he would destroy Nancy Terrell.

For all she knew, Hamm would do the same.

It was up to her.

She dialed the travel office within DIA and asked for information on airline shuttles. (She told them to book a ticket on the eleven-thirty flight.)

Jack Coriolanus accepted a telephone call from Colonel Storch at eleven o'clock. "Hello, Winnie."

"How closely is DeMott tied into this thing?"

"She's a friend of the man. And she uses a lot of public telephones whenever she talks to Hamm. Pretty damned close, I'd say."

"My source at DIA says she booked an eleven-thirty shuttle flight for today. She's already left the building."

"Where to?" Coriolanus asked.

"Montreal."

Alexi Naratsmov was not accompanied by Major Dmitri Talensk. The political officer had changed his mind about his qualifications as a First Chief Directorate field operative just before Naratsmov left the London embassy in disguise and a second decoy car.

He had arrived in Halifax, Nova Scotia, on Sunday morning as Paul Koralski, a Pole traveling on business. Under his blue pinstriped suit, he wore a padded vest that gave him a bulkier appearance, and his face was adorned with horn-rimmed glasses and a thick moustache. It was not that great a change in appearance, but he thought it enough to preclude his being spotted immediately.

Halifax was his last point of reference for Terrell, but he did not think he would now be in the area. Rather, he would have hired a car and driven south, perhaps toward Boston, which was home territory for Terrell, with many likely places to have cached the mysterious tape that had nuclear consequences.

Naratsmov had gathered airline schedules from each carrier represented at the airport, then checked into the nearest hotel. From there he called the Soviet embassy in Washington to leave his number and his instructions.

The first call came on Sunday afternoon at six o'clock. "Paul? Am I interrupting your dinner?"

It was not a secure line, of course, and he responded to the opening-code query with, "Not if it is important."

The response satisfied the caller in the embassy communications room. "This is your Washington friend."

"Go on."

"The man who dresses like a tiger telephoned his assistant."

"And they discussed . . . ?"

"Unknown. They changed telephones."

"I do not know this assistant. Who is he?"

"It is a she."

"And let us become very familiar with the assistant."

"Of course."

Early on Monday morning, Alexi Naratsmov received a picture and biography of Diane DeMott. The file was brought to him by a courier from Washington, safer than relying on the promise of American advertising. Shortly afterward, at ten-thirty, the embassy called him again with the information that DeMott was flying to Montreal. More important, and the crucial deciding point for Alexi, the wife of Robert Terrell was expected to accompany her.

It was not the direction he had expected, but it was in his general vicinity, and he thought he would be able to reach the city quickly. First, he called a contact in Montreal and ordered surveillance at Montreal International Airport, taking the time to give a full description of Diane DeMott. He used the black-and-white picture lying on the table in front of him as his source. Then, after thumbing through his airline schedules, he found a flight leaving right away that would get him into Montreal at one-fifty in the afternoon.

Hamm had checked into a Grande-Mère motel on Sunday night, but he ran into blank walls as he called the twelve supercomputer sites.

On Monday morning at eight, he had called them all again, but most did not open their switchboards until nine. By ten o'clock, after another round of calls, Bob Terrell had not checked in with any of them.

Unfortunately, he had few contacts in Canada. There was a retired DIA operative named Johnston living in Québec, and Hamm tried him. The man said he would check around, but spotting Terrell would be difficult since he did not have to pass across borders unless he chose a U.S. computer. He tried a few others in Toronto and Ottawa, but the results were unfavorable.

He tried DeMott at eleven o'clock, but there was no answer. She and her secretary were both out.

The machine in Montreal, at Larkness Research, was the closest. He had verified that Larkness rented time. Maybe Terrell was using some brand-new name. If he had to guess, Hamm would say that Terrell would have gone straight for the closest machine, and Hamm knew he could not wait much longer. He walked over to the coffee shop for lunch, and while he chewed on a tasteless chicken-fried steak, he decided he would have to shoot for Montreal, which was about one hundred twenty miles away.

Before he left, he called Arlington Hall one more time and reached DeMott's secretary at eleven-forty-five. "Let me talk to Diane."

"She's not here, Colonel."

His patience was wearing thin. "Dammit! Where is she?"

"Why, she went to Montreal. I thought you knew that."

He hung up and raced outside to his Mustang.

The tires burned rubber as he hit the ramp for the Limited Access Highway. Hamm pressed the pedal to the floorboard between each shift, trying to calculate distances and times. If he pressed the speed limit by only enough to avoid the attention of traffic cops, he figured he could be in Montreal between two and two-thirty.

He did not know how long it would take to make GABRIEL operational, but he thought that two o'clock was going to be too late.

THIRTY

GABRIEL took some time getting back into the flow of things.

After all, it had been off-line for over a month.

The program was so massive that it required twenty minutes to transfer it from magnetic tape to the memory of the Cray supercomputer. Then Terrell had to initiate the diagnostic sequence, a sub-program that sent out probes to determine that each of the other sub-programs, as well as the hardware environment, was attuned to all others, that no "bugs" had crept into the system. Then the program automatically checked its telephone accesses, dialing random numbers, remembering the lines, the microwave relays, the satellite channels available to it. There were thousands of those.

In another of its automatic operations, the program sealed off its section of the Cray's superbrain, denying access to other terminals. Only the terminal in Room 217 had control over the program.

Because GABRIEL had not been interfaced with other communications systems for a month, its memory had fallen behind on current access codes, some of which were changed daily. Once the terminal screen told him, "DIAGNOSTIC SEQUENCE COMPLETE. ALL SYSTEMS 100%," Terrell selected the option, "UPDATE CODING," and pressed the Enter key.

Terrell made himself a peanut-butter sandwich and ate it, chasing it with a can of orange juice, while GABRIEL made initial probes into communications hubs around the world, randomly testing access codes until it had the correct codes for the major networks stored in its memory. From time to time, the red light on the tape drive would flash, and the reels would jump a few inches, as the program updated its permanent storage banks, in addition to the ready-access files it kept in memory.

The sophisticated access codes for seventeen major communications hubs, both military and commercial, in the Soviet Union went into the file. Eleven in China. Twenty-four in Britain. France, Israel, Pakistan, both Germanys. Every country in the world with military, economic, or commercial importance had its secret and semi-secret communications networks opened to GABRIEL.

Like a can opener, Terrell thought.

By noon, GABRIEL was able to flash "UPDATE COMPLETE."

But it was not.

The program had never bothered storing data for

U.S. communications networks. Terrell moved to the terminal and sat in the swivel chair. Calling up a sub-menu for "DATA BANK ADDITIONS," he entered a telephone number that he knew in the Pentagon—it used to be his own—and told the machine what to search for—NORAD, SAC, DOD, CIA, Worldwide Military Command and Control System, the Defense Communications System.

While GABRIEL began to seek and memorize the thousands of new telephone numbers and access codes, Robert Terrell ate some more Wheat Thins.

He did not know how he was feeling. He felt somewhat numbed, performing a required and distasteful task because it was necessary. Blotting out as much external thought as he could, Terrell simply concentrated on the processes involved.

At one-ten, the green letters glowed on the screen: "ADDITIONS COMPLETE."

Terrell moved back to the chair in front of the terminal and called up a telephone menu, then selected the National Military Command Center in the Pentagon, accessing the Defense Communications System. From DCS, he entered the Automatic Digital Network, the prime system for data transmission. By one-twenty, GABRIEL had a direct line to a silo north of Kimball, Nebraska.

GABRIEL bypassed interlock systems that were designed to protect launch control. GABRIEL was not interested in launch.

GABRIEL conversed with the MIRV warheads and reset the barometric and radar altimeters that were fail-safe controls, preventing the thermonuclear warheads from detonating below preset altitudes.

The elevation at the silo surface was 4655 feet above sea level. GABRIEL reset the altimeters for 4500 feet.

Robert Terrell instructed GABRIEL to energize the firing circuits if the character "@" on the terminal keyboard was depressed.

He left that line open, and ran through the same process in the Soviet Union. The MIRV in Novaya Lyalya became sensitive to the touch of the "*" character.

At a quarter of two, Robert Terrell instructed GABRIEL to dial the White House.

When the telephone at his elbow rang, he picked it up.

"Situation room. Captain Davidson."

"Captain Davidson, my name is Dr. Robert Terrell. I wish to speak to the President." He had a frog in his throat, and the words came out sounding funny to him.

There was a long pause. "I'm sorry, sir. The President is not currently available."

"Captain, you pass my name to the President or the Chief of Staff. I will call back at two o'clock."

Terrell hung up.

Diane DeMott arrived at the Larkness Research Unlimited building at one-thirty.

"May I assist you?" the receptionist asked.

"I need to see Dr. Terrell."

"Dr. Terrell. Let me check." She ran a mauve fingernail through a logbook, then said, "He is not to be disturbed. I'm sorry."

DeMott produced her DIA credentials. "I'm from his office, and I have important information for him."

The receptionist was nearsighted. She leaned forward across her desk to study the picture and the data on the laminated card. "Well, we were not aware of his association. I suppose it will be all right for you to go up. Room Two-one-seven."

She took the elevator, got off on the second floor, and walked in cushioned silence down the silver hallway. Room 217 had a closed door, with drapes drawn over a window next to the door.

DeMott knocked on the door.

The heavy door muffled the voice. "What is it?"

"Bob, it's Diane." The silence of the corridor made her conscious of her volume.

Nothing happened for nearly a minute.

Then the drape over the window was pulled back. Bob Terrell stared at her for a full minute, then closed his eyes.

"Bob! Open up!"

She heard the lock clack over. Terrell opened the door, held it protectively against him, and peeked out.

DeMott thought he looked distraught. His dress shirt was wrinkled and sweat stains circled his armpits. His eyes, under the thick lenses, were too wide, too alert, and there were dark circles under them. His hair was much longer than he normally wore it, and it needed combing.

"What are you doing here, Diane?" Terrell asked, opening the door a little wider.

"You've got to come home, Bob," she said. "Nancy needs you."

DeMott moved to where she could see past him, her gaze captured by the terminal monitor. A string of abbreviated codes and queries was printed in green capital letters on the black screen. "You've got it up and running? Shut it down, Bob! You've got to stop!''

Terrell's eyes flashed toward the tape drive, and she followed them to see the big reel mounted there. That was GABRIEL.

He stood undecided for a moment, then nodded. ''It's running.''

''I could grab that reel, and it would all be over, Bob.''

''No. The operating program and the data files have all been loaded into the computer's memory now. In fact, the program has locked out other access. Only this terminal can control it.''

DeMott did not know the Cray operating systems, or she might have tried to wrestle with him, try to reach the keyboard and erase the memory. ''What's next, Bob?''

''Do you know what I'm doing? You don't, do you?'' His voice had a whine in it, like a little boy begging for understanding.

''I think you want to control the world's nuclear weapons.''

''But for peaceful purposes, Diane. For peace!'' His whole face seemed to glow with his resolve. ''I'm going to force the superpowers to dismantle their systems.''

''You can't possibly last, Bob. By yourself, alone here?''

''I'll do whatever it takes.''

''You're going to run into resistance you don't expect. You can't control every system by yourself, all alone. What's to keep a frightened Politburo, once they know about you, from launching a strike from sea?''

Terrell grinned broadly at her. ''The fact that, if

they try, they lose Moscow. I can read all of their military messages, you know."

"Suppose the Soviets don't believe you?" she asked.

"They will."

She gasped with the sudden knowledge. "You're going to demonstrate the power?"

"A missile silo in Nebraska and one in the Central Urals."

"That will be murder," she said, "not salvation."

"It's necessary. People will need to be convinced."

"Please don't hurt us," DeMott said. "Think about Nancy, Fred, and Beth."

"I'm doing this for them. And for everyone else. Now, go. Tell them that I love them."

Diane tried to stop him, but he slipped out of her grasp, stepped back, and pushed the door shut quickly.

The lock clicked loudly in the hushed hallway.

The active First Chief Directorate operative in Montreal had picked up DeMott from the moment she deplaned from her TWA flight. When Alexi Naratsmov arrived, he quickly spotted the agent who was waiting for him, but who did not know him. Naratsmov made the approach with the latest password that he had. "Am I interrupting your dinner?"

"Not if it's important." The man was nondescript in a brown suit, but the yellow carnation in his lapel had identified him.

They went into the men's room together, and Naratsmov accepted a Walther automatic, a fine weapon. Checking to see that they were alone, he examined the ammunition clip, then worked the slide. "And the woman?"

"She went to a place called Larkness Research Unlimited. It is located on Boulevard St. Laurent."

"What do they do there, at this research place?" Alexi asked.

"It is a computer service for persons involved in research. I do not know what kinds of research."

A computer tape, then. "Do you have a car for me?"

The man passed him a set of keys, a parking ticket, and a bundle of currency. "A blue Peugeot, Section A of Close-in Parking, Row Six."

Naratsmov found the car without difficulty, and he took the Côte de Liesse into the city center. Just before two o'clock, he parked the car across the street from Larkness. Dodging cars, he crossed the boulevard and entered the building. The receptionist offered assistance, but Naratsmov declined.

"I am waiting for someone, if that is all right."

"Have a seat," she told him.

He had no more than seated himself on one of the oddly shaped sofas than the elevator door opened and DeMott stepped out. DeMott was better-looking than the picture he had seen in Hamm's file had led him to believe.

Naratsmov got up and moved toward her, loosening the knife in its wrist sheath.

She recognized him—her eyes went wide and white—and froze in place.

Alexi Naratsmov smiled at her.

THIRTY-ONE

As he had done every half hour since the CIA Gulfstream had dropped him and his agents at Cartierville Airport, northeast of Montreal International, Coriolanus called in to Langley, identified himself, and asked for the deputy director of operations. The DDO had involved himself personally and was monitoring the information flow.

"He's left the building, Mr. Coriolanus. Hang on, and we'll switch you."

The special assistant waited impatiently, frowning at the two agents standing outside the telephone booth. The booth was situated outside the operations office, close to where Decker sat waiting in a car. He hated not having a better headquarters, a better communications setup.

He hated not knowing more. DeMott was somewhere in Montreal, but no one knew where in the hell it was. No one knew where Hamm or Terrell was. One of his two agents stationed at Montreal International had called to tell him that Alexi Naratsmov had arrived on a flight out of Halifax, but in attempting to follow him, the agents had been broadsided by some asshole in a brown suit and a yellow carnation. All Coriolanus knew was that Naratsmov was running around the city in a blue Peugeot.

"Situation room. Colonel Storch. That you, Jack?"

"What the fuck's going on? I want the DDO."

"He's here. Shit! We're all here. The President just got off the phone to Montreal."

"Goddamn! What's happening?" Coriolanus was unnerved. He was sitting right in the middle of Montreal, and did not know what was going on.

"GABRIEL is operational." Storch had a catch in his voice. It stumbled.

Coriolanus shut his eyes. "No. Where?"

Storch gave him the name and the address.

"I'll get right down there."

"Hold on! Jack, any wrong moves, and we lose a silo. So do the Soviets. We both lose a chunk of the population."

"Shit!"

"Terrell has his finger on the trigger. We've called the Canadian prime minister, and he has cleared the Larkness building."

"Jesus Christ! What's next?"

"Terrell says he has to contact the general secretary," Storch said.

"Son-of-a-bitch!" It was going to be worse than

Coriolanus had imagined. "No one's in the building? Who's in charge?"

"The Montreal cops are sealing it off, as far as we know. Guy named Harvey Larkness owns the company, and a police chief named Margeaux is supposed to be on the scene."

The wheels were spinning in Coriolanus's head. "I can cut power to the computer. That'll put him out of business. Bastard."

"No good," Storch said. "There's an emergency generator in the building."

"Can we cut off power to the missile sites?"

"Terrell says that GABRIEL will read our intentions, and he'll blow a warhead. We don't know what site he's picked. If we shut down the system, we're vulnerable to a Soviet strike. They might take advantage of this."

"You believe him?" Coriolanus asked.

"I believe him. He can also tap the hotline, so he'll know if the President calls the general secretary, and he'll know what's being said."

"I'll call you back as soon as I get down there." Coriolanus slapped the phone on its hook and raced for the car. He piled into the front seat as the two agents fell into the back. "Hit it, Decker!"

Hamm crossed the Prairies River on the Northshore Autoroute coming into Montreal. The traffic had been heavy all the way from Grande-Mère; he had developed a whole new vocabulary of swear words particular to Canadian drivers.

From the map spread open on the passenger's bucket seat, he had already located his exit at the interchange with Boulevard St. Laurent. It was eleven miles ahead, according to the road sign he just passed. The city loomed ahead, the autoroute snaking through it.

An interchange with the Boulevard St. Jean-Baptiste came up, and Hamm saw a Consolidated Freightways eighteen-wheeler lumbering up the ramp, ready to take the outside lane. Three more trucks were spotted in the lanes ahead of him, all destined to cut his speed from the ten miles above the limit that he had been holding.

He cut to the outside lane and stomped on the gas pedal.

The needle came quickly up to ninety miles per hour; he passed the CF semi before it had a chance to block him.

And in his rearview mirror, he saw the red and blue strobes pulsating.

Shit!

Hamm pressed the accelerator to the floor. The speedometer read one hundred thirty by the time he reached the next interchange. He ignored the pursuit, concentrating instead on quick lane shifts, flying around the slower traffic. Angry horns took fire on him. The exhaust pipes thrummed behind him.

At Boulevard Papineau, another cop joined the chase, coming off the ramp a fraction of a minute too late to cut him off.

Coming up on St. Laurent, Hamm waited until the last second, then switched from his lane to the outside lane, directly in front of an airport limousine. The Mustang fishtailed, tires squealing, as he braked and downshifted, taking the curving exit ramp.

The two police cars smoked rubber as they attempted to slow and get to the outside lane.

Hamm shot off the ramp onto the boulevard at over sixty, flashed through one red light, then slammed on the brakes when he saw the police cars blocking the boulevard ahead. They were strung across all lanes of traffic, and uniformed police were frantically setting up barricades. Emergency lights flashed everywhere. All traffic was stalled.

For a moment, he marveled at the pace with which the police had moved in order to snare a speeder.

Then he realized they were corraling the block in which the Larkness Building was located.

Traffic was jammed up tight, and Hamm did not even try to park. He killed the ignition and piled out of the car. He ran the block and a half to the barricade. Cops were everywhere, turning away sightseers and gawkers.

Hamm trotted across the street, parallel to the barricade, looking for a vulnerable spot.

He ran into Roy Decker. Decker did not look cheerful.

"Where's Coriolanus?"

"He's with some police chief," Decker told Hamm. "Come on. He'll want to talk to you."

Decker flashed tin and got them past two Montreal policemen and inside the quarantined area. There was a police van at mid-block, parked in front of the entrance to Larkness Research. A crowd of uniformed and plainclothes cops hung around it, along with an equal number of political bureaucrats. Coriolanus was in animated conversation with a Canadian who stood two feet taller than the CIA administrator.

Hamm was not going to screw around with Decker or Coriolanus or any other handicap.

"He doesn't want me."

"Oh, yes, he does, Colonel."

Checking the front of the building, he saw two uniformed cops standing to either side of the huge double doors. They appeared apprehensive. Frontal assaults were often the most unexpected, and quite often effective.

"He wants GABRIEL."

Decker looked puzzled.

"I'll get it for him. Here. Hold this."

Decker looked down at his hand just as Hamm straightened his fingers and jabbed him in the solar plexus. It was not a hard blow, but the breath went out of the man in a whoosh, his face purpled, and he collapsed on the curb.

Walking purposefully, Hamm crossed to the sidewalk, strode down to the steps in front of Larkness, and started up them. The two cops came to attention.

Hamm threw his coat flap back and pulled the Python free. "Which one of you is the bravest?"

Neither. They wilted against the granite facade, holding their arms clear of holstered weapons.

"Hey!" someone yelled from the street.

"Hamm! Goddamn it! Hamm!" Coriolanus spotted him.

Pulling the heavy door open, Hamm stepped inside, closed the door, then locked it.

A lot of people were yelling outside by then.

There was no one in the lobby, and he headed straight for the reception desk, leaned over it, and found a sign-in sheet. Dr. Robert Terrell was in Room 217. He searched the desk for anything else that might help, but found nothing.

Someone started banging on the front door.

Spotting a stairway door next to the elevators, Hamm ran to it, pulled it open, and descended to the basement. There were a lot of storage rooms, marked as such, a cafeteria, and in the back, one room marked "Mechanical Systems" and another marked "Electrical Systems."

He entered the last room.

The walls were cluttered with circuit breakers, junction boxes, and a wide range of innocuous switch boxes. A workbench along one wall held tools and electrical parts. Hamm picked up several items, including a magnetized screwdriver and a pair of pliers, and dropped them into his pocket. Then he moved along the wall, reading the labels on switch boxes. He flipped several.

The last breaker he came to was labeled "Master Building Power." If the Larkness Research setup was anything like any major computer center, it would have an emergency backup, so cutting the breaker would serve no purpose other than to alert Terrell.

"What the hell." Hamm pulled the handle, and the basement went dark.

Robert Terrell was pacing, taking short little steps, never moving more than three feet away from the keyboard. The cryptic characters on the monitor screen were menacing, far more menacing than anything Alexi Naratsmov had ever faced before.

Terrell was crying unabashedly, the heavy drops dripping from his jaw.

Naratsmov stood with his back to the locked door, and he still held his knife in his right hand. The pistol was in his coat pocket, but both weapons appeared to be useless. A white-faced Diane

DeMott sat where Alexi had told her to sit. Her hands were wired tightly with clothes hangers Alexi had found in the bathroom.

DeMott's voice had gotten them inside the room, but Terrell held the superior hand.

It was not what Naratsmov had expected. Forcing DeMott back into the elevator, DeMott had begged him not to intervene, saying it would cost millions of lives. He had not believed her, of course.

It was the wild-eyed Terrell who had changed his mind. After unlocking the door, Terrell had leaped back to the computer and held his hand over the keyboard.

When Terrell ignored Naratsmov and called the President of the United States, and had been put right through, Naratsmov had believed.

Terrell paced, waiting.

Someone in Red Army headquarters was trying to locate the general secretary. Terrell was going to talk to the general secretary. Even Alexi Naratsmov had never done that.

Naratsmov turned slightly to face DeMott. With the knife point, he indicated the tape mounted on the drive. "You are certain this . . . this computer program will do what he says it will do?"

DeMott looked up at him. She did not answer, but her expression was affirmation enough.

Walking across the office to peer once again through the bronze windowpane, Naratsmov could see yet more policemen filling the street. He must make a move quickly and get out of there, with the computer tape. He walked over to the couch.

Terrell reached for the keyboard. His eyes were

maddened, Alexi thought, and they kept straying to DeMott.

"Stay where you are!" Terrell shouted.

"You may proceed, Dr. Terrell. What do I care about a few people in your county?" He stopped directly in front of DeMott.

"You'll kill your own people in the Urals!" Terrell shouted.

Naratsmov shrugged. "We have too many mouths to feed as it is. And you are going to kill them, anyway, are you not? Your only concern, Dr. Terrell, is the timing."

"Goddamn you!"

"What is your concern for this woman?" Alexi asked. Going down to one knee, Naratsmov reached out with the razor point of the knife. One by one, he snicked the buttons from DeMott's blouse.

DeMott pushed back into the cushion of the sofa, her eyes wide with horror as she watched the knife point.

"Stop that!" Terrell screamed at him.

Terrell almost jumped at him, then remembered his computer terminal. The man was torn between Diane and the terminal. Which would he choose?

"I will stop—as soon as you shut down the computer and give me the tape." Alexi used the point of the knife to flip DeMott's blouse open. Then he cut through the band of her bra. Her breasts tumbled free, and he touched the point gently against one nipple.

DeMott tried to disappear into the couch, yet she was afraid to move. Her shoulders trembled. "Bob!"

Terrell moved toward them, stopped, went back

to the terminal. ''Oh, damn, Diane! I can't. I can't. Think what it means to the world.''

DeMott moaned, ''Bob, please.'' Tears were streaming down her face.

''She's your friend, not mine,'' Alexi explained.

He found DeMott's collarbone with the tip of the blade and drew it gently along the surface of her skin. A trail of blood droplets followed the point as the skin parted.

Naratsmov was prepared for more surgery, but then the lights went out.

Except for the terminal monitor, which blinked just once.

Hamm used the stairs to reach the second floor, keeping a hand on the steel railing to guide him in the blackness. He eased open the door on the landing and looked in on a vacant hallway. Two emergency lights near the ceiling of the corridor cast bright beams. Moving onto the carpet, he pulled the Colt from his belt and padded silently down the hall until he reached Room 217. Carefully, he tried the doorknob.

It was locked.

A drape on the inside of the window was drawn. Hamm moved back to Room 215 and opened the door. The light from the hall gave him a picture of the office layout. Would 217 be the same? He had to hope so. Where would Terrell be? At the desk? On the couch? In the bathroom?

A woman moaned, the terror muffled by the door.

Hamm moved back to 217, took two steps back, raised his foot, and slammed it into the door, next to the lock.

The wooden jamb splintered and the door flew open, whipping around to slam the wall with a bang.

Like a microsecond Polaroid snapshot, Hamm had the picture. An agonized Terrell was crouched at the desk. Diane was on the couch, heels dug into the carpet, head thrown back against the wall.

Alexi Naratsmov jerked upward and around, his right hand flying up, gripping a knife. The look on his gaunt face was less one of surprise than anger.

Hamm fired once. The heavy slug hit Naratsmov an inch in front of his right ear, and the left side of his head exploded. The impact blew his body back onto Diane, along with the skull fragments, blood, and gray matter.

Diane screamed.

"Steve!" Terrell shouted. The deafening roar of the Colt still echoed off the walls.

Hamm ran to the sofa and rolled Naratsmov's body onto the floor. His frozen right eye stared up at Hamm.

He checked Diane. Her chest was covered with blood, but a close examination told him the slice on her skin was superficial.

He turned back to Terrell. "Shut it down, Bob."

Terrell was crouched by the desk, his shoulders hunched forward, protective of the keyboard. His right hand hovered over the controls. "I can't, Steve, I can't! It's in motion."

"Shut it down."

"You can kill me. I'll still prove what fools we all are." Terrell uncurled his fist and touched two keys in the upper row with his fore- and middle fingers.

Hamm walked over to the tape drive, studied it

for a second, pushed a rewind button, and watched the reels spin. When the tape was rewound, he opened the Plexiglas cover and removed the loaded reel. He held the reel against his side, against the pocket in which he had placed the tools from the electrical room.

"It doesn't matter, Steve," Terrell told him. "The program's in the machine."

"To hell with it, then," Hamm told him. "You want another Brandvlei, Bob, push the key."

At that moment, Coriolanus and his men burst through the corridor.

He fouled up Hamm's psychology.

Robert Terrell panicked and pushed the keys.

WASHINGTON, D.C.

EPILOGUE

Lieutenant General Eugene Kuster put the Chivas Regal bottle back in his bottom desk drawer, then lifted his glass and took a large swallow. His Adam's apple bobbed.

Hamm drank from his own glass and savored the taste.

"You took a hell of a chance, Steve."

"It was the only chance available to take, Gene. The whole premise of GABRIEL was based on communications. I just shut off the telephone system."

Kuster set his glass in the middle of the desk blotter and rotated it slowly. "And Bob Terrell?"

"Nancy's found a place near Boston for him. He may be in therapy for quite a while. That's after Coriolanus and his bunch get through with what they're calling a debriefing. Diane is helping Nancy move next week."

"And of course," Kuster said, "there won't be any publicity on this. Terrell's damned lucky we can't afford an airing of the facts in a public trial. There's a real sense of relief in the White House, but it may be a year before the Strategic Planning Group gets back to normal."

"That means the security task force has yet to come up with a new plan," Hamm guessed.

Kuster grinned at him. "What do you expect? Consensus?"

"Hell, no. I understand the bureaucracy."

"Just keep your mouth shut about it, will you?"

"Is that an order, General?" Hamm took another swig of the Scotch.

"I can make it one now. I've got you back in my shop. But you start flapping your jaw, and Dilman will have you back counting widgets."

Hamm tilted his glass and finished the Scotch. "In that case, I'll go hide out for a few days."

"I didn't see your request for leave cross my desk."

"Oh. You mean there's paperwork involved?" Hamm smiled at his boss.

"Hell, I don't even want to know where you're going." Kuster immediately changed his mind. "Yes, I do."

"I promised a man I'd clean up his cabin in Canada if I got to use it for a couple of weeks."

"And you're doing this good deed alone?"

"I might have a little help." Merrilee said she liked the woods.

Hamm reached for the door handle, but he was too slow. The door whipped open, revealing a very flustered Jackson Coriolanus. "You son-of-a-bitch!"

"Me? Or the general?"

"You, dammit! That tape's gibberish."

"I'll be damned," Hamm said. "It must have been too close to the magnetic screwdriver in my pocket. Too bad."

With his right hand, he gently pushed Coriolanus to one side and stepped through the doorway. He was looking forward to a few quiet days on the lake.

Watch for

PRESSURE POINT

the next GABRIEL *novel coming in December from Lynx*